About the

After a career in the high-tech world of bioscience research, Nick recently took a chance to change gear and refocus his creative energies. Working from his home in the wilds of the Norfolk-Suffolk border, Nick now divides his time between writing, running workshops promoting the mental health benefits of wood-carving and his passion for making and selling hand-carved cups, bowls and spoons.

BEYOND THE SANDBAR: HOW THE STORM OF WAR CHANGED IDENTICAL TWIN BROTHERS

Nick Gosman

BEYOND THE SANDBAR: HOW THE STORM OF WAR CHANGED IDENTICAL TWIN BROTHERS

Vanguard Press

VANGUARD PAPERBACK

A CIP catalogue record for this title is
available from the British Library.

ISBN 978 1 784659 96 7

Vanguard Press is an imprint of
Pegasus Elliot MacKenzie Publishers Ltd.
www.pegasuspublishers.com

First Published in 2021

Vanguard Press
Sheraton House Castle Park
Cambridge England

Printed & Bound in Great Britain

Dedication

This book is dedicated to my grandfather, George Whitton, his twin brother, Great Uncle Fred, and the thousands of other men and women who fought and died for our freedom from tyranny in WWII.

Acknowledgements

I want to thank the staff and curators at the Forces War Records and their sister organisation, Forces Reunited, for their help in tracking down George and Fred's service records and for advice on the circumstances of Fred's incarceration in German POW camps. I also would like to thank the Whitton family for providing me with what remains of George's personal affects from his war service.

Preface

The dark days of 1939 to 1945. Watching Remembrance Sunday parades, many of us experience sorrow for the huge sacrifice laid at the altar of freedom and are often overwhelmed by the sheer scale of suffering. Some of us might remember a grandparent, great uncle or aunt that fought, and perhaps died, in World War II, but what was it really like to live through those years at the tip of the Allied spear facing Nazi Germany and its Allies?

Much has been written by historians about the two world wars of battle strategy, commanders, numbers of troops and casualties, but what lies behind these cold statistics? Fortunately, many veterans have written of their experiences and there are now many authoritative volumes that collect together anecdotes from old soldiers in an attempt to get a clearer picture of events from the perspective of those with direct witness. What then can another book on WWII add to this authoritative and factual body of work? What is missing in much of the current literature is that it often fails to engage a new generation of adults who have grown up in an age of the Internet and social media. Whilst many young adults honour and respect the sacrifice of a previous generation, they struggle to see its relevance in their daily lives. WWII is for them, grainy black and white figures on a flickering screen. A number of recent movie dramatizations have been highly successful in bringing to life past events and characters; however, screenplays leave little room for the viewer to imagine what it would be like to be there, to have taken part. In common with young adults today, many of the men and women who lived through those times were emotionally and experientially unprepared for total war. What did they really feel and think when events forced them to do the unimaginable and bear terrible hardship and suffering?

My maternal grandfather, George and his identical brother, Fred, were in their early twenties when they fought for their country in WWII. In that fateful year of 1939, Fred was already in the regular army whilst George volunteered for the RAF at the outbreak of war. Their journey in the subsequent five years took them down two very different paths. Whilst Fred was captured in France and spent the war in prisoner of war camps in Germany, George served with the RAF Air Sea Rescue Service in Malta and North Africa picking up pilots who had bailed out over the Mediterranean.

Family history records that George and Fred returned from the war as two very different men. My journey to better understand what had happened to them started as a mind experiment. What would it be like if I could see through George and Fred's eyes and experience what they experienced, know what they knew? I could then appreciate better how their experiences might have changed them. The book 'George and Fred' is the result. Whilst it is, in part, a journey by its author to understand more about what his ancestors might have experienced, the book is also an attempt to re-imagine WWII for a social media generation focussed on events happening in real time.

What follows is a fictional story based on factual events composed from intertwining snapshots, or vignettes, of action as the protagonists' grapple with those events as they unfold. Often full of fast-paced action, each vignette contributes to answering a single central question: how could their experiences shape and transform twin brothers both mentally and physically to an extent that they could no longer recognise each other as the same person they knew before the war?

Prologue

At the outbreak of WWII, my maternal grandfather, George Whitton and his identical twin brother, Fred, were in their early twenties. On his return from the war and in the years before his death, George often spoke of his time on a boat sailing around the Mediterranean. Hearing these stories as a nine-year-old boy, I thought it sounded fun and exciting; George's anecdotes were amusing.

However, I remember little about Great Uncle Fred, who led the life of a recluse, except that his brooding presence and austere appearance was in stark contrast to George's ebullient personality. How, one might ask, could they be identical twins? I can only once remember seeing them together during a visit to Fred's little annex where he lived at Bamburgh Castle on the wild Northumbrian coast. Fred's sombre demeanour, spartan living quarters and friendly spaniel, Shotty made a strong impression on me.

Delving deeper into George and Fred's anecdotes and personal effects from their war years, it became clear that their story illuminates two aspects of WWII that are often overlooked, namely the Siege of Malta and the war in the Mediterranean in George's case and the fate of the forty thousand or so men of the British Expeditionary Force (BEF) sent to bolster French forces resisting the Nazi invasion who were left behind after the Dunkirk evacuation.

Whilst a fierce aerial conflict (which became known as the Battle of Britain) raged between the RAF and Luftwaffe, in the skies over England in the summer of 1940, the Italian Air Force embarked on a savage campaign to bomb the tiny island of Malta – then a British protectorate and an important strategic base for Allied resistance in the Mediterranean – into submission. From the summer of 1940 to the end of 1942, Malta became one of the most intensively bombed areas during the war. Needless to say, Malta's meagre air defences were stretched to the limit during this time and many pilots found themselves bailing out over the Mediterranean.

George served with the Maltese division of the RAF Air Sea Rescue Service and their courage in going to the aid of downed British and also Italian and German pilots during that time is often overlooked. Similarly, the long march into captivity of Fred along with more than eighty thousand British and French troops that fought a desperate rearguard action is often overshadowed by the story of the evacuation of the bulk of the BEF at Dunkirk. Forced into surrender at the earliest stage of the war, many of those captured in France in 1940 would spend the next five years in prisoner of war camps in Germany suffering physical and mental deprivations that left deep scars on many of them that they carried with them for the rest of their lives.

Whilst honouring two members of my own family, what follows also honours the courage and sacrifice of the many thousands of servicemen and women who fought for our freedom from tyranny.

'I shall miss this place in the interval that sits between living and death. Dying is an abomination, but immortality would be much worse. The Fates put us all in the firing line between a rock and a hard place. All that any of us can do in this life is to at least make the best fist of it we can.' Anon.

Fred, Monday June 3rd, 1940, village of Franleu about ten miles west of Abbeville

The silence is almost deafening after the mad dash we've made towards a small copse in sight of a church and a few abandoned houses. The heat is stifling. Fine white dust particles settle on the knees of my fatigue trousers. It's one of those moments where everything quiets for a few seconds and I can clearly hear the chirrup, chirrup, chirrup sound of the crickets and my own heartbeat. Do you know you can tell the temperature in Fahrenheit by counting the number of chirrups in fourteen seconds and adding forty? Why is it these ridiculous facts come to me at times like this? I purposely tap the back of my head on the drystone wall behind me as a punishment and to bring my mind back to focus on the task in hand, namely, to get my unit into some cover.

We've had a panzer tank and about twenty or more German infantry firmly sticking with us all afternoon. To our left, I know there's a small detachment of French under Captain Guerrot, so we have a chance to flank the enemy who's sticking to the trees in the small copse ahead of us and try and make it to the village, probably Franleu, not far from Abbeville, perhaps hole up in the church where we'll be less exposed. If we could join up with the larger French forces in Abbeville, I'm hoping we will stand a chance.

I look down; my left hand is shaking involuntarily. I lean slightly away from Geddes who's sitting next to me; I don't want him thinking I'm losing it.

'You all right, sir?' There's concern and questioning in Geddes' voice.

'Quite all right, Sergeant Major. Ask Nightingale and a couple of the others to set up their Bren guns at the far end of this wall; there's definitely a sniper working from the trees somewhere over there and where there's one there's more. I want them to lay down suppressing fire while we work around that open ground to the right; I think I see some ditches we can use as cover, otherwise we're sitting ducks in the open.'

'Right, sir!' Almost to confirm this, a shot ricochets above our head, dislodging a piece of the wall above our heads. 'He's an accurate bastard, I'll give that to him that, sir.'

With that, Geddes crawls away on his stomach to get Nightingale and the others into position. He's immediately replaced by the youngest in my unit, a very bright lad called White.

'Where do you want us, sir?'

'Just stay put here for now. I've asked Nightingale and a couple of the others to lay down covering fire, while we move around this open ground to get over to that church.'

'Right, sir.'

'The Germans are as reluctant as we are to be caught in open ground, so they'll be keeping their heads down too. Once Nightingale's in position, we're going to move along behind this wall to our right and flank Jerry in the wood over there. Pass the message to the other men that we move on my signal.'

'Yes, sir.'

'Oh, and White, ask Davis to come over. I've got a job for him and that formidable Enfield rifle of his.'

'Right, sir.' He winks at me and crawls off down the line. White's got his head screwed on, so I know he'll pass the messages on correctly. I watch as the men's eyes turn expectantly in my direction. I nod and attempt a reassuring smile, but it probably comes out as a grimace.

Davis moves up and swings his Enfield rifle off his back and begins performing checks on his magazine and moves some spare cartridges into his belt. He's focussed and I'm momentarily envious of his composure.

'Okay, Davis, here's what I want you to do. Set up at that little gap midway up the wall over there. You've likely spotted where that Jerry snipers located?'

'Yes, sir, I believe he's behind one of those trees about midway along the copse.'

'Good lad. I want you to try and take him out before we make our move into the village.'

Davis simply nods, no further questions. He's a crack shot, but the distance must be close to two thousand yards, near to the effective range of the Enfield rifle and the abilities of even a marksman like him. All eyes are on him.

As he settles into his firing position, his eyes flick around, no doubt checking wind direction, assessing its speed. He chambers a round. Crack, more dust from the top of the wall.

'Your time's going to be soon up, mate.' One of the lads behind me being wishful. Another one on my right, O'Callaghan I think, has rosary beads in one hand as he cradles his Sterling submachine gun in the other; salvation and retribution contained within a single person.

Davis is making his shot; he breathes in and out a few times, then in followed by a long out. Total concentration, then, a single shot from his high-powered rifle.

'I got him, sir.' A simple statement, but with huge consequence on our situation; a little morale boost, one less Jerry sniper to contend with. I imagine the distant German soldier, also probably very young, with a surprised look on his face as his breath is knocked out of him; I don't feel any sympathy.

'Good lad, great shooting.' The others in the line smile and nod. He gets a slap in the back from his mates. Time to make our move. I punch my elbow down with five fingers held up; we go in five seconds. Nods all around. I successively count up to five on my fingers, then signalling the men forward, we crawl or stoop our way along behind the wall. As we do so, I can hear small arms fire to our left; Guerrot's got the message. At the same moment, I signal to Geddes to have the boys open up with the Bren guns. A cacophony of gunfire ensues, and all hell breaks loose.

Holding my Stirling submachine slung on its strap I motion the lads to continue crawling along the narrow ditch. I stop and, with a couple of the others, set up covering fire while Nightingale brings up his Bren gun crew. I keep them moving while we continue firing. A couple of Germans fling their arms up in the overacting style you get in boys' playgrounds of the 'bang, bang, you're dead' variety, only with them, they really are dead.

We've almost made it to the comparative safety of the churchyard. A burst of fire with the distinctive sound of German MP40s and heavier machine guns. A cry from behind me. One hundred yards away, behind us, a young lad, probably Carter, has been hit. I push the men on; nothing we can do for him at the moment. I get the unit into the graveyard.

'He's still moving.'

'It's White.'

'I can't leave him, he's from the same village, I know his family.'

'White! Get back here.'

Too late. White is weaving back down towards the

end of the wall where Carter is lying propped on one elbow. Grabbing him by his free arm, he gets Carter on his feet and both of them are doing a kind of three-legged race over to us. Nightingale and the others have opened up with the Brens. White's throat suddenly sprays blood; he's only a few yards from me. I instinctively start to go for them trying to shoot into the trees on my right. I'm punched hard in the midriff; the wind is forced out of me like someone's struck my solar plexus. I drop to the ground completely unable to get up. Heavy gunfire now; Jerry has me in their sights. A rushing sound of feet on grass; it's Geddes. He's come back for me. He turns me on my back, and I make to speak, but no words come out. He shoulders my body like I weigh nothing, and he starts running. The pain is excruciating, and I watch my hands flapping uselessly on his broad back for what seems like minutes, but it is only probably a few seconds. I'm gently lowered in the doorway of the church, sitting propped up while others are trying to get the church doors open. Geddes' concerned face appears in front of me with that of our medical orderly, Jimmy Pile. My head's swimming.

'Its gone through the meat of one of your love handles, sir.'

'I didn't know I had love handles.' I smile. Rumbling begins to emanate from the street behind us, it's the panzers.

'Sir! Two German tanks are approaching the church.' Boom, a whining sound then crump followed by heavy machine gun fire.

'You're not kidding! Mister Geddes, lay some fire down on the men that'll most likely be following the tank.' Another high-pitched whine, crump! Followed by more heavy machine gun fire.

'We're out of ammo, sir.' Nightingale's voice.

'Me too, and me.'

'Well, it was fun while it lasted, Sergeant Major.' We give each other a look.

'I'm not leaving you, sir, if that's what you're thinking.'

'Wouldn't dream of it, Richard.' I use his first name; we may as well drop the formalities if we're about to die. Jimmy's done a good job bandaging my wound, enough for me to get to my feet with Geddes' help and stand unaided. I unholster my Webley revolver and some of the others that still have theirs do the same. We begin emptying them at any targets that present themselves until they're empty, a futile gesture really if truth be known. Click, click. This is it.

A group of German soldiers' approach around the back of the churchyard, but since there's no return fire, they make the obvious conclusion that we're out of bullets.

'British soldiers, lay down your weapons and you will be spared.' A German accent. Holding my service issue white handkerchief (is that why the MOD issue them?) I slowly walk with Geddes and a few of the men to the gate, happy in a way not to stay in the graveyard, quite literally, forever; White and Carter will be though, rest in peace[1].

'Hands where I can see them, Lieutenant.' A German officer wearing the grey uniform and long overcoat of a Wehrmacht captain, holsters his pistol and separates himself from the front of a group of his men and walks nonchalantly towards us, stops a couple of yards away from me. His men begin collecting up the lad's weapons.

'I'll take that, Lieutenant.'

Pointing at my Webley. 'You and your men put up a good fight, but as you can see, further resistance is futile.' He gestures with his right arm at a tank standing opposite. He then salutes. 'Your war is over, Lieutenant.'

'Sammeln sie ihre waffen und papiere. Schnell!' The German captain's men round us up, and, with hands behind our heads, we set off down the street in a column towards who knows what.

---

[1] This vignette is based on a real WWII action in the village of Franleu. Corporal John White and Private Carter are buried in the church cemetery at Franleu. Their graves are tended to this day by local people on behalf of the Commonwealth War Graves Commission.

Fred, Tuesday, June 4th, 1940, Abbeville road near the Somme River

Dawn is breaking. The sun, like a sullen red eye, appears over the horizon spreading a liquid golden light under a huge bank of cloud hanging over the flat plains of Northern France. In a distant time before the war, I'd have said it was beautiful. Whilst we're not penned behind razor wire, we're captives, since, without weapons or the means to escape, we're de facto prisoners of the Third Reich. As we're not locked in a cell just yet, we had the 'pleasure' of spending a night under the stars in a ditch at the side of the Abbeville Road.

The military machine that is Nazi Germany rises early. It's five a.m. and tanks, military trucks, half-tracked armoured personnel carriers and motorbikes are already creating a steady flow of traffic heading to and from the coast. A truck full of enlisted German Army men passes and several take the opportunity of spitting and jeering at us. By and large, the Wehrmacht officers have been fairly professional, sticking to the 'rules' so to speak, but out of their sight, their men are abusive and savagely aggressive.

Yesterday, after our surrender, we had a couple of

heated encounters, one of which resulted in Corporal Davis being struck in the face with a rifle butt. I thought for a moment he'd be shot, but I'd placed myself in front of him and demanded to see their commanding officer. Fortunately, the German soldiers backed down. These incidents, and separation from other British forces, are bound to be sapping the men's morale.

Another wider concern for the ongoing war effort back at home is the amount of British Army equipment we've seen abandoned; the scale is truly staggering. Such losses must surely be cripplingly expensive to replace even if we get the chance to do so before Hitler gives the order to invade. Ironically, it turns out we've been sheltering not far from an abandoned Bedford truck, actually a butcher's van painted green, one of the hundreds commandeered by the army as transports for the expeditionary force.

Compared with our motley collection of ancient rifles and other equipment that wouldn't be out of place in a museum, the sheer quantity and variety of armament and transportation the Germans have is incredible to behold. I never signed up to our home-grown propaganda that suggested the German military machine paraded by Hitler at rallies was largely fake; here, however, is the unalloyed truth passing by in front of our eyes.

'Let me take a look at that wound, sir.' Jimmy Pile gently raises up my tunic. 'It looks like the wound's stopped bleeding, but you'll need to take it easy to avoid it opening up again. I can give you some morphine for the pain.'

'You did a bloody good job binding me up, I really appreciate it.' I wink at Jimmy and get a smile out of him. 'But I'll pass on the morphine; we're going to need to keep that back for a more serious casualty.'

While we've been speaking, a group of young soldiers have stopped in front of us. They're wearing camouflaged battledress and the distinctive Totenkopf (skull and crossbones) cap badge of the Waffen-SS, the militarised arm of Hitler's self-styled squad of bullyboys.

'Auf deinen füßen, beweg dich!' The lead man, who is shouting loudly, makes his point by kicking my boot. Geddes, who's next to me, rises quickly with his fists balled. The soldiers shift the muzzles of their machine guns to point at his chest, I can hear the safeties clicking off. 'Wir haben den befehl, jeden zu erschießen, der widerstand leistet. Bewegung! schnell!'

'I'll thank you for some assistance, Sergeant Major.'

'Oh sorry, sir, quite forgot.' Geddes hitches me onto my feet.

'Gehen sie weiter auf diese weise.' The German soldier indicates towards Abbeville, 'und fahren Sie nach Abbeville, wo sie mehr von ihren erbärmlichen Britischen soldaten treffen werden.' the last few words are spat out, so clearly not complementary.

'Sir, he's telling us he has orders to shoot anyone

who resists and that we need to walk towards Abbeville to join other prisoners.' Prisoners of war, POW, it's hard to accept that our war service has ended when it'd only just started; however, Nightingale's knowledge of German and French is going to be useful.

As we walk in the direction of Abbeville, I can see a group of Junkers 88s circling the town like huge, satiated, black vultures. As we watch, clutches of bombs drop out from their bellies. Clearly, the French forces are still putting up some resistance. Surely the poor blighters can't hold out much longer. As we near the Somme River, we spot a group of half a dozen corpses by the side of the road. A couple of carrion crows have landed nearby, and they reluctantly flap into the air as we approach. A young British soldier, lying further away from his comrades, is still alive. Pile and O'Callaghan check his wounds. He has a huge patch of gore on his midriff. On closer inspection, I can see that some of his intestines have spilled out into the inside of his tunic.

'What regiment are you with, lad?' O'Callaghan stoops low to hear the soldier's reply.

'The 2/5th Battalion, Queen's. Christ it hurts! Am I going to die? Please do something, please!' His staring eyes and anguish are heart rending. Some of my lads look away, no doubt thinking his fate could all too easily be theirs.

'We've got you, lad.' Out of sight of the young soldier, Pile turns to me and shakes his head. 'I'm going to give him something for the pain.' I nod, but I know it's futile, at the same time; we can't just leave him like this. Pile gives him a double dose of morphine and the anguish drains from lad's-stricken face. He must be only seventeen or eighteen; I feel a surge of disgust for the army recruiters coaxing lads in their teens to sign up, giving them rifles and then sending them off to war with just ten weeks basic training under their belts.

The men sit nearby, and a couple of the lucky ones that still have them, offer cigarettes around. Nobody comments on the risk we're taking by stopping. Pile feels the lad's neck.

'He's gone, sir.' O'Callaghan, who's been holding the young soldier's shoulder to comfort him, closes the lad's eyes with the palm of his hand and crosses himself.

'In the name of the Father, and of the Son and the Holy Ghost. Rest in peace. Amen.' Some of the more religious of the men cross themselves and murmur in unison with O'Callaghan. Leaving his body along with those of his fallen comrades to the carrion crows makes my stomach turn, but we've no choice if we ourselves are not to become a target of roaming German patrols.

We pass other corpses, mostly French, discarded at the side of the road like so much human carrion. Approaching Abbeville, we join a group of weary British soldiers at a hastily constructed checkpoint at the Somme Bridge. Despite the circumstances, we're happy to see them.

'What regiment?' The sergeant salutes.

'Twenty-fifth Infantry, the Northumbrians. We were trying to make it to the coast, but not a chance with the Second Panzer Division blowing everything to kingdom come. We got cut off and ran out of ammo. The Highland Regiments have come off worst; I heard they were blasted to pieces by tank and artillery fire yesterday. We think the French have chucked it in. Nothing we could do. Earlier today, we saw a large group of French rounded up, including their captain, and simply machine-gunned, anyone still moving was bayoneted. So much for the Geneva bloody Convention!' The sergeant's face shows the strain he's under keeping it together for the sake of the others in his unit, it turns out their captain was summarily executed in front of them as an example.

'You should ditch that pip on your shoulder, sir; it could get you killed.' Geddes is probably right, but I'm not going to give it up. If I'm going to die, I'd rather do it on my own terms.

'I'm going to chance it. There's low enough morale as it is without me mistreating my uniform.' We both laugh uncontrollably at this for some strange reason. After providing our name, rank and serial number to the guards standing in a gap between a row of army trucks, we cross the Somme River in the gathering dusk and join a large group of other prisoners who have been penned in a makeshift barbed wire corral in what appears to be the grounds of a rowing club. There's no food, water or shelter for the five hundred or so men standing there or wandering around and stamping their feet. Others have lost their battle with exhaustion and are lying on the bare ground sleeping.

We bump into Captain Guerrot whose unit fought with us yesterday in Franleu. He's dishevelled, his expression and features are those of someone who's been completely beaten. I salute and then shake his hand. Seeing that I might need his services, Nightingale appears at my shoulder.

'Bonsoir, Lieutenant. Nous nous retrouvons dans les circonstances les moins heureuses. Je crains que la guerre soit finie pour la France.'

'I think I've got that; the French have capitulated, yes?'

Nightingale nods. 'Near enough, sir.'

'Ask him what happened to his unit.'

'Capitaine, qu'est-il arrivé à votre compagnie?' At first, I think he's not understood, but then I realise that he's struggling with his emotions.

'Je suis allé au combat ce matin avec quatre-vingts hommes, il ne reste que cinq personnes, une vingtaine environ sont morts au combat et le reste a été exécuté devant mon visage.'

'He says that what remained of his unit, some fifty men, have been executed in front of him by the Nazis.' As I look into Guerrot's eyes, I know there's nothing I can say in reply. Pain, anguish and shame sweep across his face in a maelstrom of competing emotions.

Summoning my schoolboy French, all I can think

of to say is, 'Je suis vraiment désolé pour vos hommes, Capitaine,' which seems somewhat trite and inadequate in the circumstances. So, I offer the hope that the perpetrators will be punished for their crimes. 'Les Nazis vont payer pour ce qu'ils ont fait,' to which the captain simply shakes his head and walks away into the gathering gloom.

George, Monday June 3rd, 1940
Dover Docks

To describe our train carriage as full would be an understatement. It's beyond full; it's a tin of sardines and we're the sardines. Our crafty plan to stay with our cousins in Ramsgate and get the train to Dover has backfired somewhat, since it seems that everyone else has had the same idea.

Mother is in a buoyant mood; however, I've seen this before in the past few weeks. As it's become increasingly clear that all was not going well for our boys over in France, the mood in the house has been up and down like a rollercoaster. Mother's been champing at the bit to get down to Dover ever since the evacuation from France started, but my father argued that we'd be simply adding to the chaos by actually going to Dover. But I understand Mother's need to be doing something, anything, even if it's futile, so here we are!

'George, pass me your cup. I'll pour you what's left from the Thermos, it can't be long before we arrive at Dover.'

'You have the rest, Mother. If we try anything more complicated, likely we'll just end up pouring tea on our neighbour,' I reply, nodding at the moustached chap in the rather dapper bowler hat jammed against my mother's opposite shoulder. The fact is, I've been dreading making this trip as it's only ever likely to confirm one thing: Freddy's not coming home.

We've slowed to a jolting, squealing stop at Dover Marine Station. A vast sea of heads and shoulders pass by our window dappled by shafts of bright sunlight that stream through the station roof. It'd be a glorious day for a trip to the beach, arm-in-arm as we used to do on the white sands at Whitley Bay, with cake and a cuppa at the pier. But we're not. Instead, we're fighting our way through a thronging crowd to wait for Fred to be disgorged unscathed from the belly of some huge ship, like Jonah from the Whale; it seems like a far-fetched fantasy.

We've had no word from Freddy for weeks and with the MOD keeping tight-lipped on the deployment and fortunes of the BEF, there's been little news. But with newspaper reports of the German forces overrunning France and Belgium pushing all before them, it's been a foregone conclusion for a while. Well, the cat's out of the bag now! Daily newspaper reports and the fact that there's been a plea from the Admiralty for anything that floats and anyone who sails to get over to Dunkirk to bail out our forces is a pretty good indication that the show's over. Just this morning I read in the *Newcastle Journal* that the evacuation is being called the Dunkirk Miracle! Surely only we British can talk about abject defeat as being something miraculous!

As we push through the crowds of soldiers, we look out for the uniform and cap badges of Freddy's regiment, the Royal Northumberland Fusiliers. Moving out of the station building and onto the quay, crowds and little knots of soldiers emerge from a destroyer and a large merchant navy vessel tied up at the quay. British soldiers with caps and berets, French and Belgian solders in their distinctive tin helmets jostle by us. A stretcher party passes with its occupant's head cocooned in filthy bloodstained bandages. Other walking wounded, the stragglers, creep past; young men converted into doddery geriatrics, all youth sucked out of them by the war. It feels like these are the last of our lads that'll get out before the door to freedom finally slams shut.

My father spoke about the haunted stare you'd see on the faces of soldiers coming back from the front; their body is here and now, but their mind still lingers on scenes from the trenches, terrible scenes that no one should have to endure. But here we are, doing the same again just over twenty or so years later. In my mind, I try to imagine what it would be like to be trapped on a beach with little, or no, cover, nowhere to escape to but the rolling breakers where there could only be the solace of giving yourself up to a watery grave. Perhaps it would be better to drown than face the agony metered out by the shrapnel from artillery shells and heavy machine guns.

Beaches have always been friendly places,

somewhere to be with your family for a Sunday stroll, but the war has turned them into merciless killing fields. I try to picture Freddy on a beach with his men. I can feel his presence, his smile; I suddenly know he's still with us somewhere out there over the grey sea and feel some inward measure of solace. Mother, however, is becoming increasingly distraught, trying to rush ahead in a vain attempt to see if Freddy is among any of the bedraggled groups of men, surely now the last remaining flotsam and jetsam of our crushed and defeated army.

'I can't see him anywhere. We were told that there wouldn't be any more boats coming in from France. God, George, do you think Freddy's been left over there?'

I catch my mother's arm as her legs seem to finally give way under her and she crashes to the ground in a deflated heap. A group of lads come rushing over to help me get her back up onto her feet, to comfort her.

'My son, I just want to find my son!' Mother's nervous energy of the last few hours has finally collapsed into a pit of despair; I knew it would be futile to come here, but I couldn't let her do it on her own and she was determined. Her eyes are wide; her delicate features are racked with anguish and her green eyes are red and bloodshot. Huge, visceral sobs of grief and loss rack my poor mother's body stinging my own heart so it feels like it would break as well.

The group of lads are strongly affected by my

mother's plight and stay with her, trying to comfort her with well-meaning platitudes and reassurances. Perhaps they see the love, pain and worry that their own mothers must have gone through and may still be going through. It's as though her grief has triggered emotions that they've been holding back for days and weeks, finally opening the dam, the deep well of despair, or perhaps even shame. I can see a couple of them are holding back their own tears.

'What regiment is he with?' One of the lads, who turns out to be a captain, is addressing me. I make to salute but realise I'm not in uniform.

'Apologies, Captain.'

'No need for formalities here on a day like today, lad. He's a second lieutenant with the Royal Northumberland Fusiliers.' The captain ponders this for a while, like he's scanning through a checklist he's memorised in his head and finally continues. 'I think a fair chunk of them were cut off in Calais. The word is the town was surrounded by the Tenth Panzer Division during an engagement that tied up the enemy. Their action likely saved thousands of lives at Dunkirk; they're heroes every one of them!' The captain's own voice breaking on these last words. Regaining his composure, he continues. 'It's likely your brother is mixed up with the Thirtieth Infantry and the Third Royal Tank Regiment, a fair few French and a group of our stragglers from other regiments including the Northumbrians. My guess is they'll have been forced to surrender; it'd be the only card left for them to play. I'm sorry, lad. My advice is to get your mother back home and wait for further news of your brother. I'm afraid It's going to take weeks to sort out who's missing and where. It's a total bloody mess!'

Fred, Monday June 10th, 1940, village of Loivre just outside Reims

'Raus! Raus! Beweg dich!' Several young Wehrmacht soldiers are marching around what might euphemistically be called our camp, although it can more accurately be described as where we dropped to the ground exhausted last night. I make the distinction between Wehrmacht[2] and Waffen SS[3] since the latter have been consistently ill-disciplined and vicious in the treatment they've metered out and have caused me the most concern for the safety of my men. All I can think is that the SS, brainwashed by Nazi Party propaganda, are part of a self-selected group of the weak-minded that have formed around Hitler's rhetoric of hate and scapegoat-ism.

Every day is the same, waking from sleeping on bare ground, we walk in the blazing sun and driving rain for up to forty miles. At least the exhaustion at the end of the day gives us sleep. Our forced march and lack of food is beginning to take its toll on our health. Every

---

[2] Wehrmacht: the regular German Army.

[3] Waffen SS: the militarised branch of the Nazi Party's Schutzstaffel (SS) paramilitary organisation.

man in the group of fifty or so Northumbrians and a mix of men from various Highland regiments that we've stuck with over the last week, are hungry and dehydrated, but the worst of it is lack of sleep. We've also had a couple of dangerous run-ins with groups of roving SS soldiers; I need to watch Geddes and a few of the younger men like Davis as they've got a tendency to lose their cool.

Although our fifty are marching with a large group of mostly French and Belgians, I've noticed that British soldiers appear to be on the receiving end of rougher treatment from our captors. Each day we survive is a blessing, but my heart sinks every time we encounter a group of screaming SS thugs.

My worries are momentarily pushed aside by the welcome approach of our medical orderly.

'Hello, Jimmy! Doing your rounds of us sick old men!' Jimmy feigns amusement, but his face is a picture of concern and worry.

'Your wound looks like it's become badly infected. All my wound dressings and other supplies have been confiscated so all I've got is some strips of clothing that I've boiled and dried, but, quite frankly, everything is filthy.' Jimmy dips in his pocket and brings out what looks like some charcoal from the fire we were able to light last night. I watch while he grinds it and mixes it with some water from his drinking bottle into a paste.

'Don't look at me so strangely, sir! This is a makeshift poultice to try and draw out some that infection.'

'You are truly a genius of improvisation, Doc!' I wince as Jimmy carefully applies the charcoal paste to my wound and covers it with a boiled rag.

'You need to leave that on there for half an hour, or so, until its done its work. Then I'll clean and re-dress it. I'm going to try and reapply the poultice over the next few days and see if we can get that wound to close. I've another concern.' Jimmy looks me in the eye, and I know what it's about. 'It's Corporal Wishart. He's been behaving very irrationally; his angry outbursts are a worry as they're attracting the German's attention.'

'I know, I've had a word, but I don't think I'm getting through to him.'

Jimmy continues, 'I also caught him cutting his wrists with a sharp stone the other day.'

'Point duly taken. I'll have a chat with him today. It's not helped by the fact that his commanding officer's dead and that he's being ignored by lads in his own regiment.'

Jimmy takes his leave to finish his rounds by checking a few of the lads' feet. Some have lost their boots altogether and have resorted to tying rags to their feet; needless to say, they're covered in sores.

Rain clouds are gathering overhead, and it looks like another day of thunderstorms lies ahead. Thanks to road signs, many of which have been left in place, I know that we're outside the village of Loivre on the Marne Canal, which means we're not far from Reims, a place where we fought only a few weeks ago, mounting a rearguard action in the face of superior German armour.

At the side of the road, we pass three makeshift wooden crosses decorated with daisy chains of the sort a young girl might make. I imagine a kindly French farmer and his wife digging the graves for these men. Like the food that's sometimes hastily forced into our hands as we pass through a village or is left on a wall by the roadside, these acts of compassion, often undertaken at great personal risk, are reminders of basic human kindness that acts like nourishment for our souls.

The epitaph on the grave markers is hastily painted in French. 'Soldat Britannique inconnu, repose en paix.' Rest in peace, amen to that. My mind travels back to scenes of mechanised slaughter that wouldn't be out of place in a Faustian nightmare. No quarter was given by the SS Panzer divisions as retreating men were machine-gunned and dropped in their hundreds, so their corpses littered a countryside still haunted by the men killed on these same fields in the last war.

I'm beginning to wonder whether, like Faust, the whole German nation has made an unholy pact with the devil, when a plume of dust kicked up by a speeding vehicle as it veers onto the sandy verge to avoid a group of POWs ahead of us draws my attention back to the road. Stopping near to where we've momentarily paused in the already stifling heat, an officer steps out of the gleaming staff car he's driving. As he approaches,

I can see he's wearing the black uniform and insignia of a Waffen SS colonel. As his eyes travel over us, I notice a vicious scar on his jaw and lower portion of his face and an Iron Cross at his throat.

Our eyes meet, and like a wolf that's found its mark. The colonel walks briskly towards me. Deciding to be as courteous as possible, I salute as he stops in front of me. 'Guten morgen, Herr Oberst.' However, the German officers not impressed.

'Das ist Obersturmführer für sie, Leutnant, und ich habe keine lust auf höflichkeiten!'

Nightingale, responding to the commotion, walks over to offer his help. 'He's a lieutenant, Colonel, not a colonel, sir.'

I'm beginning to see that my attempt to mollify the situation may have backfired. 'Bring deine männer in den truck da drüben, ich habe etwas arbeit für sie zu erledigen.' With that, several German soldiers begin rounding up a group of us and herd us over to a truck standing nearby.

'He's saying he has some work for us, sir.' Nightingale is by my side as I painfully try and stay ahead of the rifle butts being thrust in our direction. I have a nasty feeling in my gut about the developing situation; it seems all too similar to rumours we've heard of the atrocities being committed by a German army that seems drunk on victory and the power to decide our fate.

About ten of us are forced into the truck and we

follow the colonel's staff car for a few minutes before stopping by a bridge over the Marne canal. Climbing out of the truck, we're greeted by the stomach-churning stench of death and the hum of flies. A group of twenty or so dead German soldiers are lying in a field. Nearby, the bloated bodies of British and French soldiers are piled up and partially submerged in a stagnant pool created by a bend in the canal. A couple of German soldiers start passing around shovels, so it's clear that we're expected to form a burial detail. Being conscripted into forced labour could see us being worked into the ground so I resolve to make a stand, but I know it's a risky strategy. Looking around at the men, I can see that nobody's rushing to start digging.

'Nightingale, please translate for me, "You are aware, Colonel, that the Geneva Convention is very clear that prisoners of war should not be forced to work."'

The German officer angrily replies, 'Dann kann ich sehen, dass Sie eine Überredung brauchen, Lieutenant!'

'He's saying something about persuasion…' But before he can finish his translation, our guards suddenly grab hold of Nightingale and the colonel takes out his service pistol.

'No, Colonel, please!' I'm immediately restrained.

The German officer replies in English. 'Then who is it to be, Lieutenant?'

'I'm the senior officer here; it's my responsibility.'

'No, Lieutenant, it was your mistake to question my

orders. Your punishment is to watch one of your men pay the price for your insolence.'

At that moment, O'Callaghan steps forward and stands resolute in front of Nightingale. The colonel is surprised but accepts O'Callaghan's offer of his life instead of that of the younger man.

'I admire your bravery, taking your comrade's place for an execution.' However, to show that he still maintains the initiative, the colonel makes the man he has condemned wait while he has his men assemble with their rifles. O'Callaghan, standing erect and steady awaiting his fate, defiantly meets the German officer's gaze and shows no fear. Out of the corner of my eye, I can see some of the men holding their heads in the extremis of despair. I can't believe this is happening, but I'm restrained by two German troopers and my weakened body is no match for them.

'Colonel, please, I beg you, don't do this! Your actions are not worthy of the German Army or the Knight's Cross of the Iron Cross you're wearing!'

My words fall on deaf ears and, in the intervening silence, I can hear O'Callaghan reciting the Catholic devotional prayer.

'Hail Mary full of grace, the Lord is with thee; blessed art thou amongst woman, and blessed is the fruit of thy womb, Lord Jesus Christ.'

Crack, crack, two shots ring out and O'Callaghan slumps forward. The bullets hitting O'Callaghan's body feel like they've pierced my own flesh and my legs give way from under me. I'm momentarily paralysed by a tidal wave of despair and anguish. I instantly worry about appearing weak in front of the men, but my body fails me and there's nothing I can do.

Job done, the firing squad begin to walk away, but I can clearly hear O'Callaghan's laboured breathing in the deathly silence after the rifle shots. Pile must've heard it too because he rushes over to where O'Callaghan is lying. Crack. Another shot, blood spurts from Pile's head and he falls next to O'Callaghan. As I turn to find out where the shot came from, I see the colonel holstering his pistol.

'Now do you understand the futility of resistance, Lieutenant?'

'The men you've murdered are a Catholic lay preacher and a doctor in the Royal Medical Corps who was clearly wearing the armband of the Red Cross. Your action is cowardly, in violation of all human decency and of the Geneva Convention. I swear to God that, if I ever make it through this war, I will make it my mission in life to ensure that you answer for these murders you've committed here today, Colonel.'

With a snort of derision, the German officer makes to walk over to his staff car. Turning as he does so, the colonel smirks, 'it may have escaped your attention, Lieutenant, your army is beaten and has fled back to England. You, however, are a prisoner of the Reich and, with your impudence, I should be very surprised if you make it through the war.'

Fred, Tuesday June 18th, 1940, Trier, West Germany

Light shimmers and light and dark patches dance across my closed eyelids. The vapid tendrils of a waking dream plays in my mind's eye and I glance across at the open door of the kitchen in my parents' house in Richmond that leads out to the garden beyond. Summer sounds enter the room through the door; children laughing, swallows chattering and doves cooing.

This vision of domestic paradise is slowly displaced, and another image emerges, stirred by the slow, rhythmical echo of a train's wheels passing over steel rails; a languid chunk-chunk, chunk-chunk. My head nods forward as brakes hiss. Surfacing from exhausted slumber, the nightmares of my real memories flood back and, staring around the gloomy half-light of the cattle truck, I nod to my companions who are tightly pressing against my shoulders and knees that are drawn close to my chest.

'Morning, gents. I must've dropped off.'

'I swear you'd fall asleep pegged on a clothesline, sir!'

Still in dreamlike state part-way between sleep and wakefulness, Geddes' face swims in front of me, a hard, thin smile plays around the corners of his mouth that's now half-buried in the straggly beard forming around his chin. I guess I too must be pretty filthy and unkempt, but who's caring about appearances now? I answer, trying to keep the witty repartee going. My heart isn't in it, but we must keep up appearances in front of the men.

'Well, Sergeant Major, I don't know what to say about those chin whiskers, but I wouldn't let Colonel Williams see it.'

Geddes forces a chuckle, then turns his head so that the other men, just shadows sitting or lying in a moribund mass of humanity in the overcrowded conditions our lives had become in the last few days, and says, 'well, we'll be seeing about that! As soon as we get to where we're going, I'm will expect every man has a shave. I want to show Jerry that we're still in business and still a fighting force of British soldiers!'

No response. The men have become moribund and morose. Morale is at rock bottom as everyone digs deep into their mental and physical reserves to survive. Although we have no idea where we are or what time it is, I've counted three nights and four days of achingly slow progress since we were crammed into our carriage at a freight siding near Reims station. We've had no food or water since starting our train journey, so for all of us, myself included, these two vital human needs are paramount in our minds and fill every waking hour.

Another vital need is to dispose our body waste. Out of the 'kindness' of their hearts, our captors provided us, possibly eighty or more men in our carriage, with a single steel bucket that's been used by those lucky enough to be within reach of it. The rest of us have to make do with disposing of urine and faeces by various means, all foul, by manually capturing our liquid or solid waste and disposing of it out of the carriage in the best way we can either by emptying our cupped hands through the vent that runs around the top of the carriage, or by fortuitous gaps in the rotten floorboards. The stinking residue on our hands is then wiped on our clothes and adds to our generally reeking condition.

Recently, body lice have entered all our lives with a vengeance. The heat and humidity of the carriage and our close proximity to each other has meant that this new menace has spread around the men like wildfire. In between each man's desperate shifting to maintain circulation in aching limbs, we're all continually scratching our skin; some have scratched raw and bleeding patches that further adds to the misery. I'd never really appreciated what the term 'lousy' means in the literal use of the word, but I do now. In our already weakened state, the toxin released into our bodies by the combined feeding of thousands of our tiny tormentors exacerbates our general torpor.

By the way that the train is turning and jolting over an increased number of points, I'm fairly sure that we're coming into a major city station. Hissing brakes and further jolting confirms this. Grinding finally to a juddering halt, steel bolts are withdrawn, and the door of our carriage slides open. Harsh white light streams in and we're all momentarily blinded.

'Raus! Raus! Beweg dich!' The familiar shouts of our German captors bring everyone in the carriage slowly to their feet. For many, the jump down from our cattle truck is too much and, coaxed and pushed from behind, some men simply fall out and onto the ground. Taking a more cautious approach, I slide myself along the floor and drop shakily to the ground.

My infected wound has stabilised due to Jimmy and my continued use of the charcoal poultice, but it still gives me excruciating pain when I move. To my shame, I'm physically incapable of assisting less fortunate men lying on the ground who are struck by rifle butts, nor am I mentally capable of grieving for our murdered comrades. As a survival mechanism, the regret, shame and horror of their fate and the fates of the men in my unit who fell in battle over the past weeks have been hermetically sealed and lie dormant in my mind. At least the pain and suffering is over for Jimmy and O'Callaghan. Their courage and sacrifice will not be forgotten or go unpunished. I'm going to make sure of that if it's the last thing I do. However, to achieve justice for them, I know that at some point, if I survive the war, there will be a reckoning in which I'll need to, once again, relive these days of misery and despair if I'm ever going to find a resolution.

In contrast to my self-pitying state of mind, Geddes

is being proactive, collecting together what remains of our unit that has managed to keep together, just Nightingale, Allen and Davis who say little, but I know are reaching the limits of their endurance; the others are scattered to the wind. The fact that we remain together is the one positive aspect of our current situation and I hold onto it.

It looks like we've arrived at a separate freight platform away from the main station buildings. A platform sign reads, 'Trier Hauptbahnhof'. Passengers, smartly dressed men, women and children can be seen going about their daily routines, taking journeys to work, or to see friends and family. The image of a workaday environment is deeply unsettling, and our sudden appearance brings stares of revulsion and general horror and loathing as we're escorted out of the station building by our guards.

'Well, it looks like we're going to be paraded in public for all to see.' Geddes looks pensive, as well he might be. In answer to Geddes, I voice aloud my concern to those around me.

'I have a bad feeling about this, lads, so keep close and try not to fall behind.' But the fact is, we're a shambling rabble that's barely able to walk. However, I can see that Geddes is positioning himself at the front of our group of forty or so men. His voice still has the sergeant major's strength and authority despite what he must be feeling.

'Jerry thinks he can humiliate us by parading us in

front of the public, but we're better than that, better than them. We're the fighting force that held the line and fought to the last bullet and the last man. Just remember that. Jerry thinks we're beaten, but we know that Britain is fighting on and so shall we! So, get fell in and pick up that step and march like the soldiers we are with shoulders back and heads held high. Left, left, left-right-left.'

All Geddes needs is his sergeant major's pace stick! Those that can fall into step, myself included, but the effort is considerable in our weakened state. We're attracting quite a crowd of onlookers, mostly older men and women and young women with families. Red flags carrying a white cross and Swastika flutter from flagpoles fixed to some of the taller buildings like the bunting you see in village fairs back in England. The flags are a forceful embodiment of our captor's triumph and the ascendency of the Third Reich. It makes my heart sink further to see them fluttering there and to imagine Hitler and his band of cronies strutting like peacocks.

If my memory of schoolboy history serves, Trier was a place of some considerable importance in the Roman Empire and I imagine that other crushed and defeated armies have shuffled through these same streets in front of the baying Roman mob. As if to reinforce this, we pass under an ancient pair of Romanesque arches and encounter a large group of Hitler Youth who've turned out in force to taunt us, no doubt shouting slogans they've been taught.

These adolescent boys clad in their brown uniforms, the antithesis of our friendly English Boy Scouts, shout loudly and try to kick our ankles and lash out at us with sticks. The men in front keep their eyes ahead and don't give any sign of acknowledgement to this goading. The reaction of the Hitler Youth is expected, but it's the reaction of the general public that's the most disturbing. As we pass a group of women, young and old, they throw rocks, pieces of paving slab, rotten fruit and vegetables. This is interspersed with spittle and more jeering and insults. The vehemence is savage and frenzied, the people closest to us scream into our faces at the top of their voices. Fortunately, our journey through the town is short and I can see from the street signs that we're approaching Trier Südbahnhof. I'm guessing that we could've just disembarked at Trier South Station, but why do that and miss a chance to further humiliate us?

As we drop out of sight of the main street, we give in to our aching legs and the sheer fatigue of walking and revert back to shambling as we approach what appears to be the coal yards at the back of the station. The light is fading as we're directed through a pair of huge warehouse doors. The dank smell of coal and mouldering wood fills my nostrils. The guards leave us a small pile of bread loaves on the coal-strewn floor and a few buckets of water.

'Well, I don't think much of the room service in this

hotel!' I turn and meet the gaze and smiling face of what might, a few weeks ago, have been a well-turned-out officer in his mid-thirties with a moustache that's quickly disappearing into the kind of unkempt beard we all now have.

I salute. 'Good evening, Major…?'

In answer to the upward intonation in my voice, he continues, 'Higgins, Jack Higgins of the Welsh Guards.' Higgins holds out his hand and shakes mine.

'Let me introduce Sergeant Major Geddes.' Geddes salutes and nods in his direction.

'Good evening, Sergeant Major. Were you the sergeant major that got us all marching in step earlier on?'

Geddes smiles. 'Yes, sir.'

'Jolly well done! We've got to show Jerry that he may have won a battle, but he's a long way off winning the war! We've heard along the way from Belgian and Dutch civilians that Britain's still very much in the game and more than three hundred thousand lads made it out of Dunkirk. Churchill's calling it a triumph.' Raising his voice so a wider audience can hear, 'That triumph is down to all of you men standing here. Your courage made it possible by diverting Jerry away from Dunkirk. You made Churchill's triumph possible. Take strength from it and give yourselves a pat on the back! You're all a credit to our country and to the British Army!'

Higgins' warmth and humour acts as a balm, and I

can see a few of the lads with tears in their eyes smiling in our direction. I'm, once again, amazed at the power of the human spirit.

Fred, Friday 21st June 1940, Eichstätt, Bavaria

'Pack up your troubles in your old kitbag, Tommy officers, we have got a nice warm prison waiting for you.' The speaker, a smiling Wehrmacht corporal chuckles at his own joke. We've disembarked from our cramped cattle truck into yet another freight siding and are standing in an amorphous group of several hundred men outside a huge coal shed.

A more officious captain shouts to be heard over the general murmuring and hubbub. 'Unteroffizer und Offizierlager, move to the right, all other ranks stay where you are! Move! Bewegung! Schnell!'

The familiar rifle butts are being deployed. I'm sure if they had cattle prods, they would be using those with the same enthusiasm. I hang back with the remaining lads in my unit, Nightingale, Allen and Davis. It looks like Geddes and I will be staying together, at least for the time being. I have to admit that I'm mightily relieved to have his company. We exchange strained smiles and nods, but I get the impression that physical exhaustion, lack of sleep and food has reduced both myself and the men almost to the level of wild animals, capable of thinking only about the next meal or sip of water or a place to lie down and sleep.

Digging deep and working from a small part of me that clings onto, what? Dignity? The fact that we're soldiers in a beaten army, but soldiers, nevertheless. I manage, 'It's been a privilege serving with you. Things haven't gone the way we'd hoped but we know that Britain is fighting on and the war must eventually end. I wish you luck and, God willing, we'll all meet again after the war.'

I look around their faces and salute them, receiving the same in reply. Allen looks to be close to tears but is trying to hide it. Nightingale and Davis are composed, their natural introversion making them seem almost feral.

'We'll be fine, sir,' and with that, Davis salutes again and moves with the other two back into the main crowd of men who are pushed and shoved by several troopers back onto the carriages that we've just got out of. Turning our backs on them for, possibly the last time, we march around two huge heaps of coal, with opposed vast spreading tails.

As I see the abundance of such a vital fuel piled high and in German hands, I'm reminded again about Britons fighting for survival, their shipping under attack and the baying wolves of Nazi Germany standing on the shores of France staring with covetous eyes over the Channel and sizing up their next prize.

We're marched out of the train, yards along a service road, where I can see a few army transport trucks parked up ahead. I'm thankful that we're not be going to be forced to march through Eichstätt; our walk of shame through Trier is all too fresh in my mind and I wouldn't wish to repeat the experience. Closed in the dark of a canvas-covered truck, we're unable to see anything of our surroundings; however, we have the luxury of being able to sit down on a bench.

'Did anyone get a look at where we are?' My question is thrown out into the gloomy interior with little hope of reply.

'I saw the station name we're in Eichstätt. It's in Bavaria; I was actually near here at a jamboree as a leader of a group of Boy Scouts in 1936. We had an exchange camp with a troop of Hitler Youth. Hard to believe now when you think about it. Ribbentrop, the German Ambassador was very keen on making closer ties with Baden-Powell before the war.'

The speaker has a pleasant Scottish burr, and his words are full of irony. I'm tapped vigorously on the shoulder.

'Ian Cockburn, Captain, fourth Battalion Seaforth Highlanders; just call me Hobbers, everyone else does.'

There's a chuckle, so obviously the captain is with a few of his regiment. 'Fred Whitton, Second Lieutenant and Warrant Officer Richard Geddes, Royal Northumberland Fusiliers; Freddy to most people.'

'And I'm mostly known as Gedge,' Geddes chimes in. 'Good to meet you, Gents.' I like Cockburn's informal manner and mark him, like Jack Higgins, as someone I'd like to get to know better.

Our somnolent passage over large ruts, suggesting that we're being driven along a rough track rather than a road, soon has me nodding off, but Cockburn has placed himself beside me.

'So, what's your story, Freddy, how were you picked up?'

'We ran out of ammo outside a small village near Abbeville. We were flanking a group of about twenty Jerries with a French unit under a Captain Guerrot. We'd lost a couple of lads that day to a sniper, but we'd reached some cover in a churchyard; that's when two panzer tanks turned up. That, and the fact we'd run out of ammo, was it for us. We kept shooting until our guns were empty and then showed the white flag. We expected the worst, but the Wehrmacht captain we surrendered to was professional and did the right thing.'

'Did you witness any POW executions? It's become a grim pattern I'm afraid. I'm compiling an official report on responsible Jerry officers in the event that they'll be held accountable after the war. You may not have heard, but we've had reports that ninety, or so, men of the 2nd Battalion of the Royal Norfolk's were murdered on the orders of an SS officer at a farm near the village of Lestrem[4], a fair bit north of where you

---

[4] The murder of more than ninety captured soldiers of the Royal Norfolk Regiment at Le Paradis farm near the French village of Lestrem was one of several atrocities carried out

were captured.'

Pausing and letting this piece of information sink in for a moment, I nodded. 'Yes, two of my men were murdered in cold blood. One, Private O'Callaghan, under the direct orders of a Waffen SS colonel with a severe scar on his lower jaw and the other, RAMC Pile, was shot dead at the hands of the same officer. I want to put it on record that both of the men that died showed exemplary courage in the face of the enemy that warrants the highest award for bravery.'

Cockburn nods and makes notes in a little leather-bound diary he's carrying. 'O'Callaghan took the place of a young soldier randomly chosen for execution by the colonel after my refusal to allow the men under my command to assist the enemy by burying German casualties. RAMC Pile was shot whilst going to provide medical aid to O'Callaghan.'

Describing the incident to someone else for the first time, causes my emotions to almost overwhelm me yet again.

'I'm sorry, Captain, I feel so ashamed...' my voice peters out. Cockburn holds my gaze and looks into my face, briefly sharing my grief.

'You've nothing to be ashamed of. The colonel you describe sounds like a person who's already on my list, a certain Obersturmbannführer Christian Tychsen, a

---

by the SS Totenkopf Division. The commanding officer, Hauptsturmfuhrer Fritz Knöchlein, was eventually tried and executed for his crimes at the Nuremburg trials held in 1945.

lieutenant colonel in the Second SS Panzer Division[5]. We've had reports that he ordered the murder of several other POWs. Your request for posthumous recognition of Private O'Callaghan and RAMC Pile's courage is duly noted.'

Our journey isn't long, maybe half an hour, before we stop, and my rudimentary knowledge of German suggests that our driver is negotiating with guards stationed at the entrance to the camp. Slowly lowering ourselves from the bed of the truck, early evening light reflects off second- and third-storey windows of buildings overlooking a courtyard which has the appearance of an army barracks.

A loudspeaker crackles into life: 'Prisoners will place hands behind their heads and move into the building to the right for shower and delousing.' Clearly the commandant wasn't going to let us go any further before we were cleaned and washed before supper! Guards are on hand outside a large latrine and shower block area where carbolic soap and overalls have been laid out for us.

Beyond caring about our modesty, we strip naked and dutifully stand under one of the serried ranks of showerheads and clean our bodies in the cold-water jets. Looking around, it's clear that everyone's lost a lot of weight. Those firm, muscular bodies we had when we disembarked at Calais all those months ago have been

---

[5] Obersturmbannführer Christian Tychsen was killed in action before he could be tried for his crimes.

stripped of every ounce of fat and much of the muscle reminding me of the pictures, I've seen of starving African refugees in accounts of the brutal Herero and Nama genocide in German West Africa. The Germans, it seems, have not lost their taste for using starvation to quell and control their captives.

Exiting the showers, smiling guards' step forward. 'Take a nice shave, Tommy!' Gesturing to the trough-like sinks, where a band of glum-faced orderlies wearing oilskin aprons await, brandishing cutthroat razors. We are then, literally shaved from head to foot. Once we've been issued with overalls, our clothes are taken away for delousing. Although degrading, the combined effect of a shower and removal of my infested hair is invigorating.

Once in our overalls, we're shepherded into an adjoining room where a camera has been set up.

'Name, rank and serial number.'

The terse question deserves an equally terse reply, 'Second Lieutenant Frederick Whitton, 95121, Ninth Battalion Royal Northumbrian Fusiliers.' I'm handed a chalkboard and write this information onto it and stand with the board held against my chest feeling like one of the criminal classes.

'Smile, Tommy!' For some unaccountable reason, just obliging I suppose, I actually do smile, probably the only man that did that day. Somewhere in the piles of Red Cross forms sent to the British Ministry of Defence there will be a picture of me, grinning my head off at the camera!

Stepping into an anti-room, a private hands me a metal tag with Oflag VII-B pressed into it along with my prisoner ID number 387. An orderly reads my name and service number from a list, presses this into a circular red disk and attaches it to the cord along with my prisoner ID tag. The process is coldly efficient, like the Germans themselves. However, there is an upside: the MOD will ensure that my family finally get to know what's become of me.

Stepping outside into the still, clear air, it's noticeably darker now. The pocket watch given to me by my grandfather is long gone; lost, no doubt, in a ditch as I crawled my way through vast expanses of French mud, so I have no way of telling the time. Being a watch repairer, it was a pretty fancy Omega British military pocket watch that I received when I passed out of Sandhurst.

Pondering how little I have left to remind me of family and home, I tag along with a large group and we shamble down a long straight road that skirts steep embankments to our right which sweep down towards a group of five, or maybe six, long wooden huts in the distance, no doubt our home sweet home for the duration. A long mesh fence encircles the open parade ground and what appears to be a football pitch and, near the huts, a garden. Immediately outside the mesh is a double-rowed, barbed wire fence about ten or fifteen feet in height overlooked by sentry towers at its four corners.

Approaching the huts, I become aware of a crowd of prisoners beyond the barbed wire of our enclosure. Housed in a smaller enclosure with a single large accommodation hut with their heads similarly shaved, their bodies appear to be even more emaciated than ours. Some are clad in military uniforms, possibly Polish and some others in distinctive black and white-striped fatigues look almost ridiculous, like a clown's outfit, until I notice the Star of David badges they're wearing. Back in England I heard only rumours about concentration camps for Polish Jews, but confronting the stark evidence is unsettling.

Despite our almost equal state of physical deterioration and exhaustion, I feel a strong urge to communicate. Using the gathering dusk as a cover, I move towards the fence that separates us. A small group detaches from the larger crowd.

'Careful, sir, the guards will be watching.' Geddes has joined me, and I can see he's on edge, staring from one to the other of the watchtowers overlooking our part of the camp. 'They might have important information; we might not get another chance.'

'Brytyjscy żołnierze?'

'British, soldiers, yes.' Another older man in civilian clothes steps forward.

'British yes?' I nod.

Gesturing with his arms, he replies, 'We're Polish soldiers and citizens. We have been here for many months. I wish you have come for our liberation, but I can see you are also prisoners.'

A younger man with the distinctive striped uniform puts his hand through the wire mesh.

'Bardzo przepraszam, moi towarzysze, very, very sorry my friends.' I shake his hand; his grasp is surprisingly strong for a man with such an emaciated frame, but his eyes are clear and full of tears. We stand holding each other's hand for what seems like minutes, but is probably only a few seconds, though it's longer than you might think comfortable for two men shaking hands.

For a moment, I consider that he might not release my hand, but exhaustion overcomes him and, finally, he does so. His face is young but is lined and drained of colour like that of a much older man. Having released my hand, he walks purposefully away from the wire fence and the small crowd that's formed at a distance from the fence parts to let him through and closes again after he's passed. Selfishly, I wonder what we'll look like after a few months, or even years in here.

Friday 21st, night

Lying on the top berth of my steel bunk positioned under a high window, a sound from outside has awakened me from a troubled sleep and I become aware of a shaft of moonlight shining through a gap in the threadbare blanket that serves as a curtain. Looking out of the grime-covered window and over the enclosure behind the hut where we spoke with the Polish prisoners, I can see a large group of several hundred men being loaded onto trucks. The furtive way they're being dispatched at night and knowing our captors as I now do, I can only think an unspeakable fate awaits them[6].

[6] Polish prisoners held at Oflag VII-B before the arrival of Allied POWs were likely shipped out to Dachau concentration (death) camp in upper Bavaria.

George, Friday, September 13, 1940, Monkseaton, Newcastle Upon Tyne

The elements seem hell-bent on blowing the roof off our snug little terraced house, but, whilst the tempest whistles and screams menacingly, the sashes rattle in defiance forcing the tempest to make do with depositing pools of water on the windowsills instead of wreaking wonton destruction. Since the windows appeared to be holding firm, my attention falls back to the quiet ambience of our snug home and the stark contrast it makes to the maelstrom raging outside.

As usual, Mother had battled against the morning tidal surge of final demands, bills, requests for payment of rent arrears and had finally managed to scoop up what appeared to be the most pressing, placing these on my father's bureau for him to deal with on his return from the family watch repair shop. I, on the other hand, had given in to sloth and I've only just managed to crawl downstairs for breakfast. The said tidal wave, whilst temporarily dealt with, had however, left a single, crisp white envelope waiting patiently propped against my boiled egg, complete with knitted cosy.

My body suddenly jolts as if I've touched an electrical wire. The first thought that comes to me is that this is the news we've all been dreading; the official confirmation that Fred has been killed in action. Fred, my older brother by a whole ten minutes. Whilst this age difference was slight, Fred had continued to always try and stay ahead of me ever since we both tumbled out of my mother's womb together. Fred was always ahead of me in class, ahead of me in the dinner queue and, inevitably, was drafted into war service ahead of me since he'd signed up for the Territorial Army in 1937; a circumstance that, for once, I certainly didn't envy him for. Not only did Fred sign up ahead of me, but he was also part of the Expeditionary Force sent to help the French give Mr Hitler the bloody nose he so richly deserved. But that was before the bloody disaster at Dunkirk back in June when navy ships and fishing boats began discouraging their bedraggled human cargo. Operation Dynamo it was called, but there was little fight left in the bedraggled and beaten men that we saw arriving at Dover dockyard.

They'd managed to rescue about three hundred thousand Allied soldiers, but, as we'd found out, Fred was not one of them. Since his disappearance in France back in June, the whole family had barely drawn breath whenever an official-looking letter appeared on the doormat. Since we'd been notified that Fred was officially lost in action, I'd been lying awake focussing all my powers of the intuition possessed by a brother whose identical twin has gone missing, to try and feel his living presence, or his death. Time and again, my heart had told me that Fred was alive, but was this a final confirmation that I'd been wrong all along and that he'd been left floating in the surf at Dunkirk along with the other poor wretches who'd been left there? However, when I read the envelope, I see it's addressed to me, Aircraftsman Second Class, Whitton, 1282386. The sender is the MOD, No. 1 Electrical & Wireless School, RAF Cranwell.

As I breathe a sigh of relief that I don't have to go upstairs to my mother with the awful news, a new dread takes its place; it's my exam results. I've never been a great passer of exams, and, whilst I felt I'd done as much justice as I could to my wireless operator mechanic's exams, it's with bated breath that I carefully slide my finger under the flap and promptly receive a painful paper cut to my forefinger.

Briefly wondering whether I was touching the saliva of one of the many tasty WRAF secretaries that might have touched the envelope with her ruby-red lips, I use this misadventure to further put off opening the letter. At that moment, the cuckoo suddenly busts through the doors of the clock hanging above my head and starts chiming the hour startling me into hastily completing the task. Reading the starchy missive, the word 'congratulations' bounces out and hits me in the pit of the stomach.

'Congratulations, I have the pleasant duty to inform you that you have passed the Wireless Operator exams. Please report to the Guardhouse at Coastal Command

No. 1 Coastal Operational Training Unit (COTU) at RAF Silloth in Cumberland for operational training on Monday 17th September at 08:00 where you will be given further instructions.'

So, at the age of twenty-two, I'd now reached the giddy heights of the rank of Aircraftsman (AC) Second Class Wireless Operator Mechanic (WOM). The Royal Air Force needs me after all! The endless square bashing and consumption of quantities of stodgy boiled food in the Cranwell Mess hall had paid off and I'd bought myself a ticket into the war.

At COTU I would receive further training to, amongst other things, bring my Morse code skills up to scratch so I could operate the wireless equipment at the required thirty words per minute. I honestly can't decide whether to be happy or inconsolably sad; I just feel nothing and stare for some time at the typewritten words swimming before my eyes.

George, Monday 21st October 1940, RAF Silloth, Cumbria

I'm keeping my head very firmly to the front, but out of the corner of my eye, I can see Flight Sergeant McGregor's beady eyes flicking about and weaving between our serried ranks looking for a victim; I'm determined it isn't going to be me this time. The length of time he's taking to find a target indicates that we might have, at last, managed to get our kit and ourselves to the level of spit and polish expected by the RAF.

I'm just beginning to settle into the steady sway of a man standing on a parade ground enjoying an unexpected Indian summer morning, when the silence is broken by the sergeant's pedant tones and an imperceptible groan issues from the men of our flight.

'Aircraftsman Fisher, step forward, you horrible little man.'

Fishy was going to catch it this morning, poor old chap. My heart goes out to him, and visions of my cleaning the toilets with a very small brush a few weeks earlier looms into my consciousness as a possible fate for him. I resolve to sneakily toss him a bigger brush or even a broom while passing the latrines on the way to the mess for breakfast. Our sergeant continues, 'Your hairs supposed to be above your ears, laddie. You look like one of those swooning lassies down in Silloth. Right! We've got no time before Wing Commander Iles joins us, so I'm going to handle the job the noo.'

The 'oo' of 'the noo' echoes eerily around the silence of the courtyard. McGregor promptly rummages in his pocket and produces a small clasp knife. We all watch, or, in my case, crane our necks to see, while he carefully opens it and locks the blade.

'Mother of God.'

'He's going cut his throat!'

A rather severe punishment for unruly hair, but the Wing Co. is going to give one of his famous passing out pep talks and McGregor did warn us he'd be merciless on anyone not up to snuff for the occasion.

At this point, most mortals would be quaking in their RAF shoes, but I'd come to learn that Fishy is a masochist at the best of times, so probably the most able of all of us to handle what's going to happen next. Blade fixed, Flight grasps Fishy's offending locks and slices off a ragged couple of inches which promptly drops to the ground and blows away on an eddy of uncharacteristically warm air. Task performed, the old drill sergeant steps back to admire his handiwork like a petulant artist and with a slight nod, appears to be happy.

Returning his knife to his tunic pocket, he continues to walk steadily on. Down the ranks of men, passing me second from the end of the back row and returning to his spot at the front of the flight. At that moment, as though perfectly choreographed beforehand, Wing Commander Gordon Iles' tall, assured form steps from the shadows cast by the Command Offices, walks crisply over to our assembled ranks and takes up post, standing easy in front of us, slowly surveying our faces much as a proud father might dote on his family at Christmas or, perhaps, a wolf surveying a flock of sheep looking for an easy kill.

The station commander's sudden tempers are legendary, however, as quickly as the storm clouds gather, a sunny disposition is often just around the corner. A look of determination is on the commander's face as he begins his address.

'Men, your six weeks' operational training here at Silloth is almost over and you'll no doubt be eager to get on your way to your deployments wherever they may be. Flight Sergeant McGregor assures me that he's once again been able to smooth you all into some semblance of fighting readiness, but be in no doubt, the Phoney War is over, and all gloves are off, both ours and those of the enemy. Some of you will have been surprised to be getting your feet wet in HSLs[7]. I'm guessing that many of you WOMs[8] thought you'd be cruising around in the comfort of some cosy bomber for the rest of the war, but RAF Coastal Command will play

---

[7] HSL: High Speed Launch of the RAF Coastal Command Air-Sea Rescue.

[8] WOM: Wireless Operator Mechanic.

a vital role in rescuing crews that have been shot down and in the drink. Your skills with the wireless will be critical to locating and saving our lads quickly.'

At this point, the wing co. pauses for effect surveying once again, the sea of shiny peaked caps paraded before him. 'I want you to know that I'm proud of every one of you for successfully completing your training; you're a credit to the RAF and to our country. But mark my words, your skills and courage will be tested to the utmost before this show is over.'

Nodding, Iles almost imperceptibly whispers under his breath what could only be a prayer, 'Hero's all, hero's all, may God have mercy upon us.' But taking up his defiant refrain once again, he continues.

'Let's give that strutting peacock Adolf Hitler and his Italian crony Mussolini a bloody nose and make sure they pay the highest cost possible price for their hubris. Godspeed and grant you calm seas and a fair wind to carry you all safely to your various postings.'

Seeing that his commander has finished his address, McGregor promptly steps forward and issues the command, 'Flight, attention! Flight, dismissed.'

Unsure of protocol, a spontaneous cry of 'hip, hip, hooray' echoes thrice around the parade ground. I for one am unsure where the impetus for this display of joyous abandon comes from, but McGregor, for once, lets us have our moment. Afterwards, most of us have to look up what hubris means, but we're all stirred by the station commander's words.

In the high spirits that follow, McGregor must have forgotten about Fish's hairdo transgression, as he simply disappeared with the wing co. into the command offices. Full of joy at not having to get up close and personal with the gleaming porcelain of the base's latrines, Fish talks me into another one of his hare-brained swimming expeditions to the Solway, which, I have to confess, is still pretty warm considering it's October. The last few days at Silloth would be followed by a few days of embarkation leave before we would be packing off to the Personnel Dispersal Unit (PDU) at RAF Wilmslow where we'd be getting our kit for wherever we were getting posted to.

Still shrouded in secrecy, I know only that I'm going somewhere sunny since I'm going to get some vaccinations and be issued with Tropical Kit. We have all been sworn to strict secrecy about our embarkation orders. Therefore, we're only getting information on a 'need to know' basis to avoid inadvertent slips letting the cat out the bag. I always wonder what might happen if we accidentally blabbed to all and sundry about where we're being posted and what we'd been up to during training, but I, like most of us, just assume that we'd be lined up against a wall and shot.

George, Wednesday 30th October 1940, a troop ship somewhere on the North Atlantic

Heavy chop is making it difficult for us to eat our evening meal. It's a case of waiting for your dinner plate to drift back towards you, grab it, and finish as quickly as possible before it drifts away again. The violence of the ship's pitching is causing dinner plates to bump over the table lip, fly through the air in a messy arc before crashing onto the floor like steady gunfire and small explosions. I'll never quite get the hang of eating at sea!

When I signed up for the RAF, I never thought I'd be doing so much sailing. It's lucky that seasickness doesn't seem to be too much of a problem for me or Fish. I suppose Fish found his sea legs whilst training as part of the British swimming team in the 1936 Berlin Olympics, he would, wouldn't he? Actually, I've already resolved to keep very close to Fish during this voyage of mystery or VOM as I like to call it. The military loves its acronyms and VOM seems to be rather apt for what we're doing at the moment, or should I say, quite a few of my fellow passengers are doing over the side. I've got full confidence that Fish would be in a position to save my life as well as quite a few others should the ship go down. If a man can take on the might of the Nazi Aryan race in the (swimming pool) water, saving a few drowning rats like me should be a doddle!

At that point I had a none too pleasant vision involving rising sea waters rushing through cabin doors and rats scurrying hither and dither, quite literally abandoning a sinking ship. It was rather a relief when Fish broke into my reverie.

'Come on, Witty, want to join me for a stroll around the 'campus' before we have to turn in?'

I willingly accept, anything to try and shift my stodgy meal of boiled potatoes, cabbage and 'meat'. I invert the commas since it's difficult to determine what hapless member of which species we'd just eaten. In my short experience so far, I've discovered that everything is boiled in the service. Like the RAF mess at Silloth, the Merchant Navy also seems unable to get its collective head around other forms of cooking; I'd kill for some grilled steak with creamy mushrooms on a bed of sautéed onions.

Fish's use of the word campus conjures up the airy spaciousness of the sort he'd likely experienced during his (public) school days at Fettes College in Edinburgh. Spacious was definitely far from what we were experiencing now! The MV Leinster is a requisitioned Irish Channel packet steamer and none too spacious for the cargo of one thousand four hundred souls it's carrying. Part of what had become known as 'Winston's

Special Convoys' we know only that we're heading south to tropical shores as yet unknown to us.

As we left the mess deck, frequent bowing was required to move through the sea doors and some of the makeshift overhead pipework skimmed the top of my head as we pass along the crowded corridors. The cramped quarters also require us to modify the customary salute to superiors. In the RAF, the fingertips of the flattened hand are presented palm outwards onto your temple taking the long way up to the brow and the shortest way down punching the thumb down your trouser seams. All well and good when you've got plenty of room. Aboard ship, the long way up business is no good in our close confines where your outwards sweeping hand is likely to hit a bulkhead or someone passing by. So, for the duration of the voyage, we had tacit approval to make the more appropriate naval-type salute, a sort of a rather informal palm-downwards slash to the forehead.

As we walk and occasionally slash our foreheads, I cast my mind back to the previous three nights aboard in our makeshift sleeping quarters. Sleep is a rather ambitious term used for swaying like a caterpillar cocoon from the rafters in a hammock which frequently bumps into your neighbour's similarly cocooned form if the sea was rough like it was now. In fact, I'm in no hurry to head down below to join the cacophony of grunting and nasal sawing sounds that awaits us.

Our swaying stroll is taking us through the ship's

common room area where I spy a highly polished brass instrument fixed to the aft wall of the saloon. Moving closer we could see that it's an inclinometer for measuring the roll of the ship. Currently, it's showing twenty-degree swings.

'Twenty degrees, that sounds a lot!' I exclaimed.

'That'll be why we're finding it so difficult to walk, old chap!' Fish replies just as we're treated to a further lurch to one side.

At that moment, a crusty old member of the ship's crew happens to be passing and he saunters over to stand between us like a father would with his two sons in a collective huddle.

'Ach! Twenty degrees is child's play compared to the forty-seven-degree swings I've seen passing through the Roaring Forties! Fortunately for you, young laddies, you won't see the kind of huge seas you get in the Southern Ocean where you're going.'

At this, we both asked, 'Oh, so you know where we're going? We'd love to know!'

Realising he'd probably said too much and recalling the endless 'walls have ears' messages on newsreels and public information notices, he rather sheepishly withdrew and shuffled off through one of the doors that are locked out of use and restricted to crew only.

Suddenly, the ship turns sharply to port causing the inclinometer to lurch violently. Having been thrown to the floor, we were in the process of picking ourselves up again, when the ship makes another violent evasive manoeuvre. The captain announces on the tannoy that the crew should be issued with life jackets and await further instructions.

As we dash for the nearest emergency assembly point, I have the distinct impression I can hear water rushing below. Pitch black with a storm raging, would not be a good time to be hit by a torpedo. Tannoy announcements had been cheerily keeping us up to date on news of convoy and navy ships that had been sunk by U-boats, so we know it's a possibility.

Coming up onto the outside rails of the tween deck, we can dimly make out and definitely see huge spouts of water produced by exploding depth charges lobbed over the side by one of the perimeter patrol ships, probably one of the destroyers, that's weaving in and out of our fellow convey ships. The crew cheer like supporters in the stands at a football match each time a depth charge explodes and all lean over the side to see if they can make out the tell tail oil slick or debris of a destroyed U-boat.

After what seems hours (probably only fifteen to twenty minutes) of this desperate cat and mouse game, the destroyers pull back to the perimeter of the convoy and we continue on our way as if nothing had happened. We were promised calm seas and a fair wind; fat chance of that with hunting packs of U-boats cruising around underneath us!

George, Friday 8th November 1940, a troop ship somewhere in the Mediterranean

'I propose a toast to Freddy.' Mother is sitting in solemn silence with eyes fixed on my brother with an expression that might be worn by someone watching a priest deliver the last rights over a condemned man.

Undeterred, my father continues. 'All the very best. I'm sure you'll show those lads that we're all not just disappointed Scots here in the North East!' His words die away in the otherwise silent room and we dutifully follow my father's lead and sip at our glasses of 1940 Beaujolais, a rare treat during these times of rationing since the war broke out. Despite the grim circumstances, I couldn't help my mind briefly straying onto the topic of wine and how in good heavens my father had been able to obtain a bottle in the first place. Beaujolais Nouveau was French. The Germans had invaded France last year. On the plus side, November is traditionally the time when Beaujolais Nouveau is released and voraciously bought by the upper class set to show how much money they can waste on partially matured red wine. But wait, how on earth could we be sipping new season Beaujolais? I can only think that one of our seafaring cousins based in Ramsgate had somehow managed to smuggle a few cases over the channel dodging the various warships and U-Boats on the way. A less colourful explanation could be that a dodgy shopkeeper had forged the labels and was currently making a mint!

Shifting my mind away from sunny French vineyards to the murkiness of our front room, I join Mother, Dora and Freddy in watching my father's expressions changing from one moment to the next, like clouds passing over an expanse of land. Shade, dark and sun wrestle with each other for supremacy. Father finally settles on a crestfallen demeanour of the sort you see on the faces of small businesspeople when they've summoned the courage and detailed argument you need to ask for a loan only to be told by the bank manager that the whole plan has a glaring fault and you're surely bound for ruination.

Mother suddenly breaks the silence and asks the obvious question, 'Freddy, can you tell us where you've been posted? It's all very sudden and you've hardly had time to take time at home after you came back from Sandhurst.' Freddy shifts in his chair, no doubt uncomfortable within the confines of his new uniform and wishing that he'd requested leave in civvies.

Adjusting the tight-fitting shirt collar the quartermaster sergeant had deigned to provide him with, Freddy continues, 'I'm sorry, Mother, it's all very hush

hush. All I can say is that we're being deployed overseas, and all leave has been cancelled forthwith. I have to say that I'm rather relieved that I don't have to hang around before I'm deployed. I'd probably forget what I've been taught during the last year in any case.'

This last self-deprecating remark is typical of Freddy and no doubt an attempt on his part to make light of the situation, but his flippancy, for once, doesn't work on my mother and she bursts into tears accompanied by uncontrollable sobbing. My father, sitting motionless, simply stares at her hunched frame, listening to the sound of a mother's grief and perhaps, as I do, contemplates the upcoming bitter farewell at one of the Channel ports.

For her part, Sis had simply slipped quietly from the table and is probably now hiding in her room and joining her mother in her own private well of despair. I decide to do the only decent thing possible in these circumstances, namely, to do justice to the magnificent bottle of wine sitting in front of us. Reaching out to top up Freddy's glass I notice that nobody has touched their wine apart from an obligatory brush of their glass's crystalline surface on the lips before it had been returned, chastened, to the table.

Momentarily wondering whether I was committing, once again, another heartless, insensitive act by indulging in vulgar frivolity, Bacchus, or one of his pards, must have mischievously nudged my arm and, instead of pouring wine into his glass, I fumbled the bottle and wine gushed over the crisp white linen of Freddy's dress shirt and his best bib and tucker. Fred makes to rise from his place at the table, but instead, stumbles forward. Grabbing a napkin from the table, he makes dab at the wine. But, rather than the expected derogatory remarks about my clumsiness, he utters the most awful groan as if he's in the extremity of pain. Looking over to him, I can now clearly see that he's bleeding from a ragged open wound in his stomach.

Just as my mind is trying to compute how such a thing could have happened in our front room, Freddy pitches forward and crashes heavily onto the dining room table as blood continues to pour out of his wound and pool on our parquet floor. Out of the corner of my eye, I vaguely notice that Mother has fainted, and Father has gathered up the tablecloth to make a vain attempt to stem the flow of blood that is now fountaining out of Freddy's body.

Plates and glasses crash to the floor in a deafening cacophony of shattering china and splintering crystal. As if things couldn't get worse, the room lurches sideways and the table begins to vibrate emitting a soft purring noise. I become aware that the scene is darkening: am I fainting? My eyes snap open with an almost audible click. Images from the scene at the table float in front of me and I find myself lashing out at them with my arms, willing the horror to dissipate.

This state of affairs continues for what seems like minutes but is probably just a few seconds. I now realise that the crash had been caused by my neighbour who'd dislodged a teacup from a makeshift shelf and the vibrations are emanating from the engines humming away deep in the bowels of the ship. Still fending off the lingering apparition of Freddy's pallid face hanging in front of me with a surprised expression, eyes bulging, I carefully disentangle myself from my hammock strings. I drop quietly to the floor in my stockinged feet and find my boots dangling at one end of the hammock.

Picking my way through the gloomy surroundings, I head to the upper deck with the intention of taking some air to try and clear my head of morbid thoughts. As I emerge from the saloon door, a warm wind tugs at my jacket. Leaning on the rails towards the bow, I watch the waves crashing against the side of the ship. Glancing up, I notice seabirds wheeling overhead, their large, white bodies illumined by the wheelhouse lights. The skipper and his officers are silhouetted at their post in the wheelhouse and I can see them, heads inclined downwards, intently watching the crew below as they rush hither and thither shifting ropes, turning winches.

Looking up from the frenetic activity on the decks below, I notice a dark landmass lying impassively ahead. Taking a closer look, I can see pinpricks of light flickering on the still distant shoreline. An earthy, organic smell of a foreign land drifts across the briny 'landfall'. I whisper to myself, 'Where in blazes have we wound up?' A sudden feeling invades my senses. This is where I've been heading; this will be home for the foreseeable future. I test this idea out in my mind for a few moments and the notion seems both comforting and exciting at the same time.

George, Friday 9th November 1940
Grand Harbour, Valletta, Malta

I'm rudely woken by a severely aching back, thighs and buttocks. A piercing bright light slashes through the sun deck awning above my head momentarily blinding me and causing by body to instinctively recoil backwards towards the comfort of the shade somewhat like a startled cockroach. A raucous sound of seagulls adds to my confusion by fleetingly sounding like the mocking type of laughter that emanates from school bullies and impudent older brothers. I smile inwardly at this last thought, but thoughts drift back to my waking dream of Freddy the night before. Shuddering at this ghastly image, I commence my habitual staged approach to getting up by slowly bringing my head up from the wooden bench on which it had been laying and propping it up on the palm of my hand, lying like a Roman would at table.

Stage two involves pushing my back up against the ship's bulkhead, pausing briefly before commencing stage three by tentatively swinging my legs and attached feet in heavy boots firmly onto the vibrating steel floor. I've been going through this same three-stage process of waking up since I was a small boy. However, despite a lifetime of practice, what follows is always the same: a blurred image of whatever is in front of me, in this case it's an unsteady image of brilliant white and shimmering blue, a vision of paradise if you were on a jaunty trip abroad on your holidays.

As I grapple to understand where we were, my mind conjures a memory of walking across the causeway with Freddy and my father to St Mary's Island from the white sands of the beach of Whitley Bay. This comforting image of sea, sand and the inevitable ice cream at the St Mary's Lighthouse teashop, guides me towards comprehending a new reality. I'm gripped by a strong feeling, one of euphoria and dread. 'If this is likely to be my home for the foreseeable future,' I murmured, 'where in blazes are we?'

Whilst still lamenting the wayward fashion the RAF treats its loyal subjects by sending them off on a mystery tour around the globe without a bye or leave, a familiar voice breaks in.

'Witty, old chap! Where the hell have you been all night?'

'Obviously, I've been lying here,' was my irritated reply.

Undeterred, Fish continues in a jocular tone, 'If you'd had the sense to stay sleeping in your hammock, you'd know that we've arrived in Malta!'

'Malta, by jove, it's a holidaymaker's dream! Sun, sand and feisty women by all accounts.' Whilst this exchange was going on, we have entered a huge natural harbour through an entrance flanked by a colossal sandstone bastion rearing up on our right and supporting what appears to be military fort. Getting into his part as the bringer of news, Fish takes on the persona of an enthusiastic tour guide.

'Valletta, the ancient capital of Malta and home to more than half of the island's people living in the highest population density in Europe. Fort Elmo,' with a flourish, Fish sweeps his arm across to our right, 'one of the many military fortifications making Valletta one of the most heavily fortified cities in the Mediterranean.'

Cutting into his sales patter in an attempt to shut off the stream of useless facts, I exclaim, 'Well, I know who to come to for tourist information! But is this where we're getting off?'

Flummoxed by this request for useful intel rather than a barrage of facts, Fish replies rather lamely that he has no idea. We're interrupted by an announcement on the ship's tannoy requesting all military personnel to prepare for disembarkation. Whereupon I rush back to our sleeping quarters to collect my gear. Stooping to man haul my heavy kitbag from its storage locker, beads of sweat immediately spring from my forehead and begin pooling on my knitted brows. Finally wrestling my kit free, I begin to fully appreciate how damn hot it is. 'Isn't this supposed to be November?' I murmur under my breath along with another oath sworn at my unruly kitbag that's doing a very convincing impression of a wayward drunk as it unhelpfully slumps over to one side as I try to get it onto my shoulders.

At the point of leaving our quarters, somewhat perversely and despite the drama and the discomfort of the last ten days, I'm going to miss the old girl, currently the only physical link I have with England and the friends and family I'd left behind. Tottering through the bulkhead door and heaving myself and my slumbering drunk of a kitbag up the steps to the disembarkation deck, I ponder the easy nonchalance of the civilian passengers who must have descended these same steps at unremarkable destinations like Cork and Southampton that must have been plied by the Leinster before the war.

Ferryboats and their captains and crew are at once denigrated for their repetitive journeys; no voyages of discovery for them! But the Irish Sea can be treacherous nevertheless and how I envy their familiar routine. At least on a ferryboat, you knew where you were going to and from. At that moment, remaining uncertainty regarding my posting, what I'd be expected to do and whether I'd be up to the job, causes a flat stone to descend onto my stomach and I'm gripped by a momentary wave of homesickness.

Once again, my mind conjures memories of the journeys I'd made with Freddy and my parents between North and South Shields on the Tynemouth and Northumbrian ferries.

On the quay, a brusque-looking old flight sergeant with a clip board herds us into groups. 'Aircraftsman Whitton! You've been drafted to the Marine Craft Section at RAF Kalafrana. Step over there, laddie!'

Swaying slightly on the unaccustomed solidity of dry land, I lurch over to a small group of lads who have gathered by a battered old Bedford truck. Fish, who's already there, and can't contain his enthusiasm, gives me the thumbs up. Being drafted into the Marine Section meant water, which meant ample opportunities for more ill-advised swimming expeditions. The RAF didn't know what it was letting itself in for!

Tardy by nature, Fish and I manage to hang back. We're rewarded by seats on the truck near the opening in the canvas awning. Being early in the morning, the fish market appears to be already in full swing as we meander carefully around the flat-capped locals under the stern eye of a pith helmet-wearing local policeman directing traffic, carts and thronging locals who seemed to be wilfully bent upon getting run over. I guess the fish market imperative is always the same the world over; get there early and nab the best quality at the best price and get it to your customers pronto.

Although a watch repairer by trade, my father always enjoyed visiting the bustling North Shields Fish Quay to buy the familiar newspaper-wrapped treat for tea at Machonochie's kipper factory. For some reason that always escaped me. He seemed to know an inordinate amount about comings and goings at the quay and was on nodding terms with a few of the fishing boat skippers. I quietly resolved to include details of the rather more colourful melee unfolding at Valletta in my next letter home; hopefully, the censors wouldn't black out a description of a fish quay, but you never know.

Bumping out of Valletta, dust from the badly graded track plumes behind us. 'That's why nobody wanted to sit by the opening,' we exclaim to each other. We both made a mental note not to make the same mistake again. An expansive view of small fields, some possibly vineyards, others grazed by goats and surrounded by dry-stone walls opens up. The appearance is somewhat similar to the windswept fields of Northumberland, except it's extremely hot and a bright sun hangs in a cobalt blue sky causing leaves on the trees to shimmer. Lapsing once again into reminiscing, my mind settles on the carefree days of my youth and bus journeys into the country. Ah, the quaint market town of Wooler, the Cheviot Hills and the bracing aroma of fish and chips at the 'Cheviot Charlie' Café. What happy days!

'Don't you go teaching that mynah bird foul language, George, or you'll know what's coming to you!' Dear old mama always used to scold me for the language teaching skills I used to exercise on hapless Charlie the mynah bird, the café's namesake. Trying to remember exactly which profanities I'd taught poor Charlie, a huge and rather grotesque bird flapped into view making ponderous progress along the nearby coastline.

'Pelican!' exclaimed Fish, who was just about to launch into his tour guide routine again, but he mercifully falls silent as we pass through two huge and rather forbidding wooden double doors that gave the entrance to RAF Kalafrana the appearance of a prison camp. Home sweet home at last!

George, Wednesday 14th November 1940, heading SSE, ten miles off Marsaxlokk Bay

A bucking deck under my already bruised derrière is causing me some discomfort as I grip the wireless cabin table with one hand whilst attempting to transmit our position with the other. I wouldn't call my Morse particularly fast in a flat calm, but just making sense and remembering the various codes is posing severe problems! The cause of this discomfort? Skip, in his infinite wisdom, has decided that our bedding-in period is over and it's time for new crew members to get some proper training hours in some real seas. Real, in this case was to wait for a pitch-black moonless night, a wild force-six wind and an eight- to-ten-foot swell. I'm told that ten-foot waves are child's play (where have I heard that term before?) compared to the not infrequent medicanes or tropical storms that we'd been told occur during the Mediterranean autumn and winter.

I'm a modest five foot eight inches, but Fish is a lankier six foot plus and these waves would easily crash right over his head! And let's not forget the lashing rain. Glancing out the wireless cabin, I can see Cox, Tosh

Hammond and Skipper, Matt Markham are clinging onto the wheelhouse steps and peering intently ahead through the ClearView's whirling wiper blades. Skip's chiselled features caught in the wheelhouse lights are intent, but calm and collected as he gives clear orders and instructions on heading and speed to Tosh. In his turn, Tosh's weather-beaten features must have seen such conditions, and much worse, many times before. As a Norfolk lifeboat cox before the war, Tosh has already received the lifeboat service's highest award for bravery, the RNLI Gold Medal. He personifies the local lifeboat men's creed, which in his case is quite literally, 'Caister-men never turn back.'

With these two men at the helm, my feelings of unease were somewhat quelled, if not the impending nausea in the pit of my stomach! Earlier in the day, as we headed out of the cloistered confines of the coffin-like camber, the rather odd name given to our craft's parking garage at the base, the chop had already been pretty heavy as we opened up the engines to fifteen knots to cruise out of Marsaxlokk. But as we exited the relative calm of the bay and passed Il-Kalanka Point, the prow of our boat had immediately begun to smash into the wild water beyond. If anything, conditions had been deteriorating since we left with the heavy swell and lashing rain intensifying.

Turning back to my instruments, I force myself to focus on this evening's training manoeuvres. We'd received the last position of a downed Wellington bomber (bogus, thankfully) from HQ. If all had survived the crash landing, the crew complement of five would likely be in the drink ten miles south-by-south-west from Il-Kalanka Point close to Filfla Atoll, a tiny excrescence of land about five miles off Malta's western flank used by the navy for target practice amongst other things.

The point of the exercise is simple: locate the wreck, find the crew, pick them up and return to base. Deceptively simple in fact, but in current conditions, it'd be like looking for a needle in a storm-tossed haystack several miles across. In a further, and I would say, unnecessary embellishment of the exercise, three navy marine commandos who had been deposited on the atoll as part of some previous manoeuvres, were going to play the part of downed airmen to give the rescue a greater degree of realism, if more were needed, that is. The marines, who are undergoing arduous survival training, would be actually in the water, so the potential danger to them is real. As second cox, it's Fish's unenviable task to feed Tosh and Markham updates on our average speed, distance covered from base and wind speed, so our position can be plotted by Skip using a copious quantity of maps that flow over the wheelhouse chart table.

In my mind's eye, I can vividly picture the downed crew swimming around in the drink in their Mae Wests, hopefully rafted up, but without the benefit of a raft, floating helplessly in the swell like thrill seekers on a fairground rollercoaster. Travelling now hell for leather at thirty knots, we were rapidly approaching the last-known position of the wrecked aircraft. Despite travelling at near our top speed and with waves crashing over the decks, Skip orders deckhands Rupert O'Hare and Hamish McLeod to fetch the searchlight from its stowage and mount it on-deck. The chop is making it pretty difficult to extricate the heavy one-thousand-watt searchlight light from its stowage down below in the fo'c's'le. After much swearing from Rupert, a monstrous man mountain known as the Bear, and characteristic stoic silence from Hamish who, using the contrary logic of the military, had been nicknamed Verbal by the crew, the lads must have been able to drop the heavy light onto its mounting as a powerful pencil beam briefly flashed across the wheelhouse windows.

Unable to contain my curiosity even in these challenging conditions, rising carefully from my post, I glance out of the closest ClearView and was met with a vision of the craggy shoreline of Filfla Atoll rearing up in front of us like a storm-tossed ghost ship.

'Tosh, Fisher, start the square search routine pronto. The last transmitted position was one mile to the south southeast of the atoll, so I want an expanding square based on one tenth of a mile legs.'

Fish and Tosh jump to at Skip's barked orders. A tenth of a mile, or five hundred and twenty-eight feet to be precise, seems like a pretty accurate course to set given the bashing we were getting. I'd been told

Markham is a pedant when it comes to accuracy in all weathers, so I'm expecting that we might get an ear-bashing later on since I know that Skip will be checking our position changes by following timings and headings.

Amid the controlled chaos of the wheelhouse, a flare suddenly swoops into the air overhead, its brilliant light slowly descending to earth from its high point.

'Ten degrees northwest, Skip.'

Tosh offers his estimate of position and Markham nods. 'Ten degrees, steady as she goes.' Skip steadies himself on the chart table and plots our course towards the source of the flare.

As we pick up speed, Skip calls over his shoulder, 'Easy, Tosh, we'll need to keep to seaboard if we don't want to hit the reef.'

At this point, the force of the swell and crashing waves are making it impossible to move from my post, but I hastily manage to transmit a coded 'X' message to base letting Operations know we've located the crew and we will affect a rescue within the hour. Despite the mayhem and relatively short range of the onboard transmitter, I get X291-7, 'receiving you at signal-strength 7' in reply to my coded enquiry, X279, 'are you receiving me?' I imagine the wireless transmissions skimming off the waves like the little flatty stones my father and I used to skim on the calm waters off the beach at Whitley Bay. Sometimes they'd peter out after a couple of skips, but, if you were lucky, one would skim right out to sea on five or more little hops before it stalled and sank from view; a bit like radio waves out at sea, you never know how far they'll travel.

'Men in the water, men in the water! I see them!' Out of the side starboard window, I can see Rupert and Hamish, tethered to the safety lines leaning over the rails presumably trying to use boathooks to get the men onboard. A discordant sound of wet oilskins, rubber boots and general banging and thumping heralds the welcome sight of the first 'crew' member coming through the sea-door and into the wheelhouse closely followed by his two comrades. The three men have brought with them something of the wild night they'd just escaped from, blinking in the unaccustomed light, swaying slightly, their teeth chattering. Markham, with help from Fish and myself, the lads are helped below into the relative sanctuary of the aft bunkroom. Since it's behind the engines, the aft cabin is one of the warmest, and they'll also have an opportunity to enjoy, as a distraction, the copious banter and amusing expletives from the engineers, Scrap and Crabby (Rodger Tinselly and Richard Crab) to keep them entertained while we sprint off to grab them a hot cuppa from the galley.

Whilst juggling teapots, mugs and boiling water, a feeling of elation and emotion rises within me. For the first time in my life, I feel like I'm part of something big, something heroic and good. I'm impressed how the team has worked together, the sense of common purpose bringing everyone into an instant camaraderie I'd never experienced before. For once I feel like I belong.

George, Friday 16th November 1940, Strada Stretta, Valletta

'Don't they know there's a war on!' Fish is bawling at the top of his voice to make himself heard over a mangled din constituted from Vera Lynn bashing out 'We'll Meet Again' and jazz renditions most likely by Duke Ellington blasting out of various gramophones topped off with Għana, traditional Maltese folk music apparently usually shouted from the rooftops being sung with great vigour by a rotund local woman working in a café we're passing.

I inwardly congratulate myself on this nugget of local knowledge, but in truth, if you hear off-key singing accompanied by an accordion or guitar or both and you're in Malta, it's likely to be Għana! The resulting cacophony is making my head spin. I check my wristwatch; it's 21:12 on a relatively balmy evening by British standards for December and the night is young.

This evening's little excursion is all thanks to a happy convergence of circumstances. Firstly, Fish, myself and our boat's wireless operator, Allan Harris – that's Tweedy to everyone else – had all managed to wangle the coveted little blue RAF leave pass and have it signed by the CO, Group Captain Livock. I had then masterfully cadged a lift into town from one of the Motor Transport blokes. The icing on the cake was that, since it was Friday, we'd just all just received our measly six shillings from the purser. Since this was our first 'proper' leave since we arrived, we'd decided to go the whole hog and combine drinks with dinner. From day one on the island, the 'old lags' at Kalafrana had been banging on about Valletta's infamous Strada Stretta, otherwise known as 'the Gut', where all manner of entertainment could be had. In the military, there are basically only two types of refreshment; there's the vertical type, which usually involves drinking beer and the horizontal type that requires the services of prostitutes. From my understanding, both could be had in lavish quantities along The Gut.

Despite the allure of taking both types of refreshment simultaneously, I'd been trying to steer us away from Strada Stretta, with the seemingly contrary English translation, Straight Street, since I'd no intention of taking any horizontal refreshment, but somehow our senses had followed the bustle and noise all the way into the Melo Quarter of Gżira. The transition from grand, white-stone terraced houses to tawdry shop fronts had been the first indication that we'd strayed into the red-light district. Besides the music, noise and bustle, the open doorways of many of the bars and clubs are fringed by small huddles of olive-skinned young women, and not so young woman, flaunting their busts and legs in body-hugging cocktail dresses with plunging necklines. Judging by the stares from my companions and my own attention wavering in their direction, it's clear that we are going to have to be very careful to avoid being tempted by their allure.

'Prostitution brings only syphilis and sin, my boy.' I recall my father's words born out of his experience in France in the last war.

There was also our flight sergeant's cheery admonishment to us as we boarded our transport into town. 'Just remember, lads, keep Mr 'P' in your pants, but don't pee in your pants,' still ringing in my ears. We'd all seen the posters warning us of the unhealthy downsides of liaisons with ladies of the night, but surely not these fresh-faced, coquettish damsels?

'Damn!' I thought. 'It's working!' But really, would it be so bad? Having said that, a large-breasted young woman smiling intently at me from a doorway we're passing looks just like the brunette on my favourite STI warning poster 'Boobytrap'. I think I'm in love with her, so obviously the message isn't getting through to me in the way it's supposed to! Unintentionally, my hand brushes against my meagre pay packet and I'm brought to my senses. 'Just a drink or three will do us, lads. We need to be up at five a.m. tomorrow for a patrol.'

Instantly, I feel lame. Who was I, Mother Hen? Fortunately, Fish and Tweedy aren't listening as we zero in on an unusually swanky-looking bar with high and lavishly painted ceilings, that look rather like the Sistine Chapel in Rome complete with a Grecian portico guarded by two swarthy roughs with the kind of shiny suits and fedoras worn by James Cagney and his fellow Hollywood gangsters.

'Here will do!' shouts Fish. When was he ever a doyenne of good taste? His time at posh school in Edinburgh might qualify him to know which way to pass the port and the vulgarity of keeping the band on your cigar while you're smoking it, but his taste in bars and restaurants had, up to now, been lamentably poor.

As we are passing the Cagney-esque henchmen at the door, Fish turns to me gleefully. 'Well, Mother Hen, do you approve?' So, he must have heard me after all! Staring firstly up at the crystal chandeliers and trumpet-blowing cherubs on the ceiling and then around at the polished glass and chrome and brass fittings I have to say I'm impressed. We three simply stand and stare around like some local bumpkins at a fairground.

'Can I help you, gentlemen?' An elegant Maltese woman in a black satin evening dress who'd been greeting other clientele when we'd entered had silently glided over to render aid to more lost sheep who'd obviously strayed from their mother ship. Close up, our friendly greeter turns out to be rather diminutive. But, as they say, the best things come in small packages; she is quite simply, stunningly beautiful in a kind of unselfconscious way that somehow intensifies a woman's radiance.

The way she forthrightly meets my gaze immediately suggests that she's a person of standing and importance and, momentarily, I'm rather uncharacteristically lost for words, but offer, 'Apologies, but the three of us only recently arrived on Malta and are in desperate need of a drink and some dinner.'

To which she simply replies, 'Come this way, gentlemen.' Her English is good, benefiting from a sensual Italian accent. As we follow her over to a table near where a jazz band are playing and waiters swish hither and thither with little silver trays perched on their arms, I notice that well-dressed parties of local men and women are intermixed with groups of RAF lads from Kalafrana and airbases at Hal-Far, Ta' Qali and Luqa. Nodding in their direction, we sit down and peruse the menus. Unfortunately, our attractive host is replaced by an efficient and purposeful waiter who takes our order of three pints of Blue Label. As glasses of foaming ale arrive, by way of a toast, Tweedy expresses what we're all probably thinking.

'I can't believe that we're miles away from home in the middle of the Med and we're being served English ales and listening to jazz in a bar that looks reminiscent of a swanky Jesmond club! Anyhow, cheers, lads!'

But the fact is, we're in Malta, which is, quite literally, an aircraft carrier with stupendous strategic military importance in the Mediterranean theatre of a war that's very much in full swing with our countrymen and women fighting for their lives back at home. I feel a pang of guilt that we should be enjoying such an indulgent evening on sultry shores.

However, my thoughts are pulled back to the reality of our situation. We're in the eye of a storm which must surely soon break. I look around at my companions, already dear friends all; we've come through so much already. Yet this must surely be child's play; that phrase just keeps on coming back to me. We're living through the easy days before the overwhelming tempest ahead. An ancient biblical proverb springs to mind with its ominous dread; eat, drink and be merry for tomorrow we shall die.

George, Saturday 17th November 1940, twenty miles SE of Malta

'This is our first big show, lads. I can't tell you much in detail, but the navy are mounting an operation to deliver Hawker Hurricanes to Hal-Far[9]. God knows, we need those planes to mount an effective air defence with raids by the Italians expected to intensify in the next few weeks in what could be build-up to an invasion. The stakes couldn't be higher. What I can say is the planes are being flown off an aircraft-carrier somewhere in the Med this evening, so we're going to be at sea and on full alert for the rest of the day and night. I don't need to tell you how much of a risk our boys are taking to get these planes to us; it's going to be touch and go whether they make it. For those who don't, I want us to be there to show them the best of our service whether it's picking

[9] This vignette is based on Operation White, a heroic mission undertaken by the RAF to deliver twelve Hawker Hurricanes and two Blackburn Skua dive-bombers to the Al-Far airbase in Malta. The pilots flew from the deck of the aircraft carrier, HMS Argus. Unfortunately, the Argus was forced out to sea by unfavourable winds. To make matters worse, poor cooperation between the navy and the RAF also contributed to the loss of almost half the pilots as the planes ran out of fuel one by one as they were forced to bale out into the sea.

them up alive or recovering their bodies so as our creed dictates, The Sea Shall Not Have Them.'

Out of the corner of my eye, I see Tosh staring over at Skip and slowly nodding with a do-or-die look on his face that's becoming familiar. Markham has finished his little pep talk, but it had its effect on me at least. I can feel the hairs on my arms and the back of my neck prickle. Pride, but also a feeling of responsibility swells inside me. I wonder whether I'm up to the job. After all I'd literally only just stepped off the boat from England a few days ago; talk about being thrown in at the deep end!

So, saying, we'd slipped our moorings at about 14:00 this afternoon and headed out in a SE direction towards the distant shores of North Africa in worsening weather and climbing seas. To be honest, I was exhausted after our little excursion into town last night and wondered how I was going to keep up. The radiant features of our friendly greeter in the Empire Bar drifts briefly back into my mind's eye. I'm beginning to regret not having spoken to her or got her number when I glance over at Tweedy whose face appears to have a deathly pallor, illuminated as it is by the sickly glow from his wireless equipment, he looks a bit like a Halloween jack-o-lantern.

Thoughts of death are beginning to haunt me like Banquo's ghost in Macbeth. 'God, I hope they make it.' I've never seen death close up and personal, and I've no wish to. What does a person look like if they've baled out of an aircraft at twenty thousand feet into the sea with no parachute? I instantly feel selfish. If those pilots have got the guts to fly in this weather from a ship, I've got to be prepared to do what I can to find them if they have to bale out into the drink. Because it's likely to be a big show, a medical orderly, Miles Armstrong, who the crew refer to as Mother, is with us this evening and is currently preparing a makeshift operating theatre in Skip's wardroom so any unfortunate pilots we do pick up will, at least, have the best possible chance. I was never very confident with first aid in my days in the Boys Brigade; is it two breaths then thirty compressions? But what if they've drowned?

'Hold us steady on this heading, Tosh.' Markham's voice. 'Harris, keep me informed of any chatter. I want you to follow up anything that sounds like a shout, monitor all frequencies. Whitton, send a coded message to HQ and let them know we're in position; remember, our call sign for today is "Biscay".'

Both of us acknowledge 'yes, sir' in obedient unison. Time is slipping by and darkness and the weather were rapidly closing in. Almost in answer to my thoughts, a slight commotion breaks out in our claustrophobic confines as Verbal and the Bear fetch the searchlight from the fo'c'sle in almost a perfect repeat of our dry run a few days earlier.

'Fisher, fetch Tinselly, the two of you can start fixing splinter mats on the wheelhouse and around the fore and aft guns; tell the grumpy sod that the engines can look after themselves for a bit. We need all available hands-on deck; I'm expecting things to get a bit hectic. Also, ask McLeod and O'Hare to man the fore and aft guns and help keep them supplied with ammo if and when the time comes. It's likely that enemy patrols will have spotted something's going on and will have fighters up from Sicily.' Markham then addresses the rest the crew. 'I want everyone to have their eyes peeled for Macchis. Remember they'll look similar to our Hurricanes in these poor light conditions.'

'Yes, sir!' we all replied. Up to this point, I hadn't considered that the enemy might attack a rescue vessel. We're flying the Red Cross, right? What about the Geneva Convention and all that? But I'd heard reports of the enemy shooting pilots as they baled out and strafing sailors in the water. This is the true meaning of total war; nothing is sacrosanct, everyone is a target. I'd have to get used to it. Suddenly dit, dah, dah, dit pulses wrench my attention back to my receiver; X253 – what ship? I identify us with our call sign and receive 'White Knight'.

'It's HMS *Argus*, sir!'

'Tell them we're in position and standing by.'

To this message I get their coded reply. 'Effecting operation within the hour.' Then a message. 'Your distance by signal strength – three hundred and fifty nautical miles.' Three-hundred and fifty nautical miles, I thought. They're moving away from us. My God, what is the range of a Hurricane?

I turn to Markham. 'Sir, they're moving away from us. Going on our signal strength, they estimate they're three hundred and fifty nautical miles from us.'

Markham looks shaken. 'That's too far. We've travelled forty nautical miles, so the distance to base is pushing their operating range of four hundred nautical miles. We need to move back closer to base.' Markham turns to Tosh. 'Come about, one hundred and eighty degrees. I want the maximum speed we can do in these conditions to get us twenty nautical miles closer to base within the next hour; there's a real danger that our boys will run out of fuel before even getting to Hal-Far. The *Argus* must've met resistance from the Italian Navy and is being pushed off-station.'

The whine of a high-powered turbo-prop aircraft busts on our ears as a fighter plane suddenly swoops low over us.

'A Macchi, heading south-east. I think he's spotted us!' Fish's voice from the wheelhouse door is closely followed by a deafening rattle and vibration from the twenty-millimetre anti-aircraft cannon on the aft deck.

'Take cover!' Markham just manages to give the order as a hail of bullets crash into the wheelhouse followed by another burst from our cannon.

'I got him! I got him, he's going down, his engine's on fire.' The Bear's booming voice is ecstatic, almost maniacal.

'Great shooting, O'Hare!' Skip's voice is strained but relieved. I suddenly realise that Tosh didn't move from his station during the attack. Then, as the searchlight illuminates Tosh's face, I see blood pouring from a wound in the cox's cheek. Skip must've seen it as well because he says, 'Tosh, you'd better let the medical orderly look at that cut, it looks deep.' Just then, Fish enters the wheelhouse, but he's all business and heads straight over and takes the wheel from Tosh, who goes below so the MO can bind his wound that's now drenching his tunic with blood.

'Mayday, Mayday!' Two chilling words bring my attention back to the wireless. 'Pinpoint that signal, Whitton! That's one of ours.'

I get on the wireless. 'This is Coastal Command boat 107 receiving you, over.'

The pilot continues, 'Heading south by south-east about thirty miles out of Valletta, fuel gone, preparing for emergency landing, over.'

'Coastal Command boat 107, we're heading towards you, hang in there!' In reply, a static hiss issues from the wireless.

'Nothing more, sir.' I call over to Skip, 'I think he's trying to ditch.'

'He must think he's got a better chance staying with the plane; in these seas, he might just be right,' comes Skip's answer.

After what seems hours, but is probably just twenty minutes, I'm tempted from my post in the wireless cabin, by a need to be somehow involved in the search. Then an incredible stroke of luck occurs; the clouds clear briefly and the almost full moon casts its light on the ocean silhouetting a dark object floating on the water up ahead. Before I can speak, Verbal breaks his usual silence.

'It's the crashed Hurricane, I'm sure of it; straight-ahead! I can't believe we've found it.' Fish immediately increases our speed and waves crash over the bows.

'I'll take the helm, Fisher. Whitton, up on deck and help O'Hare and McLeod to get the pilot onboard.' Markham takes the wheel and Fish and I rush out on deck; the crashed plane is up ahead. It's still intact, but there's no sign of life. O'Hare shines the searchlight on the wreck, and I can see the pilot's head through the intact cockpit cover. As we approach our bow strikes the submerged wing.

'Easy, sir,' I involuntarily cry out, but as I look back, I'm horrified to see that the plane has canted over and is beginning to sink. Fish immediately sees the danger and begins removing his heavy sea boots and oilskins. As he dives in, Verbal and I grab a couple of gaffs and O'Hare shines the light on Fish who's swimming strong and fast despite the heavy swell and is now almost at the sinking aircraft.

As he reaches it, the lower edge of the cockpit cover is at water level. Verbal throws a grappling iron on a rope out to Fish who's now astride the sinking plane. Smashing one of the iron's hooks under the cockpit cover, Fish wrenches it upwards and the canopy breaks open.

'He's stuck fast and unconscious,' Fish shouts. At that moment, the plane gives up the ghost and sinks. Without hesitation, Fish dives under the water and disappears from sight. The rope on the grappling iron runs out and pulls taught.

Verbal warns, 'If the plane's attached, she'll sink us with the weight.' As if to prove him correct, the boat starts to heel over to starboard. Verbal takes a knife off his belt and starts cutting the rope.

I reach out to ty and stop him, 'What about Fish?'

Verbal shakes his head, 'we can't risk the boat, laddie. It's one man's life or all of us. Fish'll make it; he's an Olympic swimmer, right?'

The taught rope splashes into the water as it's cut. As we strain hard over the rails, Verbal jumps in with a spare Mae West and lifebelt and swims over to where the plane had gone down. A head appears above water; it's Fish with the pilot. Verbal swims out to them and O'Hare and I help get the unconscious pilot onboard with gaffs. O'Hare uses his enormous strength to carry the pilot over the deck and into the wheelhouse.

Skip meets me at the entrance to the wheelhouse, 'Whitton, do what you can to assist Armstrong.' As I follow O'Hare into the wardroom, I get the impression that the pilot is a mere boy. His fine regular features are framed by his flying helmet.

Armstrong immediately gets to business. 'Whitton, help me get the flying jacket off and loosen his clothing.' Just as I remove the pilot's flying helmet, he misses a beat. 'Apologies, her clothing.'

Straight, bobbed and surprisingly dry locks of hair drop back from the stricken pilot's face to reveal a woman's fine features. Unfazed, Armstrong gets to work. 'No pulse, no breathing.' We turn her on her side and a trickle of water issues from her lips. 'Whitton, get to work on CPR while I check her for other wounds; it's five rescue breaths then fifteen compressions then two then fifteen.'

All thoughts vanish from my head; my only focus is breaths and chest compressions.

'She's got no other injuries, but her heart's stopped. I'm going to administer adrenaline to try and get her heart going.' The doctor sets up a drip while I desperately keep going with CPR. Fatigue, or is it hopelessness, starts to kick in, but my own adrenaline is pumped up and somehow, I seem to have superpowers like some Captain Marvel comic book hero.

'I've administered the adrenaline; hopefully, that'll increase the blood flow to the coronary artery.' Whilst he's speaking the Doc takes over CPR and I have a moment to take in the macabre tableau before me. Suddenly, I feel almost like we're somehow assaulting the poor woman. For a moment I feel a pang of shame.

'Check her pulse.'

'Nothing yet, Miles,' I reply helplessly.

'I'm not going to let this woman die! She's not going to die, not like this! Get Crabby up here, now!'

I rush down to the engine room two and find Crab

bent over one of the Napier Sea Lions.

'The MO wants you to help with pilot we've picked up.'

'I fix engines, not people, lad,' came the expected truculent reply.

'I'm not sure what he wants, but it's urgent!'

Back in the wardroom, Armstrong immediately barks out his orders. 'Crab, get me a Marine battery, some wire leads, two wooden spoons and two metal spoons. Now!'

As the dumbfounded mechanic heads back to the engine room, I call after him, 'I'll get the spoons from the galley, if you can get the other stuff, Crab'.

Finding the things, I need is fairly easy, but in my haste, I bang my head painfully as I exit the cramped confines of the galley. Back in the wardroom, I'm glad to see that Crab already has the other things.

'Fix one metal spoon to each wooden spoon with gaffer tape. Good. Connect one electrical lead to the handle of each metal spoon and then I want you to connect the positive electrode to the battery. Good. Now chuck the tape to me. Whitton, remove her blouse and bra.'

I pause slightly at this but do as I'm asked. Armstrong then quickly tapes one metal spoon above her left breast and the other below her right breast. I have no idea what is about to happen next, but respond quickly when Armstrong shouts, 'Clear!' Connecting the second terminal causes the woman's back to convulsively arch, her breasts shift upwards and her body gives the impression of being in a paroxysm of pleasure. Disconnecting immediately, he checks her pulse.

'No pulse, I'm going to give her another jolt. Clear!' Her body arches again; I find the movement unnatural, oddly sexual and deeply disturbing. A groan issues from her lips and on feeling her wrist, her pulse has miraculously returned.

'My God! You've got her heart going and she's breathing.' Tears leap to my eyes and my voice breaks slightly. Armstrong takes over and begins checking his patient.

'Help me strip off the rest of her wet clothes.' Despite the fact they're as saturated as everything else, we both decide to leave her panties in place, so the poor woman retains some fig leaf of decency under the circumstances. We both finally stand back from our labours perspiring heavily.

On the captain's cot lies a brunette with a bob of glossy hair, thinly arched eyebrows; beautiful, except for the slightly blue lips, pale pallor, bumps and bruises on her cheeks and forehead. I instinctively bend and draw the counterpane up to her chin with the tenderness of a father bidding his child goodnight and then follow Crabby out of the room leaving the MO to monitor his patient.

Fred, Saturday 14th December 1940, Oflag VII-B

My father's petulant voice is ringing in my ears. 'Come on, Freddy, what's got into you, lad? You caught it; it's your fish. You need to put it out of its misery.' The white belly of a large brown trout flashes in the sunlight as it flops around in the gloom at the bottom of the boat. Gills straining as it fights for air, its eyes stare helplessly moving first to gaze at me and then at George who's kneeling next to me, anxious with his face full of fear, fingernails digging into the flesh of my bare arm in his anguish.

Turning back to the fish, I notice that its eyes are swivelling unnaturally left and right like a devilish automation. Slowly, O'Callaghan's pain-riven face replaces that of the fish; his pallid skin is glazed with sweat as he fights desperately for breath. Blood spurting from an open wound in his chest, he arches his back and his legs thrash, his heels tapping on the hard ground like he's doing a macabre Irish jig; tap-tap-tap-ity-tap-tap. The mad tapping mutates into watery sploshing and I realise the sound is being caused by water dripping from the ceiling onto a bucket on the wooden floor next to my head. I shift on my straw mattress, the springs on my steel bunk squeaking loudly, and staring helplessly into the gloom, I can still see O'Callaghan's stricken face hanging in front of me.

The waking dream is powerful and causes me to lash out with my arms in a vain attempt to dispel it. How many men have I killed or have died whilst under my command? How many more will it be before we leave this place at the end of the war? And when will that be? The dead, all the men I've killed, seen killed, or have died under my command, their faces pass before my eyes and in that no man's land between waking and sleep, they beckon to me.

I've had no word about how things are at home. Poor Mother will be worried sick; I hope this won't have a detrimental effect on her angina, and George, I wonder where he got posted after his training at Cranwell. Mulling this over, I suddenly realise why the moonlight has woken me; somebody has taken the curtain down from my window! I swing my legs down, an action that's accompanied by more squeaking, and manage to touch down on the floor from my upper bunk.

Geddes, sleeping on the lower bunk, stirs and sits up. 'Sorry, Gedge, some blighter's taken the curtains down!'

'Well, you know who that's likely to be; Arthur Fry[10]. He was talking yesterday about needing more

---

[10] Captain Arthur Fry of the Royal Service Corps was the self-appointed camp photographer at Oflag VII-B who passed his

material for the stage set for the concert he's organising next week. I'm guessing it'll be in the tailor's shop in hut three.'

I can feel my hackles rising. 'Why our curtains, why not theirs? I'm going to have a word with Arthur.' Geddes simply shrugs his shoulders and prepares to bury himself back under his bedcovers, meagre though they are. An unaccountable rage drives me outside only to find a bitter wind blowing. Why am I acting like a spoilt child? Arthur's productions will be vital distractions in the long months and years ahead, so why am I so aggrieved? It's down, perhaps, to the fact that we have so few comforts here and little to remind us of home and the lives we used to have. At least I'm single and have few attachments back home, but some of the lads have wives and sweethearts, children and family responsibilities and live-in perpetual anguish not knowing what is going on back home.

Despite feelings of self-righteous indignation, I take a moment to watch the moonlight as it gives way to the dawn and the underbelly of low cloud is glowing red, purple and gold. The stunningly vibrant hues of sunrises are one of the few compensations of life in the icebox of a continental winter; an artist would have a field day. Despite the early hour, albedo from the thick snow makes it seem lighter and the fast-flowing waters of River Altmühl sparkle in the early morning light.

---

time as a POW putting on musical evenings, plays and pantomimes.

For a moment, the accommodation blocks behind me and the lawns sweeping down to the snow-covered football pitch and the makeshift ice rink created by a large frozen pool of water, I almost think I've emerged for a pre-breakfast stroll at a classy hotel. I walk down past the garden and decide to go for a turn around the parade ground. By the time I wade through the deeper snow at the bottom of one of the banks, others have had the same idea and are wandering around in small groups.

A party of Belgians approaches, and I recognise the moustachioed visage of Henri Mestrez[11] who's become the self-styled director of Oflag VII-B's very own symphony orchestra. I'm guessing that Henri is bound to know where our curtains have gone, so I stride up to him with the intention of giving him a piece of my mind. Seeing me approach, Henri detaches himself from his compatriots and holds out his hand.

'Bonjour, mon ami, comment vas-tu ce beau matin?' Henri's friendly smile and the fact that he's speaking French to me, which I previously asked him to do in an attempt to improve mine, causes my unjustifiable rage to dissipate.

'Bonjour, Henri, et tout le monde, allez-vous pour le petit déjeuner?'

To which I receive a pejorative, 'Oui!' Since it's early morning and I'm still barely awake, my French

---

[11] Lt. Henri Mestrez is a real-life character who formed and led a symphony orchestra in Oflag VII-B.

begins to falter as Henri continues our conversation. Noticing this, Henri seamlessly switches to English mid-sentence. It never ceases to amaze me how the continentals do that, and I feel a pang of envy for their superior linguistic skills.

Looking furtively around before speaking and keeping my voice low, I whisper conspiratorially, 'We've heard that one of your chaps is building a radio set.'

'Yes, Antoine Fernand[12] has almost completed it. He managed to salvage some critical parts from radios he found in abandoned vehicles before we were transported here. He then stole the rest of what he needed from stuff lying around the camp.'

'That is an incredible bit of forethought!'

'Oui, Antoine isn't the most talkative person, but that's because he's always got his eyes open finding bits here and bits there. I think you English would call him a spiv.'

'Well perhaps not a spiv; they're rather disreputable!'

Henri chuckles at this. I'm about to educate Henri on what a spiv gets up to when a huge commotion

---

[12] Lt. Antoine Fernand, a Belgian officer, actually made a clandestine radio receiver using bits and pieces he collected around camp. It was through his efforts and those of a small team of other Belgian officers, he was able to keep POWs in Oflag VII-B informed about the progress of the war via BBC News.

breaks out and, a pig of all things, bursts out of the kitchen, and in a riot of squealing mayhem, barges through our group scattering us like ninepins in front of a bowling ball. Picking ourselves up, we're in time to watch one of the German adjutants, who looks after the commandant's office staff, running hell-for-leather after it.

The more playful among us, including Henri and myself give chase. While we're running, I see someone moving very fast from our left, from the direction of the huts at the far end of the compound. By the way he's moving, he looks like a professional rugby player. Sure enough, as we watch, he tackles the errant beast by throwing himself at the animal's midriff and the two disappear in a flurry of snow.

Incredibly, it seems like he's incapacitated the animal and it sprawls in the snow momentarily winded. The adjutant walks up panting hard and looking around hastily attaches a lead to the pig's nose ring.

'Vielen Dank! Ich muss das schwein verstecken, bevor der Kommandant es sieht!'

Chuckling at this Henri replies, 'Nur wenn Sie uns schweinefleisch geben!'

'Oh, ja natürlich!'

Turning his head and assuming a conspiratorial demeanour, Henri whispers, 'I think this pig is being kept secret from our noble Commandant Blatterbauer[13], so I'm negotiating a share of the spoils for keeping his secret.'

As the adjutant leads the animal away, trying to stay out of sight of the commandant's office, we discover that the valiant pig catcher is none other than the medic, RAMC Graham King.

'We're impressed, Graham! I didn't know you had pig-tackling skills. Is that part of your Army Medical Corps training?'

'No, but I was a fly half with the Nottingham Rugby Club before the war!'

We all have a good laugh, something I never thought we'd be doing when I first came through the gates of Oflag VII-B six months ago.

---

[13] History records that Commandant Blatterbauer was the rather odious and pompous Wehrmacht officer in charge of running Oflag VII-B.

George, Thursday January 2nd, 1941, RAF Kalafrana

'Be a good chap and flick the switch on the wireless over, Tweedy.' One of the Maltese ground crew has just turned in and we have our chance to change the channel and catch up with news from home; bad as it is no doubt. A few of us who'd been on duty over Christmas and New Year are sitting having a natter and few well-earned drinks in the NAAFI on the upstairs veranda. Yes, folks at home, it's still, just about warm enough to sit out in January, so here's mud in your eye! I quietly acknowledge my own inner toastmaster and raise my glass.

'To Freddy and absent friends.'

'Who're you drinking to, Witty? And why can't we join in?'

'Absent friends, and to my confounded lost brother, Freddy; not a word from him since last summer. I'm convinced he's okay, but he must've been picked up by the Germans at Dunkirk. He's been posted officially lost in action.'

'Sorry to hear that, mate.' Tinselly nods over to me in a rare show of camaraderie. He's a strange one, blowing hot n' cold. One minute he's your best mate and the next, he's acting all high and mighty about some feat of engineering genius that Isambard Kingdom Brunel would be proud of when he, once again, coaxes the boat's engines back into life. The last time, it was a huge dose of sea water while we were out gallivanting about after, what turned out to be, the crew of a ruddy Savia-Marchetti bomber who'd no doubt just dropped a load of bombs on Valletta.

I run my finger across the condensation on the gold hopleaf on the shiny red label of the bottle of pale ale I'm drinking and toss down the remainder smacking my lips appreciatively. There's got to be some advantages of being in the Med.

'Anyone else for another?'

Four hands show support for another beer, but Fish pipes up, 'I'll have a Tom Collins, old chap.'

'Still think you're in the varsity common room, Fishy?' I chuckle and make my way over to the bar. 'Five pale ales and a Tom Collins, easy on the water and don't spare the gin! Isn't that right, Fish, plenty of gin?'

'Fill it up for all I care, old man!'

'Coming right up, sir.'

Carmelo turns and gets to work. He smirks as he brings the tray over to our table and serves up Fish's Tom Collins in a very swish fluted champagne glass.

'There you go, sir, special for you.' We all burst out laughing as Fish hams it up, pinkie outstretched as he takes a sip.

'Spot on!' You could never accuse Fish of taking

himself too seriously.

'So, Witty.' Tweedy pauses briefly for effect. 'You never told us what exactly happened when you resuscitated that poor Air Transport auxiliary you pulled out of the drink a few weeks ago. Mother electrocuted her by all accounts. Come on, old man, you can't keep it a secret for ever.'

I roll my eyes and look over at Crabby, who looks rather sheepishly back at me and shrugs his shoulders. 'Well.'

I didn't get a chance to continue. Tweedy can't contain himself. 'I understand it involved taking her clothes off and zapping her bare chest!'

'Well, if you're going to tell the story yourself, you might as well continue, Tweedy.' I'm struggling to keep my temper; I don't want to get into some kind of lads' bragging match over the trauma that poor old Tilly must've gone through. She'd only just come out of hospital, but I'd been told she'd made a full recovery. I'd also been told that Markham was recommending that Armstrong should be mentioned in dispatches for his quick action and Fish too for his bravery.

'All I will say, is that they reckon that Mother's likely to go down in history as the first person to use electrical defibrillation.'

'What on earth is that when it's at home?' Tweedy's drunk and has obviously been told all the gory details by Crabby. I make a mental note to have a word with him in private. I was just about to divert everyone's attention, and mine, away from an in-depth discussion of Telly Burnett's ample and very fine breasts by blinding them with science and explaining that Mother had learned of the technique from his professor when he was an intern at the Case Western Hospital in Ohio when a commotion breaks out downstairs.

An air raid warning on the tannoy suddenly cuts in over the rather soothing Glenn Miller playing on the radio.

'Air raid warning, air raid warning, air raid warning!'

We wait for the same message in Maltese to finish before standing up and walking over to the balustrade of the veranda.

'Yep, they're at it again over in Valletta, poor blighters.' Tweedy points over at the yellow stain that's appeared on the underside of the sullen dark clouds hanging on the distant horizon. It's another high-altitude bombing raid. The Italians had resorted to night bombing due to the Hurricanes now stationed at Hal-Far scaring the living daylights out of them. Their targets must look like tiny pinpricks at twenty thousand feet and in next to zero visibility, they were essentially just lobbing bombs at all and sundry without a care in the world who they were killing.

I inwardly swear an oath and offer up a prayer and hope to God I'll get a chance to return to the Empire Bar and find that Maltese woman who'd been bewitching my thoughts ever since I'd clapped eyes on her. An explosion on the airfield perimeter is immediately followed by another then another.

'Bloody hell! Take cover! Down to the shelter!' I shout. Everyone's scrambling for the air-raid shelter just outside the barrack block. The wailing sound of the siren's making my blood run cold. More explosions on the airfield are interspersed with strafing bullets. By the sound of the cannons, it's likely to be Messerschmitt's and Stuka dive-bombers wreaking the havoc. I look up while I'm running and can make out the tracer fire from our anti-aircraft cannons.

Entering the shelter, I can see quite a few familiar faces in the harsh electric lights. The pounding from the air is relentless, with 'crump' sounds shaking the lanterns and causing little puffs of dust and concrete particles to rain from the ceiling. Crump, crump, CRUMP!

'Bloody hell! That was close!' comes someone's voice.

'All right, that'll do. We're safe enough down here.' An officer's voice I'm certain, trying to keep everyone calm. Havoc indeed is what's going on all around us. Shakespeare's words come to mind, 'Cry havoc and let slip the dogs of war!' And then Marc Anthony's reflection and regret for what they'd done. 'That this foul deed shall smell above the earth with carrion men, groaning for burial.' Ah the Classics. Forced to learn the ruddy stuff at school it could always be relied upon to lift the mood and offer hope at a time like this!

Why can't I remember happy times, like Freddy's smiling face after catching that ten-pound trout in the Lake District, or Uncle Albert's riotous New Year's Eve parties? In the dim light someone's coughing like a consumptive and I can vaguely make out Mother and another MO tending to a couple of lads that'd bought some shrapnel. I look around for more of my crewmates and start mentally ticking them off. Yep, there's Crabby and Tinsley; joined at the hip those two. Fish is sitting next to me; I guess people say the same thing about us. I also spot Verbal and Tweedy; the Bear's likely in the shelter by the Camber, Tosh's in the infirmary recuperating from a bad bout of sandfly fever, Mother's taking care of business so that just leaves the skip. I begin to worry about him.

To nobody in particular, I ask, 'Has anyone seen Flight Lieutenant Markham?' A short silence follows and then someone pipes up.

'I saw him heading over to the women's billet shortly before the Stukas showed up. Sorry, mate, I lost sight of him in all the excitement.'

I stare down at the earth floor and the smell of damp and a slight odour of what? Putrefaction? Probably a dead rat. I start to feel uneasy about Markham. At that moment, the Rediffusion speaker crackles into life.

'Raiders passed, raiders passed, raiders passed.' Thrice repeated like a benediction. 'Hail Mary full of grace' pops unbidden into my head. I'd heard my godmother murmur the first line of that Catholic prayer repeatedly when she'd heard about Freddy's disappearance. The rather less edifying final two lines come to me just as we were rising to shuffle out of the shelter. 'Pray for us sinners now, and at the hour of our death.'

As we emerge from the shelter, my words of prayer evaporate and are replaced by a vision of Hell like Dante's Inferno. One of the billets is ablaze and so is part of the Headquarters building and one of the seaplane hangars. Everyone's running about doing something, so we pitch in to help the fire crew deal with the blaze in what turns out to be the women's billet.

Cowed by the heat radiating out from the building, we're forced to move back by the fire crew shouting themselves hoarse over the fire alarms warning everyone that the roof is likely to go any minute. It's then I notice feet poking out of blankets that've been hastily thrown over a line of corpses in a macabre parody of a parade-ground inspection. At that same moment, another sagging body is placed on the far end of the line. 'Fall in soldier!'

The horror is messing with my head. I stare at the feet; some have lost their shoes and are bloodied, but others still have them on. There's men's shoes and a few women's with torn nylons exposing their legs. A woman stumbles past slumping forward, a harsh light from the blaze illuminates her face which is etched with pain. I rush over to her with a couple of the lads and as we support her, we notice she's carrying something in her arms. I hold her head and the other two run to find something to make her more comfortable. Looking down I notice the gore at her midriff, and I realise what she'd been carrying; it's her intestines which spill out as her arms sag onto the ground. I instinctively recoil at the ghastly sight and would have dropped the poor woman's head I'm cradling in my arms if she hadn't started gasping in pain.

As I look into her startled, frightened eyes, she murmurs something. Stooping to put my ear to her mouth, I gently grasp her hand.

'Kill me, kill me,' she gasps.

'I need some help over here.' There's panic in my voice. A medical orderly detaches himself from a chap he's been attending next to me and comes over. He checks her pulse and breathing.

'She's gone, mate, she's gone. So sorry, mate.' Sorry seems such a trite word for what's just happened. The lads return with a blanket and something to support her head, but we end up using them to cover her body. Another one to join the parade-ground line-up of the dead. I suddenly become aware that I'm staring into Markham's eyes. He's crouching next to one of the bodies in the line.

'Sir, are you, all right?' Markham looks up at me. His face is completely drained of colour and I can see he's been crying. At that moment, there are no words.

‘Tilly, she, she, was in her billet when it was hit. She’s…’ His voice tails off and I crouch beside him as he holds Tilly’s hand which has already assumed the pale porcelain sheen of the dead. A visceral sobbing and dry retching sound is ripped from Markham’s throat as a paroxysm of grief racks his body.

I turn away, completely numb and leave Skip to his grief. There’s nothing I can or do or say that can comfort him; I feel completely empty.

George, Wednesday 14th January 1941, RAF Hal-Far & Luqa

Lady Luck has smiled again and I'm indulging in a little ritual affectation inherited from my Uncle Albert by ostentatiously breathing condensation onto my fingernails and then burnishing them on my tunic. My uncle used to love doing this and, for me, it means, 'That impressive thing I just did? I'm so good that it's caused me no more trouble than dulling my manicure a bit.'

'Well, Witty, what's making you so damn self-satisfied?' asks my neighbour, a rather disgruntled mechanic accompanying our cargo of crates containing the disassembled remains of poor old Faith, Hope and Charity, our Gloster Sea Gladiator biplanes and erstwhile courageous defenders of Malta; sobering to think that before we got some Hurricanes, they were our only defence against the combined aerial onslaught of Hitler and Mussolini.

'The answer to that, old boy, consists of two parts. For one, I'm off-base with a legitimate excuse, namely, to acquire parts for our boat's wireless. Secondly, I'll likely have enough time in Valletta while you lads are offloading those wretched biplanes at Hal-Far, to catch a cold beer in town.'

'You could give us a hand, mate!'

'You wouldn't want me around anything mechanical. I'm jinxed when it comes to machinery!' is my very reasonable reply.

'A fine ruddy WOM you make if you're constantly jiggering your radio set.'

'Which means, old boy, more little excursions into Valletta.'

There isn't time for my companions to think of a suitably outraged reply to that as we've pulled up at the Luqa guardhouse. I promptly jump down, show my ID and flash a winning smile at the lads in the sentry box and walk swiftly towards stores before my travelling companions can say anything more about it.

One other good reason to find an excuse to be off base is that I'm still processing the horror of the air raid a couple of weeks ago. We've haven't had anything as bad since due to the heroic efforts of our Hurricane pilots, but there's a flat stone weighing on my chest I can't seem to shift. The lads have really been knocked back and Markham's withdrawn into himself, becoming detached and, quite frankly, his decisions and orders are somewhat erratic. Thankfully, Tosh's been able to take a lot of pressure off the skip, but I know the rumours are spreading that Markham's lost it since Tilly's death, poor wretch!

There's no let-up at the moment what with air raids and shouts for us to pick up crews out of the drink. I really don't know how we'll cope in the weeks and months ahead. I know the quartermaster at Luqa, Jimmy Bland; he's got a wicked sense of humour and he's a mine of information on the 1082/83 wireless set-up, so I feel a bit lighter as the double doors swing shut behind me and walk over to Jimmy who's standing behind his desk.

'What can I do you for, George? Buggered your wireless again, old chap?'

I assume the confessional tone of a supplicant. 'Forgive me, Jimmy, for I have sinned.'

'How have you sinned, old boy?'

'The tuning mechanism on my 1082's finally given up the ghost. It's usually an absolute swine to tune anyway, but it's gone completely out of whack and I reckon it needs replacing.'

'Well, it doesn't surprise me. It's rumoured that you've now taken to swearing at your wireless set. You can't abuse a piece of sensitive British engineering like that and expect to get away with it you know!' comes the expected flippant reply. 'You're in luck though. I've got a tuning mechanism I cannibalised for a set from a bomb-damaged Fairey Swordfish, one of the ones those blokes flew over from France, can you believe it?'

I nod emphatically. 'Yep, I heard about that; wonders never cease in this bloody mess.'

Then, pondering the occasional miracle that seems to happen in this little war of ours, I involuntarily open my mouth and out comes the ridiculous fantasy I'm currently harbouring.

‘I know it’s an absolute long shot, Jimmy, but could you ask around and see if those Swordfish pilots know anything about what happened to the captured British soldiers?’

Jimmy knew what I was asking. He dropped his jokey tone and plays along with my fantasy as his face becomes serious.

‘Will do, old chap, certainly I will. I’m sure the blokes that Jerry picked up are tucked away in a POW camp by now and chomping on sauerkraut and wurst; your Freddy will be fine, mate.’

‘Thanks, Jimmy, I really appreciate it.’ And I mean it. With that, Jimmy disappears through a formidable steel door rather like the kind of thing you find on ships leaving me in the homely waiting room, which is a mere front, hiding the Byzantine complexity of the engineering stores facility.

Knowing he’d be some minutes scanning shelves, locating my spare part and logging its allocation, I retreat into a comfortable leather chair somewhat similar to the type of furniture you find in a hotel lobby. Sitting down, I notice that the table had actually been rescued from, not a hotel lobby, but from the Royal Opera House razed by the Luftwaffe a few weeks ago. I’d seen the fine old building only recently as it used to grandly sit at the head of Republic Street, one of the major thoroughfares. I inwardly dread what I’ll see when I get to the city proper. Would anything be left? What about the Empire Bar?

The jokey patter that everyone habitually drops into is a veneer, and, like badly applied plasterwork, it occasionally peels away to reveal the true horror of what we're going through; our private little battles to remain on the side of sanity. A creaking sound from the storeroom's doors heralds Jimmy's return.

'Here you are, old chap,' he says, producing with a flourish a battered old cardboard box that might once have held a pair of shoes. Genuflecting slightly as if receiving some great prize or book of wisdom, I thank Jimmy profusely and turn to go.

'Don't worry, George, Fred'll be fine.' His fatherly smile is strangely reassuring as if someone who can navigate the RAF engineering stores must be some great seer or privy to the secrets of the universe.

'Thanks, Jimmy.'

Flapping back through the double doors I re-emerge into a slate-grey day with clouds scudding menacingly above threatening rain, or worse. I hurry over to the transport pool and join some lads boarding a Bedford troop carrier.

'Where's this one going, lads?'

'HQ, mate,' was the simple reply. Perfect, Lascaris Battery, and the hush-hush war rooms that are being constructed there, is in the centre of Valletta. All I have to do is to hop off and walk a bit over to Strada Stretta.

Entering the city proper from the south-west really gives you an appreciation of what a dense metropolis Valletta is. Almost as soon as we start to enter the outskirts we're dodging around piles of white bricks and pulverised rubble strewn everywhere as though some crazed demolitions company had gone berserk. Walls pitted with shrapnel holes and smashed windows abound. Around one corner, is a grand old tenement with its façade dropped neatly in front of it leaving the floors, furniture and wallpaper intact, rather like a giant doll's house. Around the next, several huge buildings are gone except for a single corner here and there rather like sea stacks I'd seen in Dorset where we'd spent family holidays, God! Such times seem so far away from this apocalyptic scene.

Since this is mid-afternoon, mothers are cooking lunch on charcoal burners in makeshift corrugated iron villages that have sprung up in the ruins of the city. Children play around bricks that have been neatly piled here and there to form catacomb-like passages or trenches like you'd see in Ypres or the killing fields of Verdun where my father served during the last little shindig with the Germans. The most pitiful scenes are the desperate; wild-eyed groups of people, families probably, clawing at the rubble of what was most likely their home, looking for loved ones. I look away, ashamed that they might think I'm staring whilst they live through their own private little hell.

Within sight of Grand Harbour now, we swing inland a bit and pull up in front of HQ. Jumping down, I notice the discreetly hidden mechanical excavators associated with construction of the underground war rooms soon to be filled with a vast army of people plotting the swarms of enemy bombers that appear nightly over the city. Taking leave of the transport, I head towards the centre, passing the Grand Harbour Hotel which is amazingly intact considering that its neighbours are now just piles of bricks.

My sketchy knowledge of the city is being stretched to the limit, but like frogs that return to the same pond every year, I eventually swing into Saint George's Square and thence onto the Strada Stretta. At this point, my homing instincts falter slightly, and I ask a boisterous group of sailors for directions; they're wearing HMS *Illustrious* badges on their caps.

'The Empire, we've just been in there, mate! A bit hoity-toity if you ask me though. We were chucked out. Just having a laugh, you understand.'

'You was totally out of order with one of the girls in there, Mick,' chimes in one of his mates.

'Yeah, but they didn't have to frogmarch us out of there like naughty schoolboys!'

Not waiting for an argument to ensue, I begin walking in the direction they'd come from. I couldn't blame them for letting off a bit of steam; the *Illustrious* had been badly damaged whilst tangling with some Stuka dive-bombers and was holed up on Malta for a while. I have a hearty regard for the *Illustrious*, since it was, she who accompanied our troop convoy here. She'd also recently added to her battle honours giving Mussolini a smack in the eye by sinking a battleship and badly damaging two others just before Christmas.

Turning into the Strada, the area around the Empire Bar & Restaurant is still remarkably intact, however, the surrounding taller buildings are badly damaged. The consequences of lobbing high explosives around can be uniquely weird. Depending on how the blast is directed by buildings or even people standing around you creates a kind of lottery of consequences in which you can be completely unscathed whilst the bloke next to you is blown to smithereens.

Quickening my steps, I enter the palatial lobby, nod at the shiny suited chaps at the door and then wait to be seated by the polite notice asking me to do so in both Maltese and English. By the most incredible stroke of luck, the woman of my dreams floats towards me smiling. I experience the odd sensation of having known her for years, or is that because I'd been fantasising over her for weeks?

'RAF yes? The RAF is always welcome here, less trouble than the British Navy! Illallu ballu! Is it a table for one? Just drinks, or would you like a menu?'

'Just a Hopleaf Pale Ale, please.' I don't think my frugal service pay will run to food. Looking around the place is pretty deserted. There'd been heavy bombing the night before, so I'm guessing that everyone's keeping their heads down, it's just us mad dogs and Englishmen who're out and about.

Just as I'm composing some corny chat-up line to ingratiate myself, the woman herself brings my beer over with a plate of little pastries.

'Pastizzi, little parcels of cheese,' she replies to my enquiring glance. 'In Malta, we love food, so we never have just a drink.' She promptly heads back to the bar but returns to my table with a glass of mineral water just as I'm biting into one of the pastizzi which turns out to be remarkably greasy with pastry that's similar to a sausage role.

'Ylena.' She offers me a small hand covered with rings.

'George,' I say simply. Ylena continues with answers to a few more of the questions I'm about to ask; is she reading my mind?

'I'm the owner of this place; took over after my father died. There are no sons in our family and my mother is too ill and my sister and brother too young, so the honour fell to me.'

'It's my first time in Malta, my first time anywhere outside Newcastle actually,' I offer rather lamely. I stare around the room where we're sitting, looking for inspiration, and glance at our reflection in a huge mirror mounted behind the bar and angled slightly downwards; a man and a woman sitting together at a table talking to each other. I like what I see.

'So, Mr George, what do you do? Are you a fighter pilot?'

'No, but I rescue aircrews that have been shot down, a bit like an ocean-going ambulance.'

She raises a delicate, plucked eyebrow, appears

impressed and nods once, like a confirmation of some kind.

'I hate the war and what it's doing to us. If the British stay, the Nazis and my own countrymen will bomb us. If the British leave, the pig Nazis will lord it over us. I've heard what they're like in France. Like you English say, we're between a rock and a hard place.'

'So, you're Italian?'

'A way back, yes, but our family have lived on Malta for generations. I have no sympathy for the Fascisti and their squadristi cowards who go around murdering and torturing for some stupid political ideal!'

I watch her eyes flash and her jaw set as she forms her words; what a woman… For some reason, as a supportive gesture, I briefly and gently touch her arm. She stops mid-tirade. Half expecting, she might pull away, she instead looks directly into my eyes and holds my gaze. It's something that's never happened before with women in my hometown; they always avoid looking directly at a man's eyes for fear that it might be misconstrued. I can see the person behind Ylena's eyes is one of searing intelligence, defiant and courageous, a compelling mixture. I smile at her.

'I'm talking too much. And we've only just met!' While we've been chatting, the place has been filling up; army bods and a few chaps from Kalafrana one of whom nods over at me and smiles knowingly. Blast! This'll get around base like wildfire! I make a mental note to have a quiet chat with them and explain, but what though? That I'm talking to an attractive woman in a bar? Or is it my not so gentlemanly intentions that I'm feeling guilty about? My focus returns to Ylena.

'I can't stay much longer, I have to get back my billet, but I want to see you again. I'll need an excuse to get off base again though.' However, Ylena immediately comes up with a solution to my dilemma.

'In two weeks, we're holding a big farewell party here. The rumour is that the damaged aircraft carrier in the harbour [HMS *Illustrious*] will sail for the US. They'd normally have a big party like this at one of the big fancy places near the harbour, but most are bombed out. The navy parks its ships, and the Maltese suffer, Alla jgħinna! I will tell my boys at the door to let you in and give you a guest ticket if you can get into town.'

I liked, very much the idea that Ylena was interested; all that boyish charm and good looks wasn't going to be wasted after all!

'I'd like that. It's very kind of you. But how do you know I'm not some mad seducer?' I throw out another smile, which she catches immediately.

'How do you know that I'm not a mad seducer too?'

So, like a vaudeville double act, I reply, 'Let's be mad seducers together and to hell with the consequences!' We both start giggling at this and at that moment, Ylena leans over and pulls my face towards hers and pecks me gently on the cheek. I whisper, 'That's a first for me, kissed by a beautiful woman I hardly know.'

'I'm Maltese, I know what a man needs. It's obvious that we're attracted to each other. We're living through a war when any moment could be our last so let's skip the preliminaries.' A slight American twang, again she answers my unasked question. 'I went to business college in Boston, sometimes my American English pops out unexpectedly!'

I look down, and we're holding each other's hands across the table. Nodding at her I make a move. 'Okay, I'm going to love you and leave you. It's likely I can get a lift back to my billet with one of the chaps at the bar.'

Ylena's brow crinkles slightly. 'How can I contact you?'

'I'm stationed at Kalafrana, RAF Coastal Command.'

'Kalafrana, yes, one of my cousins is a mechanic there. I'll send an invitation to the captain's party with him.' I briefly feel like a schoolboy hatching a plot to play truant from school.

'Right, until then.' Ylena draws me close and kisses me on both cheeks. 'It's okay, in Malta even the men kiss each other!'

'But the Maltese men don't look like you, Ylena.'

Fred, Monday 3rd March 1941, Oflag VII-B

Slowly letting myself down from my upper bunk, I steal a glance at Geddes' pocket watch on the chair by our bunk. Six a.m., give or take; it's still pitch black and bloody freezing. I quietly curse the fact that it's my stove watch and the damn thing looks as though it's gone out!

The hut's like an icebox as I quietly negotiate the clutter of boots in the corridor between the sleepers in their bunks. I know that if I make too much noise, I'll stir up the wrath of my hut-mates. Mind you, some of the lads really know how to snore, and so any added noise I might make would seem inconsequential in comparison. Passing Ernie Hart's bunk, I notice he's sitting staring at the stove. As I pass him, he states the obvious.

'The ruddy thing's gone out, Freddy, you're not going to be popular!' He chuckles to himself. 'I'll come and help you. I'd hate to see a young officer strung up so early in the morning.'

I enjoy hearing Ernie's Geordie accent; in the dark, his voice sounds quite a lot like George's. Ernie's a dab hand and he soon coaxes the stove back into life, our faces illuminated now in an orange glow from the dancing flames. Ernie drops his voice further to a whisper.

'I guess you know that Arthur Fry's doing a rehearsal for his production of 'Gaslight' this evening.'

'Yes, I'd heard. Funnily enough, I saw it with Mother and George when it was premiered in London during a spot of leave. It's a pretty murky tale of deceit and madness with plenty of red herrings and a sting in the tail; I'm thoroughly looking forward to it!'

'Damn me, you've seen it already! Well, what you don't know is that I've landed the part of the police detective, Rough. Wallace Finlayson, who's been playing Rough in rehearsals, has been taken to hospital with a badly infected tooth and suspected blood poisoning from an abscess. Really nasty; he's in a pretty bad way.'

We both ponder this. It seems incredible, but it's like being back in the Dark Ages, where you could, quite literally, die of something as trivial as toothache or an in-growing toenail.

Ernie continues, 'I used to do some amateur theatricals with the St George's Players in Morpeth years ago before I joined the army. I happened to tell Arthur this a few weeks ago, and Bob's your uncle, I'm having a try-out as Finlayson's stand-in this afternoon. Why not come along to the rehearsal? You know the story anyway and you can let us know how we're doing compared to the professionals.'

'I will; wild horses wouldn't stop me, old chap!' Looking up from the stove, it's now getting light and we bundle ourselves into our greatcoats and cap comforters and step out into the crisp chill of the morning. Despite being early March, the temperature outside feels like it's set firmly well below zero with a cold wind blowing off the snow-capped peaks of the Bavarian Alps in the distance. A certain tang in the breeze suggests it might snow later on. The dry, powdery snow squeaks under our feet as we walk over to the kitchen to see what, if anything, is on the menu (as if we didn't know already).

Strolling along the Lagestrasse, we have a clear view of the inner gate and I spot the Red Cross parcel van as it arrives at the gatehouse. Ernie and I look at each other and quicken our pace as this almost mythical beast makes its way towards Block one. Our fellow inmate's ears must be trained to hear the characteristic sound of its whining gearbox as the whole camp has suddenly come alive and even the died-in-the-wool 'sack hounds' have dragged themselves out of their bunks.

Hastily set-up tables are dragged outside and the whole Strasse is suddenly filled with a heaving mass of humanity, all bent on getting hold of a coveted Red Cross parcel with its tins of delight! To a POW, there can be no more welcome sight than the Red Cross van, our only lifeline with the outside world carrying the possibility of receiving letters from home.

Since we're almost at the head of the queue, we're

amongst the first to get hold of a coveted parcel from the orderlies who are, try as they might, hardly able to keep up with demand from the ravening hordes! Most of the eight hundred blokes in here must be heading over as the huts empty and the courtyard fills with excited men. Sorting through accompanying mail, I spot a parcel addressed to me. My heart misses a beat; I recognise my mother's handwriting.

Tearing it open, a woollen sweater and a couple of large tins of shortbread drop onto the table. The sweater is almost certainly my mother's handiwork and I fancy I can still smell her perfume on it as I pull it over my head. A letter, opened by the British censors of course, drops to the ground. Opening it, my mother's untidy scrawl covers the page, and I can hear her voice in my head while I read her words:

'Dearest Freddy. I hope this finds you well and in a good spirits despite your awful circumstances. The MOD took ages before confirming your POW status and even longer before we found out where you are being held. I've hastily put a few things together for you and sent them to the Red Cross office. I will make sure I'm better prepared next time and write you a longer letter. I know you will be keeping yourself busy and your sense of duty to your men will keep you going, but you must remember that you are always in our thoughts and prayers. George has been posted to the RAF Coastal Command in Malta. We got a letter from him last week. He seems to have met a Maltese girl; his letter is full of it. We just hope he is not getting in over his head; these Mediterranean women can be fiery. Uncle Robert and Aunt Mae have been asking after you constantly, and so have Frank and Melissa. I will try and get your father to include a note to you next time, but you know he's not much of a writer. Keep your chin up, son. All my love and best wishes. Mother.'

Reading the spidery scrawl, I can picture my mother sitting writing at the kitchen table with the Rayburn burning merrily in the corner by the sink. Small chunks of the letter's contents have been blacked out by the censor; likely they're details of George's posting. I sit heavily on the billet doorstep and stare at her words, reading and re-reading them. Home and the rituals of family life seem like they're a million miles away; I even find it difficult to remember my mother's face.

Pulling out the Red Cross printed postcard I've been issued with, my heart sinks. I'm only able to include a few words on how I am, nothing more. At least my poor mother will know I'm okay, so I pen my message. 'I'm fine and spirits are good. Love Fred.' Oh well, better than nothing I suppose! Whilst writing my paltry message, I become aware of a chap almost collapsing on the step beside me. Turning to see who it is, I notice he's got his head in his hands, a letter clasped to his chest and his face is in extremis of emotional turmoil. I don't know who he is, but I can guess what's happened to him. It's almost certainly a 'Dear John' letter. There's been a couple in our hut and the effect is devastating.

Slowly, my neighbour reads his letter again, his shoulders heaving as he spits out his grief. Turning to me, I can see he's trying to keep his emotions in check, but his eyes are wild and full of the kind of impotent anger that only a prisoner can experience when he receives news of a situation, he's utterly powerless to change.

'My whore of a wife has gone off with someone else. Don't bother coming home, she says. I'll kill him if I ever get out of this bloody hole.'

His vehemence makes me believe he would if he ever gets the chance. Before I can offer any response, most likely platitudes that would be of little solace, he gets to his feet and storms off towards the huts at the far end of the camp, briefly dropping out of view behind trees in the small garden in front of my accommodation block. I can now see his dark figure clearly against the expanse of snow on the football pitch as he crosses to the other huts. My heart goes out to him.

'What's wrong with him?' Ernie reappears beside me brandishing his Red Cross parcel and a couple of letters.

'He's just had the dreaded "Dear John" letter from his wife.'

Ernie taps his own letters on the palm of his hand. 'These two are from my wife. I'm a bit reluctant to open them because I know what they'll be about; lack of money to feed the family. I committed the cardinal sin of not making arrangements at my bank before going overseas to ensure my service pay could be accessed by Beryl. It's all a huge mess and it seems there's nothing I can do about it. The bank's solution is for me to open a joint account; fat chance of that stuck in here! At least she's getting some help from the SSFA[14] and the Red Cross, but the MOD's doing absolutely nothing to help.'

'Sounds like par for the course.' I wish I could find some further words of consolation, but I know that, as far as the MOD are concerned, we're out of the game and out of the country, so out of sight, out of mind. As far as they're concerned, the country's fighting for survival and we're just so much dead weight.

'Come on, Freddy, it's almost time for rehearsal. Let's wonder over to hut four so you can meet Arthur [Fry] and the other players and see how we're getting on.' Ernie fishes a wad of papers out of his inner coat pocket and brandishes them. 'My lines! Quite a few, so I'd better do some swatting while we walk over.'

As we enter, I can see other members of the cast

---

[14] SSFA: Soldiers, Sailors and Air Force Families Association is a UK charity that assists families of service people to this day. It's a fact that the British government did little officially to assist families of POWs in WWII despite the dire financial predicament they often found themselves in. It has, however, to be remembered that WWII occurred in a time that predated the welfare state. Therefore, the MOD simply regarded financial issues of their service people to be a private family matter and not their responsibility.

huddled around the stove at the far end of the hut. It's the first time I've been in hut four, but as the huts at the far end of the camp are all the same, it's a bit like déjà vu since they're all exactly identical inside. There is one noticeable difference though, a small area around one of the bunks is completely cordoned off with a makeshift arrangement of curtains. Passing this structure, I can hear snatches of a conversation. 'Well, that's very interesting, Mother, I hope you're going to have a word with him about it.'

'I will, dear, just as soon as I get a chance.' It's as though there's more than one person cosseted within the curtain walls: most peculiar. As we approach the group around the stove, Arthur stands up and shakes our hands and I introduce myself.

'Glad you could make it, Ernie. I hope you've had a chance to take a look at your lines!'

Unable to contain my curiosity concerning the curtains, I nod in their direction and ask the obvious question, 'So what's going on with the curtain arrangement over there? Its sounds like there's a male and female couple?'

'It's Bob Farrell. He built his curtain contraption several weeks ago and he pretty much stays in there most of the day. He's got it looking a bit like a living room, with a couple of chairs and a table.' Lowering his voice, Fry continues, 'The poor chap is almost certainly going insane. We're letting him get on with it at the moment, but it's disturbing the other lads in the hut, especially when “they” have arguments.’ Fry addresses the group. ‘All right everybody, let’s get started. Okay Mike [Mr Manningham] and Brian [Mrs Manningham], you’re on.’

‘What are you doing, Bella?’

‘Nothing, dear. Don’t wake yourself.’ Pauses.

‘What are you doing, Bella? Come here…’

Sitting on the side lines watching the rehearsal, I can see everyone’s engrossed in the script, so my eyes wander back to the other, private play being enacted within the walls of the curtained ‘room’ at the other end of the hut. A shaft of light from above the enclosed area illuminates Farrell’s hunched form as he sits on his bed. As I watch, he rises, walks to the other end of the bed and begins gesticulating with his hands whilst he’s speaking.

Only when living in the close confines of a prison can you observe the unravelling of a human mind at such close quarters. In his case, Farrell’s mind is quite literally, splitting apart and conjuring alter egos to inhabit a life in which he’s become a character in his own play.

A burst of heavy machine gun fire stuns everyone into a silence in which I can hear my ears ringing. Looking around, we all gather our composure for a few seconds before rushing outside into the garden. At the bottom of the wire netting fence opposite, a dishevelled figure is slumped on the ground like a rag doll. Cordite smoke issues from the middle of the three guard towers.

In the complete silence, I can hear the rushing sound of water from the Altmühl and the jacking of rooks that've been startled from the trees opposite.

We walk slowly towards the fence, raising our hands to reassure the guards that we're not up to something. Graham King, the RAMC, is running over from my hut, but we can see that it's futile; there's an entry wound in the front of man's skull. I now realise it's the same chap who received the fateful letter from his wife earlier in the day.

'Poor bugger! At least it was quick.' Ernie passes me, kneels beside him and places his forefinger on his neck. 'He's gone.'

Graham arrives and repeats the process, feels for a pulse, draws the same conclusion. 'I recognise him, it's Holmes from hut eight. He was only twenty-two.'

Ernie articulates what we're all probably thinking. 'Looks like it's suicide by guard.' However, I know that's not what'll go on his service record; it'll show that Holmes died during an escape attempt. At least that way his family will get some death in service payments. The hard-hearted among us always see suicide as an easy way out, but there's nothing easy about taking a decision to end your own life.

Kneeling beside his crumpled remains, dense flurries of fine snow blow around us whitening the red gash in Holmes' shattered skull like a benediction.

'We'd better move him to the hospital before the snow covers him. Who'll give me a hand?'

Myself, Ernie and a couple of members of the cast lift the body. It's remarkably light; just skin and bone like the rest of us. As we trudge back over the deepening snow, it's almost like we're still in character acting a part in some tragic play.

Fred, Friday 20th June 1941 Oflag VII-B

A raucous group of shrieking swallows and swifts glide effortlessly in the sky above us catching insects lofted into the air on the early morning heat. 'Little Spitfires' I call them, God! I wish they really were Spitfires, raining hell down on the heads of these German goons! It's both familiar and strange to see them; familiar since they always remind me of lazy Sundays taking tea in my parents' garden and strange, because I'm seeing them a million miles away from Newcastle, or Britain for that matter, and from the point of view of a 'guest' of the Third Reich' as we're euphemistically called by Major Higgins[15], no doubt a little joke on the part of our ebullient SBO [Senior British Officer].

This morning roll call is being officiated by Feldwebel-Leutnant[16] Steiner himself rather than one of

---

[15] Major Jack Higgins of the Welsh Guards was the Senior British officer (SBO) who was well remembered for his good humour and leadership in Oflag VII-B. In prisoner of war camps, each nationality appointed a senior officer to represent each faction in dealings with the guards and other German authorities.

[16] Feldwebel-Leutnant: Warrant Officer.

his unteroffizers[17] with the result that the whole process is taking way more than the usual hour. From my position in the centre of the second row, I can see that the old soldier is leaning heavily on his stick, suffering from the rising heat and, no doubt, jip from his old war wound. Steiner's okay and he and Geddes, being of equal rank, similar length of service, also sharing a similar loathing of the odious Commandant Blatterbauer, have struck up something of a cautious friendship.

This morning, the count is unusually thorough; guards walk up and down the rows, one NCO checking the prisoner number on each man's ID tag and the name and service number on his disk and the other, carrying a large roster, checks off the details. The pair stop in front of a man in the third row of the Belgian and French group. A long discussion ensues, and the man is removed from the ranks and led away by a couple of other guards towards the commandant's office, most likely for interrogation.

The corporals, their count and re-count finally completed, meet in front of us and confer with Steiner for several long moments.

'Either their arithmetic's up the spout, or there's been an escape.' Geddes bends again and continues to whisper, 'There's been a rumour that a couple of Belgians might have got away and this confirms it. I bet

[17] Unteroffizers: Non-Commissioned Officers, or NCOs.

they've been using ghosts.'

I nod. 'Makes sense, they must have one or more of their group hiding out to take the place of real escapees; clever! But risky. Switzerland is four- or five-days march, but if they've got a few days start, they've got a chance.'

Steiner's face creases into a look of irritation before barking out his orders. 'All prisoners, return to your quarters immediately, where you will be confined until further notice!'

Steiner turns and follows the detained prisoner and heads towards the commandant's office, where he'll no doubt get an all mighty bollocking for having 'lost' some of his POWs. We, on the other hand, are unceremoniously shoved with the butt of a rifle or threatened with the sharp end of a bayonet, back towards our huts. Looking up, I can see the flaps of the sentry towers opposite the parade ground have been latched open with the closest one giving us a charming view of the business end of the guard's MG 34. We've all heard too many of those to wish to hear it again so we're passively taking the hint and heading back to our huts. It's about ten in the morning and, in our long absence, the heat has already caused our barracks to become stuffy. The guards close and bar the windows and doors, which has the immediate effect of increasing the unpleasantness of an already stuffy atmosphere.

'Well, I suppose that's put paid to the football game this afternoon.' Ernie's prediction is likely to be true.

The last time we had an escape, we were confined to our huts for forty-eight hours without food and water. As the day wears on, the heat climbs higher and is joined by the uncomfortable humidity of a Bavarian summer's day. By common consent, the smokers amongst us are refraining from lighting up, but I can see that nerves are frayed as a result.

The approach of German voices and jackbooted feet heralds a new development. The latch to our main door is wrenched back, Gedge's shoulders tense in anticipation. A group of six Waffen SS troopers' step through the door and take position either side of a small group of our regular guards that includes an elderly chap named Schmidt who I can recognise by his huge paunch and dishevelled lock of silver hair. He's sweating profusely and obviously under some duress. Not waiting for further explanation, four of the SS soldiers, probably in their late teens, early twenties, proceed to go through our belongings very thoroughly whilst the remaining two remain by the door and train their MP 40s on us, making a show of cocking and locking a round into the chamber.

'Raus, beweg dich! Hände, wo ich sie sehen kann!' I can see Gedge's hackles rising and, as he stands slowly up from his bunk, he slips his wristwatch into his sock and steps into the corridor. Even after the deprivations we've suffered in camp, his considerable bulk is still a menacing presence even to the tall and very fit young troopers. One of the youngest looking of the group, probably a lad of eighteen, points to Gedge's foot.

'Your clock give it to me! Now! Schnell!' When he doesn't respond immediately, the trooper, bristling with rage, un-shoulders his machine pistol, plants the muzzle firmly in Geddes' gut and draws back the cocking handle. The young soldier's haughty expression and his forefinger on the trigger convince me that he's not going to back down. Geddes hardens his stance and triangulates his feet into what might be the start of a defensive, and fatal, move.

A tense staring match ensues, and I hold my breath, a graphic vision of what a burst from the machine gun would do to Gedge's gut and those standing around him at such close-range flashes through my mind. I'm about to try and intervene in some way but a small disturbance deflects my attention.

'Was passiert hier?'

All heads turn towards the door to watch Steiner as he walks falteringly up the corridor, stick tapping loudly on the wooden floor in the silence to stand behind the young trooper who petulantly replies, 'Dieser Gefängene versteckt etwas.' A look of utter distain registers on the young Nazi's haughty visage, but he's outranked and has no option but to allow Steiner to approach; however, he doesn't stand down.

Moving close to Gedge, but keeping an eye on the young trooper, Steiner speaks quietly to him in English, 'Whatever it is, can it be worth a bullet? Not like this for a soldier who has done such distinguished service.'

Steiner meets Gedge's eye soldier-to-soldier and solemnly nods towards the long row of medal flashes on the old sergeant major's tunic.

'I know you have courage, Sergeant Major; that is not in question.' He nods again at the distinctive white and red flash of Gedge's Military Medal. Apparently mollified by Steiner's words, Gedge reaches slowly down, retrieves his wristwatch and shows it to Steiner, who nods.

'Es ist nicht illegal, eine armbanduhr haben.' The young trooper opens his mouth as if to say something, but the old soldier stares him down, making a point of adjusting the Iron Cross hanging at his throat; the message is received, and the younger man backs off. I involuntarily breathe a noisy sigh of relief. The search continues, and in the end, they content themselves with confiscating all the plates and cutlery we've laboriously made out of tins from our Red Cross parcels because, 'there are too many and may be being horded for an escape attempt.'

It's early evening and we've finally been released from our huts. I accompany Gedge and Ernie in a walk over to the mess for a much-needed bite to eat. Nobody's saying anything about the incident with the wristwatch. There have been some murmurings of descent at my sergeant's stand, with some saying it was irresponsible since it's likely that others would have been killed in the crossfire. There's some truth in this and, in any case, it's well known that once the SS start shooting, they find it difficult to stop. I've shown my full support, but it was damn lucky for us that Steiner appeared when he did.

Approaching the mess building, a throng of POWs milling around blocks one and two is becoming agitated. A sleek black Mercedes Benz limousine has pulled up at the commandant's office just outside the inner gate; full regalia, with swastikas fluttering on the wings. Everyone's craning their necks to see, so I nip up the steps of block one and find a window that overlooks the courtyard in front of the commandant's office. Two Gestapo officers emerge from the Mercedes followed by a couple of lower ranked officers who take up a flanking position opposite the car. The Belgian escapees follow, swiftly putting their hands behind their heads. Blatterbauer emerges with three prison guards and an exchange takes place. The Gestapo officers follow the commandant into his office and the Belgians are marched through the inner gate.

As they enter the camp, I can see they're grinning despite their obvious exhaustion and when they give a victory 'V', the whole camp cheers, and, for good measure, there's a chorus of 'For he's a jolly good fellow!' The mood of the camp lifts. Even though the Belgians have been recaptured, they've snatched a victory from defeat. The information they'll have about the surrounding lay of the land will be invaluable for future escape attempts.

Henri and a few of his compatriots join me at the

window. They're grinning like idiots.

'Well, your blokes have certainly given the Germans a run for their money!' We enjoy the moment, backslapping all round, but we all know there will likely be hell to pay after Blatterbauer emerges from his roasting from the Gestapo.

George, Saturday April 12th, 1941, Bahrija

For some unaccountable reason, we're 'enjoying' a brief respite from bombing. The theory goes that the Italians, being religious, are observing Easter, a bit like the eerie silence my grandfather said that fell over the battlefields of Ypres over Christmas 1914. None of the enemy have dropped in for a football match though. After the slaughter and destruction of the past few weeks, I doubt the Germans would be treated with the largesse they got back then though.

I pat my tunic pocket; the little blue leave pass nestles in there, only the second since I arrived here, so I'm feeling exceedingly happy with myself. Another bit of luck is I've been able to purloin a sturdy BSA motorcycle from the motor pool after making a vague promise to drop in and pick up a couple of magnetos at Hal-Far on my way back on Monday morning.

A rough, dusty road spools away from me into the distance with gulls wheeling above my head as I follow it around Marsaxlokk Bay. Such has been the intensity of bombing recently that Ylena, her twin sisters and her mother have evacuated Valletta to live with her grandparents in the little village of Baħrija on the northwest coast. An aquamarine blue sea stretches away to my left, broken only by white breaking wave crests on a series of reefs about a mile out. The air has an almost crystalline freshness to it this morning as my mind follows Ylena's hastily drawn map. Rather than following the main road, I turn onto a twisting coast road passing the little fishing village of Dingli where traditional high-prow fishing boats sit quietly within the protecting arms of the harbour walls.

As instructed, I turn inland to Mtarfa and take a left on the main road to Baħrija. I stop in a small square and spot the quaint little church I'm looking for, St Martin's Chapel. There, sitting on the wall by the church gate is Ylena, who pushes herself off and runs towards me, her long, raven-black hair streaming behind her. A flood of emotion flows through me as I push down the motorbike stand and wait while she approaches. A couple of old village women cast a glance in our direction; what do they see? A radiantly beautiful young girl meeting her soldier beau perhaps. They smile and nod in our direction.

Ylena stops a short distance in front of me, walks slowly over and, on her tiptoes, reaches up for us to embrace, while I bend slightly. We meet somewhere in the middle. No polite pecks on the cheek this time, but the full nine yards; I feel quite overwhelmed.

'We'll need to get that uniform off you when we get back to my grandparents' farm! You'll be so conspicuous.'

'Perhaps if we're somewhere away from the public, Ylena. My leave pass is conditional on me wearing my uniform, not civvies I'm afraid.'

I can hear fretfulness in my voice, but she tosses her head. 'Well, you could have brought a car for our first proper date!' She laughs and gets on the back behind me, her slim arms snake around my midriff in another embrace. She whispers in my ear, 'Now I have you, my Englishman.' The motorcycle starts first kick. 'Head past the church and take a left. The farm's about five miles from the village in a little bay, very romantic.'

She squeezes me again as we head out of the village past a few shuttered shops, another small square and down a narrow dirt track. A perfuse carpet of purple, yellow and pink flowers stretches away from the track, softening an otherwise bare rocky landscape. Here and there, white-flowering almond trees and prickly pear bushes add to a starkly beautiful foreground with the azure blue of the Med in the background.

I wonder if I'd remembered to pack my little Kodak camera. I'd got the bug for photography when my mother found a battered Kodak six-20 in a pawnshop in Jesmond, and I've had it with me ever since. Wartime is not a good time for budding photographers since what you can photograph is pretty strictly controlled, but I've got one or two of the lads and our boat.

Ylena is enjoying the motorcycle ride, cheering and giggling every now and again when we go over a bump as though she's on a fairground ride.

'Here, the farm on the left.' We stop by an iron gate in a high sandstone wall. 'Wait, here, I'll grab the keys to the place where we're staying. We can drop off your motorcycle and walk down to the beach. I want to show you my little secret.' She flashes a smile as she creaks open the iron gate, skips across the inner courtyard to a large wooden door and disappears from view.

Seeing Ylena in this informal rustic setting is totally different from the, what would I call them, dates, we've had so far at the Empire. I'm experiencing a sense of guilt, but I can't suppress a strong feeling of euphoria. Guilt, why? That we've snatched a brief moment of happiness away from death and destruction? I conjure a vision of Markham's grief-wracked face as he holds Tilly in his arms. Is that what inevitably happens? How can it be possible to be happy during a war?

Ylena re-emerges brandishing a heavy iron key like the sort you'd see on a jailor's belt and swings herself back onto the pillion seat.

'Straight on, past the end of the wall, you'll see a track to the left, that'll take us down to the stable cottage.' The track takes us through the beginnings of a large vineyard. Ylena waves to a couple working in the field. 'My grandparents. They grow Ghirgentina grapes that produce some of the best frizzante [sparkling] wine on the island. You'll need to try some; it's a bit like champagne.'

The cottage is, as the name suggests, an annex to the stables at the far end of the enclosed farmhouse yard.

A group of flustered hens run hither and thither as we approach the front door. Inside, a musty odour of disuse pervades the dark interior. 'I'll open the shutters and air the room.' I follow Ylena into a back bedroom where she's made up a bed covered in a white lacy counterpane. It's like my room at home and I suddenly feel an overwhelming homesickness.

'It's lovely, Ylena,' is all I can manage. Perhaps to reassure me, she kisses me again.

'Come on, George, let's walk before it gets too dark.' Back out in the dazzling sunshine, Ylena takes my hand and we walk down a well-worn path towards the sea which, after a while, begins to drop down towards a small, enclosed cove fringed with a crescent of brilliant white sand like you'd see in Cornwall. 'Here is our little secret hideaway.' As we walk, the sand squeaks under our feet like cold snow. 'We call it the whispering sands. Even the beaches talk too much in Malta!' I pull her gently to me and we kiss fully on the mouth, taking our time over it. 'Wait,' she whispers, 'come over here. There's a little cavern in the rocks where we won't be seen.'

Stepping onto the warm rocks, and around a little rock pool, the base of the cliff to our right opens into a shallow cave. Ylena is prepared. From her shoulder bag, she takes out a couple of glasses, a bottle of white which she carefully places on a flat rock and spreads out a coloured woven blanket on a small rocky pedestal where we sit down. She's not finished with the luxuries though. With a little flourish, she brings out a jar of olives in oil.

'This is too much, Ylena, so kind of you. I can scarcely remember the last time I had a glass of wine, thank you!'

Ylena's face lights up with pleasure. 'Before we have our wine, I think we should take a little swim?'

Smiling, I say, 'But I haven't brought my costume.'

As she starts removing her blouse, Ylena replies, 'Neither have I.' Slightly taken aback, but in no way rushing to stop her, I watch Ylena remove her clothes. It's an unselfconscious process that ends with her simply removing her panties and bundling everything into a large towel before she walks over to where I'm standing. 'In Malta, it's rude for a man to remain clothed when his woman is naked.' She titters and begins opening my service belt buckle whereupon my rather ill-fitting shorts slide down to my ankles.

The sight and feel of her smooth olive skin and her unselfconsciousness overcomes my reluctance and I finish the job she's started with gusto. Taking my hand, we carefully step off our rocky plinth and onto the warm sand. Equally warm breakers grab hold of our feet and draw us into the surf; we're both at chest height before we give in and launch ourselves into the water. Waves break over our heads. To our right, a shoal of fish suddenly breaks from the surface of the water in a frenzied thrashing.

'What on earth is that?'

'Watch and you'll see.' Two grey-coloured fins pop up in the water that look ominously like they belong to a pair of sharks. Reading my mind, Ylena brushes my shoulder reassuringly. 'Not sharks, dolphins! The dolphins come here to catch tonn far-xewk [yellowfin tuna] with their streams of bubbles. Trapped between them and the shallow beach, they have nowhere to go. The dolphins work together to catch fish, it's amazing no?'

As the frenzy begins to die down, I follow Ylena back to our 'table' and we towel ourselves down. Wrapped in my towel, I open the bottle, pop the cork and pour us both a drink.

'Cheers!' Ylena clicks her glass on mine.

'Saħħa!' We sit. Ylena hasn't wrapped a towel around herself or put any of her clothes back on. Instead, she puts her glass down and pushes me gently back. My shoulders are caressed by the warm rock. Opening my towel, she stretches the full length of her naked body on top of mine. Our tongues meet and play together, while her hand gently strokes my penis. Part of my mind can't believe this is happening, whilst the part of my body being massaged by Ylena responds accordingly. Ylena opens her thighs and rocks her pubis on my naked penis for a while, using the opening of her vagina to caress me. The sensation is overwhelming, and I tremble slightly. Ylena moves her face back a little from mine and smiles. I'm consumed momentarily in the liquid brown of her eyes. I want her.

'I've just had my period and I'm very regular,' she breathes. Reaching down, I feel her hand guiding my penis into her opening. These are unchartered waters for me, but Ylena skilfully manoeuvres my penis until it's fully inside her. She closes her eyes and sighs; our mouths close around each other's again. I imagine that the pleasure can't get more intense, but then Ylena starts to rhythmically move her pelvis up and down and in slow circles. I dig my fingertips into the flesh on her hips and buttocks which spurs her to pick up her pace, her tongue reaching deeper into my mouth.

All thoughts of what's occurring around us evaporates. There is just our bodies and our pleasure.

'I'm going to…'

I make a move to take my penis out of her, but she responds, 'No, keep it there, I want you to fill me.' My back involuntarily arches and the muscles between my legs contract hard over and over, emptying myself inside Ylena while she continues rhythmically moving her hips. Keeping me inside her, she rolls to one side and I shift my body on top of hers, this time my hips work independently of my mind, thrusting over and over. My penis doesn't get soft.

Holding my bucking hips with both hands, Ylena encourages by thrusting. 'Harder, George, do it harder,' she whispers and begins moaning and keening in my ear and gently biting my lobe. Feeling my penis in contact with Ylena's insides keeps me hard and I thrust my length in and out around a constricted bend in her vagina. After a while, I ejaculate a second time. Ylena grips my buttocks almost painfully as she has her own orgasm, a pulsating clenching of her vagina triggering my third crashing ejaculation. My penis finally begins to soften. Ylena holds my buttocks in her hands and we continue to kiss deeply until my penis drops out of her. I roll to her side, physically drained. Holding her hand in mine, Ylena's face appears above me.

'You were fantastic, my English lover, just what I needed.'

'It was what we both needed, Ylena, my love.' I notice that the word love for this young woman slips easily from my lips for the first time in my life.

April 12th, evening

'You have sisters?' We're eating home baked Lampuki Torta which has been brought to us by Ylena's grandmother, a lovely kindly woman in her late seventies who wordlessly looks at us both, nods knowingly and smiles.

'Yes, younger twins, Tamyra and Thwayya.'

'I have a twin brother, Fred. We think he was captured in France and is now in a German POW camp. We've had no word from him, but I know he's still alive. I feel it here.'

I touch my heart and Ylena places her hand over mine. 'I used to feel jealous of my sisters for their closeness. As little girls, I often felt like I was spying on their little secret world, one that I could never be part of. We are very close now. The war has brought us together; at least something positive might come from it.'

'I sometimes almost feel I'm in physical pain when I think of Fred and what might be happening to him in captivity.'

'I can be part of you now and know your brother. Feel your instincts, if you know he is here,' she touches my breast again with the palm of her hand, 'then he is still here on this Earth.'

Ylena rises, takes my hand and leads me over to the bed where we strip naked again and meet under the covers. We lay on our side facing each other and Ylena eases her arm under my torso and around my waist, cupping my buttocks and pulling me towards her. I'm responding again as she hitches her uppermost thigh around my waist. Her leg gently pulls me into her groin. I slide my penis into her again and we thrust against each other. We make love like that so we both orgasm again and again until our bodies are sated and drift off into fitful sleep.

George, Tuesday 22nd September 1941, forty miles SE of Pantelleria Island[18]

My head nods forward violently, almost making contact with the wireless in front of me. The sultry sound of little wavelets lapping on the hull of the boat has once again sent me to sleep. Feeling a little stupid, I glance across to where Skip is standing at the chart table and make to apologise.

'It's all right, Whitton, we could all do with getting into our bunks.' Markham chuckles to himself and returns to his charts. We're in virtual darkness with the instrument lights and lamp from the skipper's chart table the only sources of illumination. It's reminiscent of Christmas Eve night, when I would sneak downstairs and hide in the living room in the hope, I'd see Father Christmas. There's that same hushed air of expectation now.

Our much wished-for present is to be part of a naval operation to capture a damaged German U-boat they've

---

[18] Pantelleria Island, part of Italy, was a strategic base for Axis (Italian and German) air forces, including radar, during WWII.

been chasing since it slipped past the Strait of Gibraltar three days ago. All Skip's told us is that we need to be on hand to pick up survivors and that the U-boat captain is likely to scuttle his craft rather than risk capture. For this reason, the small and unobtrusive size of our boat may be missed by their ASDIC [sonar]. The reasoning appears to be that if the German captain feels he's still got a chance to escape, he might not scuttle his craft. Needless to say, close contact with the enemy means that side arms have been issued to all the crew, even Mother, so it's in the balance whether we shoot them or save them. Personally, I couldn't hit the side of a barn at thirty paces; I'd probably have more chance of hitting someone if I simply threw my revolver at them!

For once, the Med is as calm as a millpond which is a great blessing because we're currently maintaining our station on a sea anchor to save fuel as we're right on our five-hundred-mile range. Dit, dah, dit, dit, the familiar tones come to me like the whisperings of a lover; Ylena's full lips on my cheek spring to mind but are then swept away when I realise it's our call sign followed by X291 [what's my signal strength?] I tap out X291 + 5 [signal strength 5]. I immediately get back, X218, [I have something to communicate] followed by a coded message, which I note down and pass over to Skip.

'It's HMS *Marigold*, sir.' Markham takes the torn-out page from my stenography notebook and turns to ponder its contents using his codebook. 'Okay, everyone, the enemy is close, and torpedoes have been in the water. I want everybody to be on high alert; we aren't going to get a better chance than this to capture an intact U-boat and prisoners with valuable information. Be warned, they will be armed, and U-boat crews are known for their fanaticism and they may be unwilling to surrender.'

A mental picture of the captain of a U-boat in the dreaded Nazi wolfpack sailing underneath us is unsettling. A huge flash and explosive splash off our starboard sends me involuntarily crouching down over my desk. There's another and then another, the *Marigold*! Depth charges are being lobbed over the side a little under a mile away. The wolf being brought to bay by the British Navy bloodhounds.

'All hands, action stations! O'Hare and Macleod, get up on deck and see if you can spot anything.' I glance over at Fish standing next to Tosh who's wearing his usual dogged expression. We look into each other's faces like people who are likely not to make it through the next few moments and then turn back to our instruments.

'Wake in water, wake in the water! She's surfacing!' O'Hare's booming voice. 'Fish, Whitton, get those splinter mats up!'

As I wrestle with the uncooperative corpse-like bulk of the starboard splinter mat, I catch sight of a submarine conning tower creating a wake in the sea ahead of us. Some of the crew are issuing from the top of the tower and taking up position on what you'd suppose was the deck. As we watch, six men throw themselves into the water and make to swim over to us. The dark briny envelops them, and the small splashing motions of their arms seem pitifully ineffectual in the open sea. These will be our first German visitors. For some unaccountable reason, I'm trying to think of German phrases, but the only ones I can come up with are from boys own comic books, like 'hände hoch' and 'achtung minen', which on the face of it are probably going to be handy!

'Stow the splinter mats. Everybody stay calm and keep your wits about you.' I'm beginning to wonder if they'll simply try and take our vessel hostage. There's likely to be more of them than us and they're cornered; will we be the captors or the captured? But then I remember O'Hare out on the front deck with our twin .303 machine guns trained on them. A huge wild-eyed Irishman with a big machine gun in his hands is a pretty convincing deterrent!

As the German crew approach our boat, I help Macleod to throw the scramble net over the side; there's clearly just six survivors out of a complement of twenty-five. As they drag themselves onto the scramble net, nobody's helping them. I feel a pang of pity; after all they're men just like us. As the first reaches the deck, Skip trains his .38 on him and glancing over to the wheelhouse, I spot Fish standing in the doorway with a Sten gun; he'd always told me he's a crack shot on pheasant shoots. However, Fish's usual jocular expression has been replaced by steely determination; I have no doubt he'd open up on our prisoners if there was any funny business.

The men assemble on the deck, three in fatigues, two dressed as lieutenants and the sixth in a senior officer's uniform. All are pretty bedraggled and shivering with the cold.

'I'll take that gun, Major.' Markham uses his pistol to point to the major's holster. The major shoots out a defiant look and assumes a haughty manner.

'Ich bin sicher, es wird nicht funktionieren, Captain, es ist voller wasser.'

'Nevertheless, Major, bitte,' Markham insists with his pistol pointed at the German's midriff and shows he's not bluffing. The major complies by bending slightly and opening the flap of his holster; in doing so, his Iron Cross appears from under his tunic. 'Vorsichtiger, Major, very carefully.'

Fish moves from the wheelhouse door and takes up position to our left so he has a clean shot at the major should he try anything. Macleod takes the sleek, black Luger pistol proffered by the German officer and sticks it in the back of his trouser belt.

'Setz dich und lege deine hände hinter deine köpfe.' Dutifully, our prisoners sink to the deck and place their hands behind their heads. I'm thinking that Skip is full of surprises; I'd no idea he could speak German, but it's certainly handy at the moment! A hissing sound emanates from the stricken U-boat. Then, out of the corner of my eye, O'Hare dashes across the deck, dives into the water and thrashes across the few yards to the sub, clambers aboard and starts climbing the conning tower ladder.

'Whitton, take the Sten from Fisher. Fisher, get in there after him and do what you can to help but don't go in after him. I don't want to risk both of you in this mad scheme!'

Fish doesn't need a second telling, hands me his Sten and winks. 'It's cocked and locked, mate, so watch where you point it.' Fish promptly dives in and follows O'Hare's heroic action. I know O'Hare worked as a ship's fitter in Rosyth before the war, if any of us might know his way around a sub it'd be him. It dawns on me that he's trying to recover ship's orders and other vital intelligence. Onboard our vessel, such things are kept in the skipper's wardroom, but were the hell would that be on a German U-boat is anyone's guess.

Our prisoners look tense and I can see the major looking at his men and then at those of us with guns, but I can see the fight has gone out of his fellow countrymen. Instinctively, I shift the muzzle of my machine gun towards the major. A commotion breaks out over on the U-boat, O'Hare emerges with a steel briefcase.

'I found the wardroom. I'm going back to the comms room. I've seen their encryption device! I'm gonna risk it, sir.'

'O'Hare, no! Get back here!' Markham shifts his attention to O'Hare. The major lowers his hands and shifts his attention to the briefcase that Fish is holding aloft like a football trophy.

'Hände hoch!' The major looks puzzled; probably my terrible accent, but he gets the message. O'Hare disappears again and just as he does, the sub makes a further lurch towards Davy Jones' Locker.

'God damn it! Fisher, get down there and drag him out if you need to!' Markham's eyes look wild, his face contorted by anxious frustration. The U-boat is giving up the ghost and looks like it's going for its final dive. Fish pops out of the conning tower like a cork from a bottle just as the last few feet slip beneath the waves and swims away from the vortex forming around the craft as it disappears with the handle of the steel briefcase in his teeth. As Fish scrambles onto the deck, we stare at the 'hole' in the ocean made by the sub. I can't believe O'Hare's gone. How could a man mountain like him just disappear?

A scuffling behind me, the major lunges at my legs and I topple over, dropping the Sten, which clatters onto the deck. Markham wheels around and sees the German officer diving for the machine gun. Everything seems at this point to slow right down. The major reaches for the Sten, I try to throw myself on top of him, but he manages to grab the stock and bring the weapon down on my head. The blow is glancing, but it makes me roll to the side where I collide with Markham's feet.

Bang, bang, bang, bang. A pause as Markham gets up close and gives him two more in the head, bang, bang. I look away from the horror as the back of the German's head explodes. Dazed, I manage to recover the Sten, and watch the five other crew, no movement, no fight from them to be seen. During all the excitement, it's got fully dark.

'Whitton, get those men below. Fisher, great work, great work.'

'I'm sorry about O'Hare, sir. I just couldn't get to him.'

Fish's voice breaks and Markham nods and simply says, 'I know.'

Tosh has taken up position at the wheelhouse and is holding his service revolver in front of him. 'Move, move, inside.' We leave their dead officer on the deck and assemble in the wheelhouse.

Regaining control of the situation, Markham points towards the bows, 'Tosh, Macleod, take these men down to the fo'c'sle and lock them up. Whitton, message the *Marigold* that we have six prisoners and have captured valuable papers that will need to be taken into custody by Intelligence.'

I got on it and received a reply in plain language. 'WL DO OC WTHN T HR,' which translates as, 'Will do, old chap, within the hour.' I blow out a sigh of relief and lean back in the wireless operator's chair and spot Markham jiggering the lock on the briefcase.

'Skip? Shouldn't we leave that for the eggheads in

Intelligence?' Markham wheels around. I know he's been erratic since Tilly's death and losing O'Hare is going to be another blow that's got to be clouding his judgement.

'I've got to know it was worth losing O'Hare. They'll never tell us anything once we hand this over. I've got to know.' His voice tails off and he shifts his attention back to the briefcase. Tosh, Macleod and Tinselly have joined us on the bridge and they gather around the skip as he triumphantly holds aloft a typed and signed letter. 'I knew there was something unusual, a senior officer of the Wehrmacht aboard a U-boat. It's a letter to the Head of the Wehrmacht, Adolf Hitler, from Rommel himself!'

Mein geschätzter Fuhrer.

In der nordafrikanischen Kampägne ist alles für uns verloren. Die Italienischen Streitkräfte unter Graziani sind schlecht ausgebildet und unfähig und. Ich bitte daher mit Respekt um Verstärkung und weitere Lieferungen, um mein Afrika-Korps so schnell wie möglich zu unterstützen.

Die besten Wünsche

Erwin Rommel, General Deutsches Afrika Korps

Heil Hitler!

Which roughly translates as, 'My esteemed Furer. All is lost for us in the North African campaign. The Italian forces under Graziani are badly trained and inept and therefore respectfully request reinforcements and further supplies to support my Africa Corps to be made available as soon as possible. Best wishes, Erwin Rommel, General, Deutsches Afrika Corps.'

Our deceased major was probably a senior member of Rommel's staff. 'And look!' Skip holds up a booklet and reads from its front page.

Streng geheim!

DAS ENIGMA-ALLGEMEINE VERFAHREN

(Der Schlüssel M Verfahren M Allgemein)

Eingetragen in die Secret Book List der 59. Patrol Flotilla unter der Seriennummer 66

Oberkommando der Marine

Berlin 1940

Then, noticing that none of us knew what the hell he was saying, he said, 'It's a top-secret instruction manual for an enigma machine! It's an almost mythical beast, but it's a device the Germans use to encrypt their messages. Our Intelligence is going to be all over this.'

'Skipper, it's the *Marigold*.'

We all turn and see Tosh peering out of the wheelhouse window at a Morse message from a ship's signal lamp.

Markham nods, 'send them okay to come alongside, Tosh. Macleod, Fisher, bring those prisoners back up on deck.'

Being a mere corvette, the *Marigold* doesn't tower above us like a frigate or a destroyer, but what with a rising wind and a heavy swell the height difference between the two craft makes the transfer of our captives and the dead major rather awkward, but Macleod and Fisher finally get them onto the *Marigold's* scramble net and the body of the major is unceremoniously hauled on deck with a rope.

Reversing away from the corvette, I flop down on my chair. What a night's work! And then it hits me again; O'Hare's gone like he never existed.

'Can I have everyone up on deck, I want to say a few words for O'Hare before we leave his final resting place.' We all follow Markham out onto the deck and brace ourselves on the bow rails. Markham's holding a small pocket New Testament. 'O Eternal God, your ocean is so wide, and our boat is so small. Please welcome into your Kingdom our dear shipmate. Fair winds and following seas, Rupert. There can be no grave marker or place to grieve in the vast emptiness of the ocean, but we take solace in the knowledge that our shipmate will be in the company of the bravest and finest that have served our country and have upheld the highest values of our service. Rest in peace my friend, rest in peace.'

In my mind's eye, I fancy that O'Hare's chiselled face wearing a wry smile briefly surfaces in the black of the foaming briny before slipping back down. With that, Markham turns on his heel and walks through the wheelhouse door, descends to the wardroom and shuts the door, where I suspect he'll write a letter informing O'Hare's family of the tragic and heroic death of their only son. I wouldn't be surprised if O'Hare is recommended for a posthumous Victoria Cross; not that it'll do him much good, poor blighter, but I suppose his family might take pride in the honour once their grieving is over. My eyes begin to sting, and my vision is momentary lost in a sea of tears.

George, Saturday August 8th, 1942, Birżebbuġa

On Friday, Ylena had sent a message to me via one of her cousins, Alfredo, who delivers fresh produce and other food supplies to the base, that she'd booked us a room for Saturday night at the Oxford Hotel in the dusty and none too inviting seaside town of Birżebbuġa, just a mile or two from the base. However, my mind is definitely not on the quality of the décor or the cuisine, but on the beautiful raven-haired woman seated at a table by a window near the check-in desk as I enter the hotel lobby area.

Ylena shoots me a radiant smile and steps away from her table to greet me. She's wearing high heels, so our height difference is somewhat reduced, and I use the opportunity to slide my hands around her slim waist and briefly cup her full, round buttocks in my palms out of view of the hotel receptionist who's craning her neck to get a better view of us.

When we collapse from our embrace into opposite chairs, I notice that an ice-cold Tom Collins is sitting in front of me and there's the remains of a Scotch and soda sitting opposite. Ylena is not a passive female presence like the women back home who'd have simply waited for their beau to arrive and then expect them to order them drinks at the bar. I'm unsure whether this is because she's older than me or if it's a cultural thing, but it's endearing, and I like it.

As I compose myself, Ylena waves her glass in the air. 'Ieħor, l-istess jekk jogħġbok.' The receptionist acknowledges with a nod, pushes off her chair and heads over to the saloon. Whilst she's gone, Ylena sides her hands up my inner thighs and brushes my groin under the small table. Her face comes to a stop a few inches from mine and we kiss passionately.

'I've ordered us room service for dinner; we're going to need it after we've finished.' A devilish smile plays on her rouge lips. However, we're leaning back in a chastened pose on our chairs by the time the receptionist returns with Ylena's refill. We giggle like naughty schoolchildren at our little transgression. As her drink is placed on the table, she immediately stands, slides a silk scarf around her shoulders and jingles a key with an enormous copper fob that's been sitting on the table.

'Let's take these up to our room.' Leading the way up a steep, stone stairwell, we arrive at a door with ornate decorative wooden mouldings with the words 'Suite tal-Bridal' on a small plaque above the room number. 'I got us the bridal suite,' she winks. Swinging the door open, she throws her shoulder bag on the king-sized double bed and bows. 'Welcome, your Excellency!' Ylena titters at her own joke, but before I can say anything more, she begins removing her dress, letting it drop on the floor to reveal her white lace lingerie that frames her beautiful olive skin. Blowing me a kiss Ylena opens the door into a small room opposite the bed and says, 'I'll run us a bath,' and promptly disappears out of sight.

I slip out of my khaki fatigues, drop them on a chair and join her in the bathroom. A shower is fixed above the bath, but Ylena is now fully naked and bending over to fill the tub. No further invitation is necessary. I kneel behind her, push her open and bury my face between her inviting buttocks running my tongue between the lips of her open vagina, breathing in her scent like a fine wine. She pushes back onto me and slowly raises and lowers her crack on my lips.

'Mmmh, you seem to know what to do. Is that part of your military training in England?' Another tinkling giggle. Ylena is my first lover, but my body seems to have a mind of its own when I'm around her. Steam issues from the bath as she turns and does something totally unexpected. Caressing me through my briefs with her lips she pulls them down, then, holding my buttocks in the palm of her hands, she slowly takes my erect penis into her mouth swirling her tongue around the glans and using her hand to guide me in and out of her mouth. After a few strokes, she removes her hand and takes all of me inside her mouth until her nose touches my lower belly. I can barely speak; my pleasure is so intense, and my legs almost give way. Glancing up,

Ylena confirms I'm enjoying the experience.

Controlling my thrusts with her hands on my hips, I make love to her mouth until I'm almost ready to ejaculate. Sensing this, Ylena removes my penis from her mouth.

'Let's do the bath later, darling. I don't think we can wait.' Moving to the bed, I lie luxuriantly in the middle, Ylena follows me on all fours resuming her oral magic, head bobbing up and down above my groin. After a few strokes, she shifts again and positions her vagina over my lips. I bury my tongue deeply inside, lapping around her opening; appreciative sounds indicate I'm getting something right! Tell-tale signs of an orgasm surge into my belly and I reach down to gently remove her lips from my penis, but Ylena continues and I empty myself in her mouth.

I'm feeling deeply apologetic as she turns to face me, but her face is radiant, and she simply wipes her mouth with her palm and falls back on the bed beside me. Not wishing it to end, I position my hips over her, and she opens her legs invitingly.

'I love your English stamina.' She smiles while I glide smoothly into her vagina and then closes her legs around my waist. We lie together as she holds me inside her until I recover my erection and we continue lovemaking. Ylena whispers in my ear, 'I should let you know I'm at my most fertile time of the month.'

'I'm sorry, I should have asked or used a condom.'

'I don't care, I want you inside me. If it's my time

to bear a child, then it's r-rieda t'Alla!' She cups my face in her hands, smiles and moves her hips under me in encouragement. 'Make love to me, fill me with your love, I want you to give me a child.' Somewhere in my mind, I hear a voice telling me what a bad idea it would be to get Ylena pregnant, but another whispers, 'I love her, I want her, we'll work it out.'

Having ejaculated a moment before, I'm able to vigorously thrust inside her without feeling like I'm going to empty myself again right away. Perhaps realising this, Ylena detaches herself from me, turns on her front and tucks a pillow under her hips and opens herself invitingly with her fingertips. I bury myself inside her again; the sensation of my belly resting on the open cleavage of her buttocks while I plough into her causes a wave of pleasure to wash over me.

Sensing that I'm about to cum, I make to pull out of her. Ylena whispers, 'Please, empty yourself, fill me, I want you inside me, I love you.' As if to reinforce her words, Ylena reaches back behind her and grasps my thrusting thighs causing me to ejaculate hard until I'm completely spent. I imagine my essence flowing deep inside her and into her womb; I've never felt so happy in my life.

We lie together for a few minutes and I caress her body, tracing her shoulder blades with my lips, repeating 'I love you' over and over. Tears well up in my eyes and I experience emotions I've never had before, a man's love for a woman. Ylena turns, tears in her eyes too, but smiling, and reaches up to pull me into an embrace. I draw the covers over us and we slip into oblivion together.

August 8th, later in the evening

A bustling sound and words at the door pervades my slumbers. I wake with a start. Ylena's smiling face appears above mine and she kisses my lips.

'Dinner has arrived, darling.' A tray with two plates rests on our bedside table. On each plate, a large grilled fish looks up accusingly from a bed of shredded white cabbage, tomatoes and sliced lemon. 'Lampuki. I thought you needed to try a traditional dish. We Maltese get very excited about the start of the Lampuki season; these are, no doubt, fresh from the quayside this morning!' A little contented sigh issues from her slightly parted lips.

I brush Ylena's cheek. 'Where I come from, kippers, grilled herring, is the national dish, it's served in a similar way.' I try some of the oily fish; it tastes similar to herring and again brings back memories of visits to North Shields Fish Quay and coming home with kippers wrapped in newspaper.

Naked, Ylena sits cross-legged in front of me wolfing her fish. 'I'm starving!'

'Me too.' And I mean it. I inwardly pray that this image of her will remain with me forever. 'You know, there's no one else for me, no one at home in England,

I mean. I've never felt like this before about anybody. You're the first, you know… I've been with. I never want to leave here without you.'

Ylena is looking intently at me. 'I know, George. You're so honest and true, my English gentleman! You must know that I've had a husband when I was very young; my parents arranged it. He was a business partner of my father. I was only sixteen at the time. After I had several miscarriages with him, he left me for another woman, but we're still married otherwise he'd take everything I have; the divorce laws are barbaric in Malta.

'When my father became sick, I had no brothers, and my mother has no head for business. I'd been bright at school, so my grandparents paid for me to go to business school in Boston where I stayed with relatives. I owe my grandmother a lot. She and my grandfather have built a business on their winery, which is one of the biggest in Malta. I run the Empire Bar, but also help run their vineyard.

'After my husband left me, I learned not to expect anything, but just live for the moment. I've never loved anyone like you George. You're my first love as a mature woman. As for never leaving each other, we say in Malta, Fejn thobb il-qalb jimxu r-riglejn – where the heart loves, that's where the legs walk. Always remember that our hearts will carry us to be with each other, my love.'

George, Wednesday, August 12th, 1942 Kalafrana HQ, 08:00 hrs

The briefing room is buzzing with rumours and counter-rumours and generally contradictory information. Where there's a void, the lads will either repeat titbits from overheard conversations or simply make something up to pass the time. I'm sitting near the back of the room, in the opposite corner near the door, my favoured spot for these things where I'm least likely to be asked an awkward question or for Skip, or another officer, to notice my dishevelled appearance.

It's twenty minutes since we all assembled with the other crews in a makeshift briefing room in an annex to the quayside workshops. It's not usual for Markham to be late for these things, so I'm thinking that something really big is happening. Through the window, I can see a Short Sunderland seaplane coming in to land in the broad sweep of Marsaxlokk Bay like a very cumbersome, white bird. I always marvel at the skill of pilots capable of landing such a huge plane on something as insubstantial as water.

During any prolonged wait, where we appear to have our fate, yet again, in the balance, my mind takes me to a happy place. Since meeting her, my favourite place, or places, are inevitably with Ylena, and this is no exception; a smile involuntarily spreads across my lips as I conjure a vision of her strong sweat-beaded back flexing under me as I stroke into her from behind. My erotic reverie is interrupted by Markham's entrance and a cacophony of scraping chairs.

'At ease, gentlemen. Apologies for my lateness. The officer's briefing was a long one, so I'll keep this brief. Our flotilla has been asked to set up a standby station about one hundred nautical miles off the coast of Sicily. The balloon has defiantly gone up, so to speak. A huge re-supply operation was mounted in England over a week ago and a large convoy of merchant ships including a significant portion of the fleet are heading our way and should be about one hundred nautical miles off the Sicilian coast by about 20:00 this evening[19]. There is likely to be heavy enemy resistance to the supply mission with a lot of casualties expected for our forces. God willing, there will be fewer than is expected, but I'm afraid it's going to get pretty hectic over the next twenty-four to thirty-six hours.

'Navy warships and Sunderlands will take care of

---

[19] These vignettes are based on a major relief mission, codenamed Operation Pedestal, undertaken by the British Navy to resupply military bases on Malta which had been deprived of basic supplies and fuel due to the ongoing siege by Axis forces. More than fifty warships, including four aircraft carriers and twenty-one submarines were involved in the operation to escort fourteen merchant ships, including the US oil tanker SS Ohio.

rescuing crews from damaged or sinking vessels, so we will concentrate our effort on picking up fighter pilots that will be flying Hurricanes and Spitfires off aircraft carriers, the *Eagle*, *Furious*, *Indomitable* and *Victorious*. Accompanying the aircraft carriers is the biggest naval force that has been deployed to the Med so far.'

For effect, Markham stops speaking and his eyes travel over the heads of people in the room waiting for questions; everyone is pretty stunned, so there are none. Markham continues.

'Although, due to the size of our craft, we'll be largely invisible to U-boats. We will be targets for enemy fighters, so all hands will be on-deck manning fore and aft guns at all times. This is an operation that'll go down in the history books for sure.' Looking over at Tosh, Markham continues, 'We will not flinch from the danger that our sailors and pilots will endure over the next few days, and, like the lifeboat men, we will never turn back.' Tosh nods in agreement at Markham's words, the steely look in his eyes has become familiar. 'If there's no questions, then let's get down to our boats.' Markham collects his briefing notes and walks from the room.

'Phew! This is a big show. It's going to get pretty chaotic out there.' Fish has appeared next to me and we walk together out onto the quay to scan the distant horizon beyond and the shimmering waves of

Marsaxlokk Bay. We're both probably wondering whether we'll make it back in once piece after this little shindig.

Thursday, August 13th, Mediterranean one hundred miles NE of Malta on station with Force Z, 06:00 hrs

During the night we've steamed into position. Dawn is breaking and aerial operations around the still-distant battle fleet have started. U-boats have clearly been active during the night as plumes of smoke trail from the floating wreckage of two ships. Radio communication last night indicated that HMS *Nigeria* and *Cairo* had been torpedoed and SS *Ohio*, a US-registered, fuel-carrying merchant ship, has been badly damaged. Hurricane and Spitfire sorties are getting airborne from various aircraft carriers to tackle a large group of what could be Junkers 88 bombers heading towards the battlegroup from the direction of Scilly. On the plus side, pilots we'd picked up from the drink yesterday have been safely transferred to the cruiser HMS *Phoebe*.

As we watch, a larger force of attendant German ME109s engage our fighters and a desperate dogfight ensues. Aircraft exhausts swirl in the cobalt-blue sky as pilots' manoeuvre around each other in an intricate dance of death. As our pilots, and those of the enemy, bail out of damaged aircraft, our job is not only going to involve picking up pilots, but avoiding being strafed by enemy aircraft, shelled by our own navy or shot at by the crews of Sunderland flying boats mistaking us for the enemy. On top of that, we're likely to come into close quarters with German Dornier flying boats as they attempt to pick up pilots and crews from planes and damaged or sunk warships.

Moving back to my post in the wireless room, I'm just in time to pick up a challenge. 'What ship?' I speedily reply.

'Here the RAF Coastal Command boat HSL-2007.' I'll certainly have my work cut out for me today. Markham gives his orders for battle stations. 'Tosh, I'll take the helm. Macleod, help Tosh get the splinter mats up, we're going to need them today. Once that's done, Fisher, I'll need you to help Macleod with the aft deck gun, it's likely to get pretty busy in the next few hours. Everyone needs to keep an eye out for enemy aircraft peeling off from their flights and coming in our direction. If that happens, we'll need to do our best to manoeuvre the boat to get the aft cannon into a suitable firing position. With so many pilots and crews in the drink, we will maintain a continual square search pattern around our allocated rescue grid.'

'Aye, aye, sir!' is the pejorative reply from all on the bridge.

'Foxtrot leader, enemy in sight angels one, two,

tallyho, tallyho!'

Various indistinct chatter follows, and then, 'Foxtrot leader, Foxtrot leader, Titch, watch your six o' clock, you've got a Jerry coming in behind you.'

'Roger that, diving.' The chatter I'm getting from the dogfight going on around the *Indomitable* battle group sounds like our lads have got their hands full.

'Foxtrot leader, Foxtrot leader, I'm losing altitude, baring one, nine five degrees.' I quickly step out on deck and check the sky to our left; sure enough, a fighter is trailing smoke. As I watch, the pilot inverts his plane and the cockpit cover tumbles into the slipstream, closely followed by the pilot.

'Skipper, we've got a pilot bailing out, on our starboard.'

'Yes, spotted him.' The boat banks hard over, but just as I can see a parachute opening, an ME109 dives down from the left and opens up on the pilot.

'Whitton, stay out there and keep Tosh supplied with ammo.' Grabbing a couple of ammo boxes for the Brownings, I run out onto the foredeck just as Tosh pivots his twin machine guns around and fires a burst at the German fighter, who's now climbing steeply to come around for another strafing run. Markham suddenly banks the boat to port and Macleod opens up with the aft cannon. The German swings his plane away from the pilot and heads in our direction. The pilot dropping into the water is now just a hundred yards away. The boat slows and comes about. I can see the pilot floating on his back in his yellow Mae West. Markham appears on deck with a gaff. More gunfire from our cannon. A flash of guns from the ME109, we all drop to the deck and Markham collapses holding his leg. I rush over to him. Just as I reach him, and I think it can't get any worse, I notice a Dornier seaplane coming into land about five hundred yards ahead. Tosh joins me with Markham.

'Tosh, stay with Skip, I'll get the MO.' I run into the wheelhouse and nearly collide with Armstrong coming the other way. 'The Skipper's been hit!' Back on deck, Markham's lying with his head cradled in Tosh's lap. He's looking very pale and in the early stages of shock.

'Give me a hand, Whitton. Cut Skip's trouser open.' Blood spurts from a huge wound in the back of Skip's thigh; it looks like the bullet has severed the femoral artery.

All I can think is, 'Christ, no! Don't let him die.' Mother applies a tourniquet above the wound, and I press on a wad of bandages to try and staunch the flow. Glancing up, I can see we're drifting towards the Dornier. Tosh makes a move to get back over to the Brownings. Markham grabs his leg.

'No, Tosh! I know they're the enemy, but they're in the rescue service, just like us.' Markham's voice falters. I can see fury in the old cox's eyes, but he won't disobey his skipper's order. The Dornier rescue crew are helping a group of men into a side door, but nobody makes any attempt to open fire on us. The Dornier's engines roar back into life, the seaplane gathers speed, bounces into the air and banks away. Armstrong feels for a pulse, his face is pale and grim.

'He's gone, I couldn't stop the bleeding.' The MO's shoulders sag in defeat. All three of us are covered in the skipper's blood. Tosh gently closes Markham's eyes and squeezes his shoulder.

'Farewell, my friend.' We carry the skipper back into the wheelhouse, past his favoured post at the chart table and down to the wardroom where we place him on his cot. Markham's face is at peace at last. The lines on his brow placed there by the responsibility of command have disappeared. Tosh kneels next to Markham; his face is taught and pale. We quietly file out of the room to give him some privacy to have a final moment alone with his friend.

George, Tuesday August 18th, 1942, Pietà Military Cemetery, Valletta

The first heat of the day causes sweat to trickle down my back and pool on top of my belt. To my left and in front, lads from our flotilla stand to attention as Tosh and Macleod lead the official pallbearers. There's complete silence as they place Markham's Union Jack-draped coffin on the grave batons, step back and salute. Tosh, who's elected to say a few words on behalf of all of us, steps forward, his usually impassive features are grief-stricken. I wonder how many times he's said a eulogy over lost sailors and crewmates during his long years at sea.

The sun glints on the gallant cox's chest of medals which includes the blue ribbon and distinctive insignia of the George Cross and striped ribbon of the Air Force Medal he earned rescuing a pilot from the water under enemy fire.

Tosh has no notes to read from; it seems he knows the words of his chosen passage from The Prophet by rote. Tosh clears his throat and begins. 'After saying these things, he looked about him, and he saw the pilot of his ship standing by the helm and gazing now at the full sails and now at the distance.' 'And he said: Patient, ever patient, is the captain of my ship.' Tosh stumbles on his words, I bite my lip, moved by the cox's momentary loss of composure. Taking a breath, he continues. 'The wind blows, and restless are the sails; Even the rudder begs direction; Yet quietly my captain awaits my silence.' Tosh stumbles again and looks over to us; a few of us solemnly nod in encouragement. 'And these my mariners, who have heard me patiently. Now they shall wait no longer. I am ready. The stream has reached the sea, and once more the great mother holds her son against her breast.' Tosh falls silent, bows his head and then salutes.

A bugler steps forward and plays 'The Last Post' while the battens supporting the coffin are removed. The pallbearers slowly lower the coffin and Markham makes his final journey down into the gaping maw of his grave to join the hundreds and possibly hundreds more, or even thousands, that will never leave this place.

I follow Fish and Tinselly as they file past Markham's grave. Not wishing to leave him without some final mark of respect, I peer into the grave. There, like a door into another world, the coffin lid bares a small brass plaque, 'Flt. Lt. Matthew Frederick Markham, CGM'. I never realised he'd been awarded the Conspicuous Gallantry Medal, or that his middle name was Frederick. I suddenly have a vision of Freddy's name on another brass plaque on a coffin miles away in some unknown graveyard, perhaps even in a mass grave in some hellhole of a prisoner of war camp.

The thought is so compellingly sad that I nearly lose my own composure.

Gathering myself together, I throw a small handful of warm sandy soil down onto Markham's coffin and follow the others towards an avenue of trees leading to the main entrance. Quite a few white crosses have sprouted up in the military section of the cemetery. Reading the inscriptions, I notice how young many of them are. There are quite a few pilots there; maybe some are lads we've picked up from the drink but didn't make it.

As we're on a small rise, the city of Valletta stretches away to our left. Gone are many of the ornate spires, minarets and gleaming white palisades, destroyed by the combined efforts of the Luftwaffe and the Regia Aeronautica. The bombed-out shells of some of the larger buildings are visible even from here on the outskirts of the city and I wonder whether it'll ever be rebuilt. As we pass into the cool shade of an avenue of carob trees, the melodic warbling of a striking yellow songbird fluttering among the clusters of large seedpods breaks the stillness and momentarily lifts my mood. As my eyes are adjusting to the shadows, I spot the familiar figure of Ylena. Her sudden appearance sends a jolt of electricity through my body. She's wearing sunglasses, an elegant grey skirt suit and a black headscarf. She's staring intently at me and steps forward smiling as we pass.

'Some of the lads are having a few drinks for

Markham at the NAAFI. Are you joining us, mate?' Fish nudges my arm. I turn to him as Ylena approaches.

'Sorry, Fish, I didn't catch that.'

Spotting Ylena, Fish nods. 'Okay, mate, I see you've got other plans.'

'Ylena, this is Blair Fisher, Alan Harris and Roger Tinselly; Ylena Bonnici.'

'I wish I could describe it as a good afternoon, gentlemen, but I know it is a day of sorrow for you. I'm very sorry for the loss of your noble captain.' The lads are momentary entranced no doubt by her beauty but also the sincerity of her words. After they shake her hand, she slips her arm under my elbow. We slow and the others move ahead. 'I had to come, George, to pay my respects to a man I know meant so much to you. If you want to join your friends, I've got a lift back into town with Alfredo.'

I'm momentarily torn, but it's an unequal contest. An evening with Ylena in her dusty little attic room above the Empire seems like an offer that's too good to refuse. We stop by Alfredo's battered delivery truck and I help Ylena up into the cab and share the passenger seat with her as Alfredo drives back into town along the rutted highway.

Stepping into the portico of the Empire Bar, we get the royal treatment from the hustlers at the entrance and the doors are opened for us. The soothing big band music of Glen Miller is playing. A few early diners, mostly British servicemen, are sitting expectantly at tables near the piano. Basking in the respect accorded to Ylena, I shake hands with various well-dressed local men standing at the bar.

We sit at a little table with a reserved sign that commands a view of the glittering tableau vivant; drinks are already waiting for us. As the pianist prepares himself on the little raised dais reserved for the opulent Steinway Grand piano, a beautiful young woman in a sequinned gown joins him.

Ylena squeezes my arm. 'My sister, Thwayya. She's an accomplished singer. I'll introduce you later.' I'm pleasantly surprised that, rather than the expected traditional Għana, it turns out that Thwayya is a Gracie Fields and Vera Lynn aficionado. 'She's learnt it all from listening to the gramophone. She can't speak much English, but she can sing in English. She's a marvel.'

I have to agree with Ylena; Thwayya is stunning and the audience are appreciative. After Thwayya's set, Benny Goodman is playing on the gramophone and we take to the floor. Ylena needs some help with her swing steps, but it's fun showing her, and we collapse in stitches whenever she steps on my toes. 'Why not just step onto my feet; that way you're always going to follow me!'

Ylena's diminutive form melts into mine and we become one person as we dance around the room with Ylena balanced on my feet to the delight of customers at the tables around the dance floor. The proximity of her body and the sharp odour of her perspiration are arousing me. Swivelling my hips into her open thighs so that onlookers can't see what's happening between my legs, Yelena looks up and smiles. 'I think I need to take care of you, or you won't make it through dinner.' She steps off my feet and tugs at my hand in the direction of a little stage door to our left.

Passing the backstage paraphernalia, boxes of lights, we skirt around a huge mirror ball that should be suspended from the ceiling. 'We took it down when the bombing started, too dangerous to have it suspended over our heads!' Opening a small door on our left leads into one of the performer's dressing rooms. Snapping on the lights reveals a bank of mirrors, a large dressing table and a sumptuous red satin chaise longue. 'My mother's dressing room back in the days when she performed here.' Looking at the chaise longue, she adds, 'I'm pretty certain she entertained her fair share of young male performers here while Father was out chasing young girls at the front of house.' She giggles.

Shaking off her shoes and removing her dress, Ylena perches on the chaise longue and opens my belt buckle and zip fastener. Struggling to get my tumescent penis out of my service briefs, she gives up and pulls them down completely, takes me in her mouth and pumps my shaft with her fist for a few strokes before positioning herself on the chaise longue on her front, resting her hips and belly on a large, sequinned cushion.

'It's perfect, no?' All thoughts of the grief I felt earlier in the day have evaporated and all I can see is the groove of her open vulva and the damp stain that's forming on the small pair of satin panties she's wearing. A flush of desire reddens my face and neck as I inhale her acrid scent.

Removing her panties completely, Ylena sighs with contentment, as I kiss her inner thighs and buttocks, and, as I enter her, she pushes her hips towards me. 'Empty yourself quickly, my love, I don't know how long we have before someone else needs this room!' Another tinkling laugh.

All the death, destruction and evil deeds I've seen in the past weeks are washed away as I stroke into Ylena's lithe body. We're making a child together, a new life that I fervently hope will live in a world that's far from the strife and suffering of war. Her soft moaning and the tightening walls of her vagina trigger a familiar warm ache in my belly. Grasping her firm breasts, I feel my release pulsing over and over and over; semen escapes from her opening producing a large milk-white pool on the red satin cover. 'Oh, Alla tiegħi! I can feel your seed filling me.' Ylena gasps and clasps her belly. 'I think I'm ovulating! This has never happened before during sex; we must make love again tonight!'

Dressing quickly, we emerge from our hiding place and almost collide with Thwayya. The women smile at each other, Ylena bends close to her sister and whispers something in Maltese, Thwayya blushes a deep scarlet, titters and disappears into the dressing room we've just vacated. 'Thwayya is jealous; I told her what we've been doing and apologise for the mess we've made!' Ylena beckons me closer. 'My darling, you've made me complete tonight; I can feel our baby already growing inside me. Also, I'm going to have our love running down my thighs for the rest of the evening!'

Fred, Monday 24th August 1942
Oflag VII-B

Well, well, I wonder what's prompted Blatterbauer to attend morning parade? Nothing good I suspect. Heads have turned in the direction of the inner gate to watch the commandant's staff car coast along the Lagerstrasse and down onto the parade ground. A large plume of white dust rises from the wheels as the big Mercedes wallows on the dirt track that connects the Lagerstrasse with the parade ground. One of the German corporals officiating this morning's headcount steps forward and opens the rear passenger door with some pomp and a Nazi salute. Blatterbauer emerges with all the hauteur of Adolf Hitler himself and gives the Führer's jaunty acceptance salute which I'm sure is overstepping the mark for a POW camp commandant. Steiner and his corporals offer the standard Nazi salute.

Seeing all this Nazi posturing and anticipating that something's amiss, Higgins walks over to meet the commandant so that the conversation can remain private until the situation has become clear. There is much inaudible shouting and aggressive arm waving by Blatterbauer, which is countered by Major Higgins' impassive stance. The commandant's tirade apparently finally over, Higgins simply nods and walks over to take his customary place at the centre of the parade ground where he's joined by Captains Cockburn, Hobkirk, Meakin, Jickling and our own company commander, Ernie Hart and a further conflab ensues.

Getting impatient to know what fate awaits us, I look up towards the sentry towers overlooking the Altmühl. Sure enough, all three have their flaps down with the mussels of their MG 34s protruding. Nearer the parade ground, guards have taken up station on the perimeter; machine pistols un-shouldered and likely cocked and locked. There's also soldiers moving around outside the perimeter fence. From where I'm standing opposite the fence, I can see that they're setting up what look like mortars, a lovely state of affairs on a sunny morning in August.

Several of the lads next to me have drawn a similar conclusion and I can see some anxious glances. In everyone's mind I'm sure there is one thought: 'We're going to be shot en masse.'

'Everybody, please can I have your attention.' In my distracted state, Ernie has approached our group, presumably to offer an explanation. 'Right, this is the situation. Orders have come down from Jerry High Command that one hundred and twenty of us here are to be manacled during the day. It's part of a reprisal for an operation by our forces where they allege that German POWs were manacled, and various atrocities carried out.[20]'

This news was greeted with some murmuring. So, British Forces captured German soldiers; which means what? Jerry's invaded England? It just doesn't make sense. Ernie continues, 'Apparently the commandant has indicated that he's prepared to have his men open fire if there's any perceived resistance on our part. For this reason, Major Higgins has ordered that the situation be played as calmly as possible.' Ernie waits for the information to sink in before continuing. 'The goons have got themselves pretty worked up about it and I wouldn't put it past Blatterbauer to carry out his threat if he's provoked. Higgins has asked that each of the companies produce fifteen volunteers to be handcuffed during the day for the foreseeable future.'

For some reason, is it boredom, curiosity? I always feel as though I need to be at the centre of these sort of things, so I find myself putting my hand up. 'Thanks Freddy, anyone else? I'm taking volunteers, but unless people step forward, I'm going to have to make a

---

[20] This vignette is based on a true-life reprisal carried by the commandant of Oflag VII-B in response to the alleged mistreatment of German officers taken prisoner during an Allied assault on the French port of Dieppe, codenamed Operation Jubilee. Later to become known as the Dieppe Raid, the operation on 19th August 1942 was intended to test German forces as a prelude to an Allied invasion. The operation involved more than six thousand troops, mostly Canadian; however, it proved to be a costly failure with 3,623 men killed, wounded or captured.

selection, sorry, but that's the way it is.'

Back at our billet, Gedge joins me with a group of half a dozen other volunteers from our hut and I give him a quizzical look. 'I wouldn't miss it for the world! Being manacled during the day just means that everyone will need to do the cooking and cleaning!' I just wag my head and smile. Dear old Gedge, he never wants to be left out of anything either.

'Right, follow me and collect your stuff. You're going to be billeted separately so the goons can fit the manacles in the morning and release you at night.' Ernie holds the door for us as we troop out of the hut with a pile of our bedding. As we do so, some of the lads offer a thumbs up and we receive a pat on the back from Ted and Andrew.

As we file out, Graham King steps over. 'We'll see you're all right, Freddy. I'll be making sure you get your rations and any medical stuff you chaps need. How's that old bullet wound?'

'Yep, it's playing up, I have to admit. It's opened back up a bit.'

'I thought so. Okay, I'll make sure you get some fresh vegetables. You're probably low on vitamins.' All I can think is, Christ! I've got scurvy in this day and age; can you believe it? If anything, the enforced inactivity might actually help it to heal. I nod to Graham; he's such a selfless chap, always thinking of others, just like Jimmy Pile, God rest his soul.

'Well, every cloud has a silver lining!'

'That's the spirit, Freddy!' Heading back up to Lagerstrasse, we join the other volunteers, and the guards take us over to the large storage hut next to the hospital; well at least it's going to be handy if we're taken ill.

We set up our makeshift beds, just a mattress on the floor, and wait as the guards fit our handcuffs. Given the German mindset around thoroughness, I was expecting leg irons and a ball and chain. 'Schnell!' One of the younger guards is angrily wrestling with a set of keys and pair of heavy-looking handcuffs and trying to fit them on my wrists. Moving closer, and hissing in my ear, 'Sie haben glück, dass wir sie nicht wie Ihre Kanadischen freunde in Dieppe erschießen.'

'Canadians? In Dieppe?' The young guard looks taken aback that I understand him; perhaps he's let slip too much?

'They are all kaput!' With that, he collects another set of cuffs and starts the process again with someone else. Gedge steps over, wrists firmly clamped in a pair of cuffs.

Holding them up triumphantly, he says, 'my mother always said I'd end up in a pair of these!' A few of us smile at this, but I think several of us reckon that wearing handcuffs might not be all the Germans will do especially if the SS get involved. Gedge then bends towards me and whispers, 'What was that about Canadians?'

'Not sure, but I guess we'll find out eventually.

British and Commonwealth Forces in Dieppe, I wonder what it means.'

Gedge shrugs. 'Absolutely no idea whether it's good or bad news; let's go over to the mess and see what there is to eat.'

A few minutes later, we're sitting hunched over a bowl of thin soup. I stir the cloudy, steaming liquid and a small chunk of what could be meat, floats to the surface. Before I attempt to pick up a spoon, it becomes clear that eating isn't going to be the only thing that'll be difficult to do in handcuffs. Irritation from incessant bites from lice is driving me crazy and I realise that I'm now totally unable to reach the spot on my back to scratch it. On top of that, I'm beginning to find it increasingly difficult to read for some reason. It's intensely annoying since I've recently managed to borrow one of the few fiction novels in English from the camp library, 'The Maltese Falcon'. Try as I might, the harder I concentrate, the more the words appear to blur on the page.

Apart from deteriorating vision, I've got the start of a headache and a fever, which is something I don't need right now. Exasperated, I shut the book and toss it on the table. It's not like me to feel down, but these last few weeks have been hard. It's almost two years to the day since we were captured. We're so totally out of the picture as far as the authorities back home are concerned. There's little news about the progress of the war, so we've absolutely no idea how long we're going to be in here. At least a criminal knows how long his sentence will be! The empty, dull lives we have here are starkly illustrated when I'm writing letters home. There seems little to say that won't be censored out which could convey the life we live in here; it all seems like such a waste of time.

A conversation between Gedge and Taff, one of the Welsh Guards lieutenants interrupts my melancholia, at the point where Gedge is describing a full English breakfast he once had in the Marine Hotel in Aberystwyth. It's a place I know very well, so I butt into their conversation, 'You said Aber? Funny that, but that place is run by the family of an army mate of mine.'

Taff smiles broadly. 'Well, you'll know what I mean about the breakfast! You'll also probably know the feisty woman that runs the place, Rowena I think her name was. She's a bit of a looker and not shy about putting it around, especially with the army blokes.' Taff winks knowingly and the conversation meanders away from the Aber and onto ex-girlfriends, but my mind lingers on my stay at the Marine. My mouth waters just imagining the crisp fried bread, bacon and fat sausages winking at me from a large white plate. However, I'm not going to mention my, probably more intimate encounter with the lovely Roanna Jenkins.

Images of that weeklong holiday after ten days of arduous training at the Brecon Beacons Army Camp enter my mind. I'm sitting by the window in the breakfast room on an unusually bright and sunny morning in March overlooking the shingle beach and the children and families playing there in the unexpectedly warm weather. I'm staying in one of the hotel's staff bedrooms at the behest of my mate Glynn Jenkins who runs the place. What I didn't anticipate was how attractive Glynn's older sister, Roanna, is. From the first evening Glynn introduced us, she immediately took a bit of a shine to me. Well, more than a shine, actually if truth be known.

'Well, Freddy, I hope the bus journey over from Brecon wasn't too arduous.'

'Not nearly as arduous as the bloody training I've been doing on the Beacons; I reckon I must've crawled through every muddy ditch and puddle the ruddy place has to offer!' We both laugh. Hearing us, the woman I spotted at the reception desk when I arrived comes over.

'This is Roanna, my big sis. She's the boss around here! This is my mate, Freddy. You'll be glad to know he's an army officer just off training over at Brecon Barracks so just your type.' I was expecting a blush or the woman to become embarrassed, but instead, she meets my gaze.

'Well, I'd say you're right there. Great to meet you, Freddy.' I hold out my hand, which she takes, but instead of shaking it, she kisses my cheek. I've always been the tongue-tied quieter one of us two brothers. Whilst George is quite the lady's man, I've always been on the side-lines. But with Roanna, a spark was there from the start.

The intense memories of that stay in Aber causes my very being to ache with a longing to be back there again and to feel her smooth warm skin on mine once more. Try as I might, the image of our encounter spools like a movie clip and will not be assuaged until it runs its course, like a favourite tune you've hummed a thousand times, it remains all the sweeter for its repetition. It's a Saturday, the hotel bar has just closed, but I've been chatting with Ro all evening. I remember the thrill of watching the other chaps at the bar, looking over at us and obviously wishing it were they who were sitting on a barstool in front of the till chatting with the lady of the house.

'Well, Freddy, that's me off shift. Do you fancy a nightcap?'

'I'd love to; a small Scotch and soda please but go easy on the soda!' I start walking over to the lobby seating area, but she has other plans and heads up the back stairs to a small set of rooms. We enter the one right at the back overlooking an alley at the back of the hotel.

'The old servants' quarters, but they make a fine place to crash when I'm too tired to walk home.' She unties her hair, which falls in big glossy curls onto her shoulders. 'I hope you don't mind, but I'm all talked out. A night serving at the bar can do that to a woman. Besides, I know you're footloose and fancy free.' She smiles. 'I'm going to run a bath; my feet are killing me. You can make yourself comfortable in here or join me in the tub.' I must have looked taken aback, because she returns to the bedroom after turning on the taps to offer further encouragement. 'You know you want to. Call me patriotic, but I think it's wrong for a soldier to go into battle without feeling a woman's touch.' My trouser zipper is opening of its own accord and so is my belt.

'Are sure you want this, Ro?'

'Does it look like I don't know what I want?' Smiling, Ro steps back, unzips her skirt and lets it drop to the ground, her blouse follows the skirt. She turns and offers me her back; even I get the hint that she wants me to unfasten her bra. Bobbing down, she removes her panties. 'Convinced now?' Her large brown nipples are hard, and they brush my chest as she helps me undress. 'Let's bathe afterwards, I'm not sure I can wait! But, before we go any further, I need to fit my diaphragm.'

Removing a small box from her bedside drawer, Ro removes a latex object that looks like a small bath cap. 'Here's another part of your education, watch and learn.' Squatting down, Ro lubricates and then deftly inserts the diaphragm up inside her vagina. 'Voila!' and takes a bow.

Collapsing on the bed the springs complain loudly. 'We're going to be making a fair bit of noise, but there's nobody else staying in this part of the hotel.' Kissing my chest Ro travels down my abdomen licking my penis head and stoking me with her hand; I empty myself into her mouth almost immediately, but, unperturbed, she continues giving me oral until I become hard again. 'You shouldn't cum so quickly next time, now, just relax, we've got all night. Let me give you something to remember and some of my own little training exercises.' She giggles at this and backs up her bottom until her opening is over my mouth. Instinctively I start kissing her thighs and burying my face deep in her vagina. Ro's moans of pleasure suggest I'm not doing a bad job for a novice! My penis is back between her lips, her tongue swirling around my glans until I'm about to ejaculate again, but before I do, she turns around and lies on top, so my erection is resting between her open thighs.

We kiss for quite some time until she reaches down and guides me into her opening. 'I've got my diaphragm in and this is my safe time of the month, so don't look so worried.' And then whispers I my ear, 'I hate using condoms. Just relax and enjoy yourself, finish inside me if you want. I promise you I can't get pregnant.'

Thrusting into her, the bed springs squeal like a veritable cat's chorus, but we're a long way past caring. My penis is so hard it actually feels like it's going to split at the seams. I climax twice. I'm startled by how loud I bellow each time. Still hard, Ro continues riding me until she also climaxes letting out a very loud scream as she does so. The sound of Roanna's orgasm echoes in my head, and I have to make a conscious effort to close out these arousing thoughts.

We kept in touch until I was posted to France. I wonder if she still thinks about me, but it seems unlikely. The handcuffs tug painfully on my wrists as I reach for some salt, dammit! Why in hell did I volunteer for this? A wave of despair hits me and I wonder whether I will ever return to the ordinary life I once had before the war. What if the war goes on for another ten years, or, God forbid, if the Germans win, will they decide to keep us captive after the war? And for how long? A new resolve emerges. 'I've got to escape.' The answer is simple and so clear, and yet, achieving that goal is going to be far from trivial.

George, Friday October 2nd, 1942, Kalafrana

'I can't keep a lid on it much longer, Witty. You were AWOL last night and the same the previous week. It won't come from me, but Tinselly, he's a slippery bugger, has got a whiff of it and he's likely to go to Skip and then your goose will be well and truly cooked, old chap.'

'I'm in way over my head with Ylena, nothing like this has happened to me before. I'm literally a newborn when it comes to women, but Ylena makes it so easy, she knows how to be with a man, takes the lead, shows me the ropes. I'm never likely to find anyone else like her. I'm completely head over heels and if we could marry, I would in a shot, but, although her husband's left her, she can't afford to divorce him, or she'd lose everything her family has worked for.'

'Has it occurred to you that she might be playing on your youth and inexperience in these things? She has everything to gain from hitching herself to a British serviceman. Think about it, Valletta has been bombed flat, we're getting supplies now, but the bottom's dropped out of the Maltese economy. Don't you see? You're her ticket out of here.' Fish's face is the very picture of exasperation and concern.

'I know you're thinking about me, but it's just not like that. We love each other.' Fish scans my face, and his features soften.

'What do I know about it? A few fumbles with the odd girl after the varsity ball and that's about as far as I've got! Now here I am acting the agony aunt and giving out relationship advice!' We both laugh and the mood lightens slightly. 'I'll get us another.'

Fish wanders off to the bar and I stare out into the night. How many times have I looked across the Marsaxlokk Bay and willed the Fates to give me a sign, a clue about what lies ahead? It's a beautiful clear evening. The enemy bombers appear to have suspended their destructive raids, at least for the moment. I suspect that the focus of the enemy has shifted since the Italians haven't invaded us and the Germans maybe have their hands full elsewhere. Monty's given the Italians a kicking in North Africa, so my guess is that the Germans are concentrating their efforts there.

Moonlight sparkles on the flat calm and a million tiny wavelets shimmer creating a silvery path that comes ashore in the harbour. It's six thirty p.m. and completely still, with not a soul about. It wouldn't surprise me in the least if the *Flying Dutchman* and her ghostly crew hove into view and the eponymous Captain van der Decken himself stepped ashore.

'Carmelo just took a call at the bar and he says the station commander is looking for you.' Fish's face is ashen; we both know what it's likely to be about. Group Captain Livock tends to deliver bad news after hours. I guess it makes sense since the base is one huge rumour mill and not being in possession of the facts is no reason to prevent a good story being spread about on the jungle telegraph. Fish and I exchange a glance; I must have the look of a condemned man, because Fish rises to shake my hand. 'Good luck, old chap' was all he could find to say, so I head off to the administrative buildings to discover my fate.

Walking across the slipway, towards the Marine Section offices, I once again contemplate the legend of the *Flying Dutchman*; sailing off in her would be the only way I'm going to escape a bollocking. In the moonlight, the imposing edifice of the station headquarters building casts a long shadow and I slowly climb the steps, my heart sinking still further into my bootstraps as I open the door into the lobby and step inside.

I clearly remember making three memorable trips to the headmaster, Mr Todd, while I was at The King's School in Tynemouth to receive punishments for misdemeanours. In two out of those three occasions, I'd managed to talk my way out of it, but I don't think it's going to be so easy this time.

The outer office is unmanned when I get to the group captain's office, so I simply step up and knock on the inner office door.

'Yes! Ah, Whitton, come in and sit down. I don't

believe in beating about the bush. I've got something rather important to talk to you about. Firstly, I should say that Flight Lieutenant Markham spoke very highly of you and had recommended that you be mentioned in despatches for your exemplary conduct during that U-boat incident back in September last year when, unarmed, you tackled a German officer.' I could see that Livock was reading from a service records file, probably mine. 'Markham was a courageous and exemplary officer; he is sorely missed.'

'Amen to that, sir.' I silently thanked Markham for his faith in me; I certainly miss him. By his demeanour and the way he shifts in his chair, I can see that Livock is going to get to the point concerning something awkward.

'It's come to my attention that you've started a relationship with a Maltese woman living in Valletta. I shan't go into detail on how this came to light, but let's just say, that your attendance and performance have been erratic over the past few weeks. You know the rules, fraternising with the local women is frowned upon. Apart from causing problems with the local populace, there's the security angle; we can't afford to risk information finding its way to the enemy. As a matter of fact, there have been a number of information leaks recently and the top brass wants a clampdown. I also understand from Flight Lieutenant Bryant that you were effectively absent without leave after Flight Lieutenant Markham's funeral. He felt disinclined to mention anything at the time, but it turns out that you spent the night off-base with this woman you're seeing.'

'Ylena Bonnici, sir.'

'Look, I understand why chaps posted overseas for months, or even years, are inevitably drawn to the local women. The Maltese women are fiery and unpredictable, but also have a reputation as being very alluring. As a matter of fact, I've already been informed that it is Ms Bonnici you're seeing. You may not be aware, but Ms Bonnici's family are very influential on the island and their business activities have come under scrutiny by the local police and the British authorities several times over the years. Whilst it can't be proved that Ms Bonnici's late father was involved directly in criminal activity, he was implicated in the Music Hall Affair in the 1930s, a very unsavoury chapter in Maltese history relating to the sexual exploitation of English women who had come to Malta to work as music hall artistes. It was alleged that certain women working at the Empire Bar were under duress to provide sexual favours to paying customers. Mr Bonnici denied all knowledge, and charges never stuck, but the allegations still stand.'

'Sir, I haven't seen anything untoward happening at the Empire and I've been there on numerous occasions.'

'That's just the point, Whitton! You must see that the Bonnici family are potentially part of a criminal element in Malta.' Livock falls silent for a moment and his expression looks strained; I can see he's prevaricating. 'It's out of my hands, Whitton. I'm really sorry, but I've been asked to have you transferred away from Malta. The recent reduction in enemy activity around Malta and a shift in focus to the North African theatre means that there's a shortage of trained people over there. As it turns out, Coastal Command in Port Said is in desperate need of experienced WOM personnel so I'm having you transferred there. I'm not going to record anything negative on your record. The matter will be closed once you're transferred and you'll leave here with a clean and exemplary record of service.'

I'm truly stunned and can't find anything useful to say in reply. It seems to be a fait accompli; Livock has had his orders and my transfer is signed and sealed.

'When will I be transferred, sir?'

'You'll be on a Sunderland that leaves for Port Said two weeks from now.' Livock scans my face and I can see his expression soften. 'I'm very sorry it has come to this. It may surprise you to learn that I too have been through a very similar thing years ago in France during our last run-in with Germany. You have my sympathy.' I stand, and salute. 'Goodbye and good luck, Whitton.'

Leaving Livock's office, I can barely make my legs function. I'm desperate to talk to Ylena, but it's too late to get transport into town and I'd only be compounding the situation. I feel like I've had the stuffing well and truly kicked out of me. Reaching the open air again, I lean on a tree standing in what passes as the headquarters gardens. Tears well up and there's nothing I can do to stop them.

George, Friday October 16th, 1942, The Empire Bar, Valletta

We've been holding each other all night and my right shoulder is completely dead, but I don't want to disturb Ylena as she's sleeping. A shaft of light pierces the curtained gloom of Ylena's attic bedroom, an unwelcome reminder that morning has come on my final day in Malta. I'm scheduled to fly at twelve noon, so there's still some time left for us to prepare ourselves.

Ylena told me last night that she'd had her period, so there's no chance that she's pregnant despite our frequent lovemaking. Our fervent hope was that she'd fall pregnant and I could somehow wangle a reprieve from my transfer to Port Said. I even entertained a fantasy that we'd be settled in the married quarters.

Ylena stirs and her beautiful brown eyes are directly opposite mine. Tears well up and fall quietly on her pillow. 'Oh Ylena, please don't cry, my darling. This isn't the end; we can keep in touch by letter. When this damn war is over, we can be together. I'll come back to Malta…'

I've run out of words, there's nothing I can say that makes this any better or changes the fact that I feel like my heart is going to break and I'll die of sadness. The

French talk about 'la petite mort' referring to the lethargy after orgasm as being like a partial death, but actually, being torn away from the woman you love is like dying. I feel physically sick. As always, we're both completely naked in bed. Despite my all-pervading feeling of grief, my libido appears not to have been affected. Ylena notices and reaches down between my legs to encourage my stiffening penis.

'I will miss this gorgeous monster! We say in Malta, "li kien, kien, li kieku, kieku". There should be no crying over things that happen; we must just accept reality and move on. So, my beautiful English lover, I want us to spend the next three hours lovemaking as though our lives depend on it!'

Easing herself down under the bedsheets, I feel Ylena's warm mouth sliding down my penis. Not wanting to miss anything, I pull the bed sheets off us and meet with her brown eyes looking directly into mine while her lips slide all the way down to the base of my shaft. I'm beginning to learn how to stop myself ejaculating every time Ylena gives me the deep oral treatment, but my toes still curl up in my effort not to fill her mouth with the semen that needs to go into her belly.

Mercifully, Ylena is impatient to get me inside her. Hitching her open thighs around my hips, she slides my penis into her opening and sits slowly down on me. Riding me slowly at first, she balances herself on my chest and picks up the pace rotating her hips with each stroke. Just when I feel like I'm going to fill her, Ylena releases me and my penis slaps down hard on my belly.

'Oh, I'm sorry, my love! But I want to give you a special little parting gift, but promise me you won't cum until you are inside me properly?'

'I'll try, but I'm getting very close!' Ylena puts her hand in her mouth and moistens her fingers with copious saliva and reaches between her legs and pushes two fingers into herself. After a few seconds, she positions her anus over the tip of my penis and sits slowly all the way down. I can see she is wincing, so I touch her arm to ask her to stop.

'It's okay, I just need to stretch myself. When we were first married, my husband didn't want children, so we had anal sex all the time; I actually enjoy it.'

The feeling is tight and after a few strokes up and down, Ylena pulls on my testicles to prevent me ejaculating. She's moaning loudly; the feeling of pure pleasure is overwhelming. Sliding off me, she lies back on the bed and pulls on my hips, her signal for me to enter her on top. I manage only a few stokes inside her before emptying myself so hard it's almost painful.

'My God! What did you do there, my love? I thought I was going to explode!'

'A little trick I learned from a woman's magazine that said that a woman that gives her body totally to her man in every way possible is certain to always keep him.'

'What sort of woman's magazines do you get in

Malta!'

'It was a French magazine. The boring old Maltese wouldn't dream of writing such an article.' She giggles in a way that I always think is absolutely adorable.

October 16th, 12:00 noon

The weather has had the decency to be correspondingly sombre and it's raining hard to match the occasion. Our prolonged lovemaking session appears to be cushioning the melancholy of our last moments together on the deserted slipway. I know the pilot and crew will be intently watching us from the flight cabin, be we don't care. We embrace like our lives depend on it and kiss deep and long trying to savour each other and to store up our love for the time we're going to be apart.

'I will write to you and make sure you have the address of my unit so we can keep in touch.' Ylena simply nods. I can see she's crying and is unable to speak. We separate and I turn one last time to wave as I climb into the Sunderland's passenger door and pull up the steps. As I look up, Ylena is walking towards the quay in the driving rain with her head down, her small form is hunched, and I feel compelled to call out to her. 'Ylena! Ylena!' She turns and waves. Waving back, I close and secure the door. It feels like I've sealed our fate as I seal the door.

Fred, Thursday November 12th, 1942, Oflag VII-B – planning

'Ernie, Freddy, Gedge, thanks for coming and apologies for all the cloak and dagger stuff; not my thing usually.' Clem Elson[21] shakes each of our hands in turn and we make ourselves as comfortable as possible on some makeshift benches. Elson has the short, lean figure of a man of action and his moustache positively twitches with nervous energy. The rows of shelves around us are piled high with the myriad of paraphernalia needed to keep a prison camp of eight hundred men running, blocking out the waning afternoon light of another cold, damp November day and the snooping eyes of ferrets.

---

[21] Captain Clement (Clem) Elson of the Royal Norfolk Regiment was a real-life figure and a serial escapee. Clem was part of what became known as the Warburg wire job, an audacious escape from Oflag VI-B over the fence using a makeshift ladder. Captured at the little village of Le Paradis in France in 1940, Clem was one of only two survivors of a massacre where ninety-nine men of the Royal Norfolk Regiment were executed under the orders of Hauptsturmfuhrer Friz Knöchlein of the SS Totenkopf (Death's Head) Division. Knöchlein was later held accountable for his crimes and was sentenced to death by a jury at the Nuremburg Trials held after the war.

I'd not met Elson since he and others, including Hamilton-Baillie, Moir and the main instigator, Frank Weldon, were transferred from Oflag VI-B for a pretty audacious breakout over the fence involving a makeshift ladder. Maybe they all got moved here because the Germans reckon that Oflag VI-B is way too close to the Dutch border to imprison such a slippery character so far north. Anyway, Oflag VI-B's loss is our gain. I involuntarily shiver at the thought of spending another winter in captivity; this is my chance to get out of here. At this point, I don't even care if I'm re-captured, I just need to feel like I'm doing something! Elson's speaking again.

'Once we bring you in on this, we need to maintain complete secrecy from everyone outside the escape committee and the digging teams until everything is ready. As you know, the ferrets are everywhere and we're going to need airtight security if we're going to make this work.'

Elson looks around us, Gedge and I nod and in unison. 'We're in.'

'Okay, here's the plan. We're going to dig three tunnels: one from Block three, via an existing tunnel under Block four and the storeroom we're sitting in; she'll be called "Betty". Another one from the communal latrine at the back of Hut eight called "Gretta" and the third, called "Rita" will go from the Block two latrine. It's likely that one, or maybe two of these tunnels will eventually act as decoys if the digging gets too tough or they're found by the guards. I'm coordinating with Frank Weldon who's leading the Hut eight digging team and with Block three digging team leader, Jock Hamilton-Baillie. Frank will be the "Big X" on this and will be in overall charge. Frank was the brains behind our quick and dirty attempt at Warburg, and he's keen to have another crack at it. Any questions so far?' Shaking heads all around.

'We're keeping the number of people in the know to an absolute minimum, even the people making the uniforms; Arthur Fry is leading on that since he's got access to material and clothing for his theatre productions. Others will take care of forging documents, identification passes, work and travel permits and the like. None of them will know the details of the plan, only that there is an escape afoot. When the time comes, we'll inform a selected group of people about the escape plan.

'One of the reasons why we didn't go for a tunnel in Oflag VI-B was due to severe problems with disposal of dirt; however, this site has some clear advantages, especially the garden and flower beds where we can scatter and dig over the spoil. Freddy, Ernie tells me that you're fairly fluent in French and have a smattering of German; that's going to be handy. Can I ask you to work with Robbie Eastman and Jonny Mansel in Hut six? Both are taking care of forging ID papers. Jonny did an amazing job for us in Oflag VI-B.

'Lady Luck has granted us another bit of good

fortune on the identification papers front. We've got some very compromising photographs from a honeypot sting on one of the guards, an odious fellow called Schmidt. A fellow inmate who'll remain nameless for obvious reasons, agreed to trap this Schmidt by offering to give him sexual favours in return for cigarettes. To cut a long story short, we've got Schmidt, quite literally, by the short and curlies and he's already supplied us with a couple of POW passes, Ausweis, and a genuine French work permit[22].'

I quietly smile to myself. So, the slimy Schmidt finally gets his comeuppance, hallelujah! 'I understand that you were a Northumbrian miner before joining the Army.' Elson smiles at Gedge.

'For my sins, sir, yes. I know a thing or two about digging a mine shaft if that's what you mean?'

'Yes, it's exactly those skills that could be vital, Sergeant Major! So, I'm going to ask you to lead on ensuring the tunnel supports are up to scratch and also to improvise a way of circulating air down there; I can see it's going to be a problem.' Elson takes another break from speaking and looks over at the three of us.

---

[22] In Nazi Germany, all citizens needed to carry identity papers. Any foreign nationals also had to additionally have a permit to allow them to work. Papers were often checked by police and other officials, including the Gestapo, whilst travelling on public transport or passing through checkpoints. Prisoners of war also needed permits, called Kriegsgefangenen Ausweis, if they needed to travel outside the prison camp to work.

'Ernie, you haven't said much, have you got anything to add?

'Not really. I don't have any more to add than we've discussed earlier about the selection of digging teams. I'll do what I can to help coordinate activities in our hut regarding positioning of the tunnel entrance in Block two's latrine. It's going to probably mean taking one of the toilets out of commission and that will cause questions to be asked.'

'If I might suggest a solution to that?' Our heads turn towards Gedge. 'I think we can improvise a flexible pipe using buckets joined together like a concertina to keep the toilet bowl connected to the sewer and some hosepipe to lengthen the water inflow to the cistern. We can then simply mount the toilet on a wooden board, which will allow us to move the toilet to one side while we're digging and lift it back into place and be fully functional the rest of the time. It should also be fully functional while we're down there digging.'

'A genius plan, Geddes!' Elson looks impressed, as well, Gedge's plan is brilliant. 'All right, gentlemen, I think that's all for now. We'll have another brief meeting once digging has started to check on progress, in a couple of weeks.'

We all file out into the dark cold air and I head over to Block four with Gedge so as Ernie can have a chat to Arthur about an upcoming pantomime that's being organised for Christmas called 'Dossing Dulcie'. Entering the second floor, there's no sign of Arthur, but there's a small group of lads gathered at the far end of the dormitory, one of whom is peering through a telescope.

'How on earth did you chaps mange to filch that?' All heads turn in my direction.

'Keep your voice down, old chap, we're doing a spot of bird watching.' There's some collective mirth at this, so I wander over for a closer look. One of the group who's been looking intently through the telescope since we came in, makes a flamboyant bow and obligingly moves to one side to let me take a look. Adjusting the focus and looking over the roof of the storage hut we've just been in, it's as though I'm standing on the balcony in front of a pair of large, brightly lit, French windows on the second floor of the married quarters opposite.

There, in full view, is a naked woman standing bold as brass at the window. She's young and slim with short mousey hair, large, heavy breasts and a long lean stomach. I can feel my penis tighten against my zip fastener as I stare intently at the thick bush of dark pubic hair between her legs and the pleasure, I imagine awaits there for any man lucky enough to get between her slim thighs. As I watch, I can see her fingers working between her legs, masturbating herself with apparent abandon for all and sundry to see. The telescope is more than powerful enough to allow me to clearly watch while she spreads herself open with one hand and uses the thumb of her other to massage her clitoris whilst pushing her fingers into the opening. Every now and again, she removes her fingers to ostentatiously taste herself and moisten them with saliva. Occasionally, she turns and bends over to give us all a better view of what she's doing and of her open vagina.

It's then I notice that she has a large cylindrical object pushed inside her anus. She's smiling broadly and clearly enjoying herself immensely as she taunts us with her body. She's carefully placed herself in the room so that a long curtain shields her from the guard tower opposite, so I assume her husband and the other Germans are oblivious of what she's up to.

I become mesmerised by the sight. I haven't seen a naked woman since I spent that heavenly sojourn in Aber with Ro. Admittedly, I got to see plenty of her beautiful flesh over the week I was there, but the sight of this woman flaunting herself for us to see is deeply unsettling and I can feel sexual frustration building; I wrench myself away from the telescope.

'Well, you don't see that very often!' Huge mirth erupts at this understatement from the audience that's been waiting with bated breath for my reaction. I'm embarrassed enough to feel myself blushing red like a schoolboy who's been caught by his mother reading a Penny Dreadful in the bathroom.

George, Monday November 30th, 1942, RAF Marine Section, Port Said

A slow but insistent flapping of canvas in a warm breeze coaxes me out of a fitful slumber and I turn petulantly on my side in an attempt to ignore the unwelcome reminder that it's the morning after the night before. Settling again, a large mote of dust from my careworn blanket settles on my nose, making it impossible to continue my pretence of sleep.

Swinging my legs over my surprisingly comfortable bed and onto the floor independently of my top half momentarily places me in an awkwardly twisted posture in which the rest of my body is forced to follow my legs causing my head to throb and my stomach to lurch. The large quantity of Scotch I'd drunk at the NAAFI bar last night finally makes its presence known. I stumble outside to answer the inevitable call of nature. Dawn is breaking and the still-cool breeze gently rocks huge bunches of dates hanging from the top of palm trees that fringe the roadway into the walled enclosure of the fort.

Moving along an alleyway between serried ranks of similar tents, my neighbours are already emerging, some looking almost as ragged as I am. The acrid stench of the latrine block meets me full on as I approach, causing vomit to rise and burn my throat. Forced to stop and to bend so as I can brace my hands on my knees, I'm forced to accept that I've been drinking more and more heavily recently. It's been a tough few weeks settling into a new posting and getting to know a new set of crewmates. Skip, Titch Pettigrew, has been very welcoming. Also, Don Latimer, the cox and his number two, Mike Prince, are great lads and they've bent over backwards to help; in fact, they're partly to blame for my lamentable state this morning! Fatigue due to an endless succession of patrols, shouts from downed crews and the general chaos caused by Monty's victory in El Alamein[23] should have blunted my senses, but I walk with ghosts. There's Markham and O'Hare, of course, but I also grieve over Ylena.

I'd never have thought it possible, but I feel anguish and despair at our parting that I've never experienced before, not even after Freddy's disappearance in France. Whilst I can somehow feel that my brother is okay and can even envisage him in a POW camp, I feel only a hopeless longing when I think of Ylena. Despite the flies and unpleasant stench, I'm forced to spend quite some time speaking into the porcelain telephone as the

---

[23] Montgomery's victory over Erwin Rommel's Panzer Army Africa in the Second Battle of El Alamein proved to be a pivotal moment in the Mediterranean theatre of war. As Winston Churchill later put it, *'Before Alamein we never had a victory. After Alamein we never had a defeat.'*

army wags like to call being violently sick. Amazingly, after the retching abates and my stomach's finally empty, I actually feel like a new man!

Walking back from the latrine block, I'm met by the already rising heat and clouds of sandflies, but also the familiar figure of Sergeant Graham making his way over to my tent, no doubt to gloat over my current state. Reaching in his tunic pocket, Graham produces an envelope, and my heart misses a beat. Ylena! I immediately change direction and walk over to meet him. 'It's a letter for you, lad, from a mate in your old unit in Malta.'

My disappointment must have shown on my face because, rather than stay for a chat and a bit of banter, the old sergeant makes his way back towards the administration building. It's only when I watch his ramrod straight back disappear across the parade ground that I wonder why he'd come to deliver the letter to me himself; very strange. Something about the letter coming now, but not from Ylena makes me uneasy. I stare at the envelope with its stamp, Coastal Command, Kalafrana, Malta and on the back, 'from: AC1 Blair Fisher.'

It's been over month since I left, and I've not had a single letter from Ylena. A pang of despair that's almost too much to bear causes me to physically sag. Back in my tent, I focus my attention back on the envelope, trying to imagine what it contains before I open it. I momentarily think about postponing reading it until later, a cop out that that wouldn't solve anything. I will myself to open it; my hands shake as I do so.

'My dear friend. I'm sorry to be the messenger carrying ill tidings, but I'm going to say it straight out. Ylena was killed along with her mother in an air raid a week ago.' The word 'killed' literally leaps out of the page and strikes me in the stomach. Killed? How is this possible? It must be a mistake. Mistaken identity happens all the time. Malta has been bombed flat for months; the authorities must be overwhelmed. It's a mistake! I look around my tent for something that might help, some kind of sign that what I'm reading isn't true, but all that happens is that I'm violently sick on my canvas groundsheet.

Fighting to recover my composure, I continue to read. 'She'd gone back to live in Valletta during a lull in bombing, no doubt thinking, as we all had, that things had settled down. Ylena's cousin, Alfredo brought me the enclosed unsent letter intended for you plus a couple of opened letters from you. Alfredo told me that Ylena had them with her when she was found. I can assure you that there is no mistake. Alfredo was distraught and grief-stricken; I understand that it was he who officially identified Ylena and her mother at the mortuary. I'm so, so sorry, George, and I apologise for my words to you in the days before you left and trying to make you doubt her. Ylena loved you deeply. The worn condition of the letters from you and the fact that she kept them with her meant that they, and you, were precious to her…'

I feel like a hammer blow has been dealt to my being and, despite the sweltering heat that's beginning to make the tent uncomfortable, I can't go outside in my current condition, so I flop back onto my bed. I'm barely able to open the letter from Ylena, my hands tremble so much. Although I've never seen Ylena's handwriting, the careful words written on a single sheet of paper inside are as beautiful as their author and I can hear her voice as I read them. It's dated Sunday 15th November.

'My dearest George. I am so sorry for not sending a reply to the two letters I received from you this week, but I am going to take this letter to the mail plane myself on Monday. The love you send in your letters to me is overwhelming and has given me strength. I was grief-stricken when we parted, but I prayed that night for you and us and those prayers have been answered. I missed my period this month and I'm sure I'm pregnant; I know the signs. I cannot find the words in English to express how happy I am. The knowledge that our love is growing inside me into our baby fills me with joy. It is helping me to cope with not having you here with me to know that part of you is growing inside me day by day.

'I am making a plan to travel to be with you. Things have settled down here in Malta and the bombing raids are lessening. Everyone is saying that the Germans are losing the war in Africa and it might be over as soon as Christmas. Please do not think that I am crazy, but I will make my plans to be with you and see what you think. I have much love in my heart for you when I write this and will write soon with news of my plans. Your ever loving, Ylena.'

I'm reading her words, but I'm scarcely able to take in their meaning; a baby, she's having my baby? Oh God! She's dead, and our baby is dead, and our love is dead. My tears start and I can't stop them. I'm startled by an animalistic sound and realise it's my own uncontrollable grief finding its voice.

Fred, Monday April 26th, 1943, Oflag VII-B – Digging

Tap, tap. I turn to Gedge. 'It's Clem and Ernie. What's the score outside?' More tapping as Gedge asks the question of Ken [Cockburn] who's standing out in the courtyard keeping an eye out for roving groups of ferrets. They've been increasing their patrols of late; no doubt the goons suspect something's going on. Tap, tap, delay, tap-tap. 'Okay, all clear.'

The toilet pedestal pushes up and I give it a heave. Ernie's head pops out of the entrance, hair covered in sand, hands braced against the vertical exit section of the tunnel like an emerging mole. He's sweating profusely and the veins on his forehead are standing out; I can almost see them pulsating. His face is ashen and he's not looking too good.

'God! This is going to kill me! It's bloody warm down there and very humid after this rain. I'm sorry, Freddy, I'm just not able to do any more tonight. We've hit a real obstacle so we're having to dig around it.'

Ernie looks beaten. He can't be in good shape since he's usually a virtual powerhouse. I just hope he's not going down with something. We're so close, about eighty feet the last time we estimated, so if we push on for another ten days or so, we should have travelled far enough.

'Give me your hand, Ernie. Me and Gedge will take over and try and push past the obstacle. It'd be a great way to end the night's digging and a bit of a cause for celebration.' It's tricky getting any purchase on Ernie's sweat-slicked forearm but I manage to ease him out of the hole, and he sits on the edge with his legs dangling. Clem follows Ernie and they both sit panting on the floor while Gedge and I strip off our clothes. We both decide to take everything off to keep as cool as possible and to avoid the incessant snagging of any form of clothing on roots and stones protruding from the tunnel walls. Gedge passes me and begins to enter the tunnel ahead of me.

'I'll have a go at the digging, Freddy. This is a job for a Northumbrian miner!' Without further ado, he lowers himself down the entrance shaft and starts crawling down into the passage below.

'Freddy, don't forget these.' Clem brandishes a stack of boards. 'We've dug a fair way beyond the last lot of tunnel supports. It's pretty loose and sandy. We can't risk going any further without supporting the roof or we might get a collapse.' Clem passes me the boards. The little wooden panels manufactured from Canadian Red Cross parcels have been an absolute godsend. Without them, we would be hard pushed to find something suitable to act as tunnel supports without arousing the suspicion of the goons.

As I take the boards, Clem takes over my task of pumping air into the tunnel using the crafty set of bellows constructed from Red Cross dried milk tins; another of Gedge's inventions. The pedestal and toilet is carefully placed back over the tunnel entrance in case we get an unexpected search by roving ferrets[24]. Crawling down the tunnel in semi-darkness, I can hear Gedge grunting and swearing some way ahead of me. I don't envy him his size in this narrow space; it must've been hellish working a narrow seam down the mine he worked before the war. No wonder he joined the army!

The dust and heat kick in and, in the flickering light of the oil lamps, I push the stack of support boards ahead of me creating plumes of choking dust in the process. I have some sympathy for the ancient Egyptian workers who toiled in the catacombs of the Pharaoh's pyramids; theirs was truly a thankless task, and, if the great man died while it was their stint, it was likely they'd be buried down there as an offering to the dead king. Speaking of burials, I reach the point where the tunnel supports have stopped. I begin fixing in place the boards from my stack just as Gedge passes me a basin filled with dirt.

'Hang on, Gedge, I want to fit these supports before

---

[24] Nicknamed ferrets by the prisoners, German guards specialising in escape detection used to roam about the camp in groups trying to listen in on conversations, looking through windows and entering huts of the POWs checking for evidence that an escape might be in progress.

we go any further.' More grunting, which I take to be acquiescence. Boards in place, I take the basin from him and fill the first bag of our shift and pass the basin back up to Gedge who's straining at some large obstruction up ahead. Some minutes pass, and finally, a puff of dust wafts back towards me accompanied by a little cry of satisfaction.

'I've moved the bugger! A large chunk of concrete no less, probably supporting the floor above!' I can't say that this news gives me much confidence. Being crushed by a collapsing floor or suffocating in a tunnel collapse. Take your pick; neither is a great way to go! Filled basins now come thick and fast and before long, I've filled twelve bags with sand, so I start ferrying these back up the tunnel to stack them at the bottom of the entrance shaft ready to be removed for disposal at the end of our shift.

'Christ!' I can hear some muffled words in German above my head.

'Ich muss pissen. Sie gehen voran, ich werde Sie in Block 3 treffen.'

'Ja, gut!' Footsteps and then creaking boards right above my head. I hear the cubicle door bang. More creaking follows and the toilet pedestal above my head shifts slightly. He's having more than a piss! I'm absolutely frozen in place; I daren't move in case the guard hears something. Urine running into the toilet bowl. I'm unconsciously waiting now for the first turd to drop; yes, there it goes, but it sounds like diarrhoea, just my bloody luck!

The first stream of shit is followed by two more. Our concertina arrangement to connect the toilet bowl to the sewer pipe is about to be tested to the limit. The inevitable flush. Water bleeds out between the ribs of the concertina of buckets fitted one inside the other, but the contraption holds! More creaking and dust falls from the edges of the removable pedestal.

'Was ist das?' The sound of the guard's heel tapping on the floor above my head.

'Are you finished in there, old chap, I need to take a dump.' Ernie's voice followed by some banging on the cubicle door.

'Use another toilet! Freches Englisch!'

'They're all-in use. If I can't get in there, I won't be responsible for what happens next; it's an urgent case.' I stifle a snigger. Despite the dangerous situation we're in and his poor state of health, he's totally not fazed by it, good old Ernie! More creaking and footsteps and then the toilet pedestal shifts again. More urine hitting the pan and then, yes, more shit! I can't believe it! It must be Ernie this time. Another flush and some inaudible words.

A few minutes pass, the pedestal begins to shift, and Ernie's face appears in the tunnel entrance. All we can do is laugh. 'That was close, Freddy old chap, that was close! Apologies for having to go myself, but the fact is, I think I'm suffering from a dose of the shits, and in any case, I had to follow through to appear convincing.'

'Well, the sewer connection held, otherwise I'd be swimming in shit by now!' Clem appears beside Ernie.

'Okay, okay, very funny, but look, we need to brace the tunnel entrance to make sure the pedestal is more solid, or the Goons are going to suspect something. We can't take it out of service now or it'll look even more suspicious.'

'Okay, Clem, I'll get onto it and use some of the floorboards we've got down here to do a better job on supporting the toilet once you've replaced the pedestal.' In my mind's eye, all I can see is an image of the ferret sitting on the toilet and then suddenly disappearing down into the pit. I burst out laughing again. This time it's infectious and Clem sees the joke.

Fred, Thursday 3rd June 1943, Oflag VII-B – Escaping

In the utter blackness that can only be had at three a.m. on a pitch-black moonless night, I look around a room full of expectant faces. Our Block two dormitory has started to fill with fellow escapees. Nodding at one or two familiar faces, I run over my cover story for the umpteenth time. I'm Maurice Dubois, a French forestry worker. I take my Ausweis [identity card] out of my top pocket and read it over again. It's an absolute triumph of counterfeiting genius by Burnie Andrews and his team.

I take a moment to marvel once again at the genuine-looking official Nazi stamp printed using a stamp cut from linoleum and the other printing on the document, all laboriously drawn by hand using pen and ink. Even if they'd wanted to, Burnie and his team of forgers had been ordered by the SBO not to escape, as their skills were too valuable. Mind you, if we're captured and shot, Burnie et al are, at least, pretty certain to see out the war.

I'm travelling with my compatriot, David Gouache, who's also a forestry worker. Said compatriot, the extremely amiable Albert Martens, is sitting opposite me and I unintentionally catch his eye whilst muttering through my cover story. Albert smiles. 'Freddy, it's going to be fine, just relax.'

'I know, Albert, but I don't want to let you down by getting us caught right after escaping because I'm unsure of the details. I've got to make certain my story is straight.' Basically, that story is pretty straightforward: we're heading over to the Schwarzwald (Black Forest) area to look for seasonal felling work. This would explain why we're heading south and east, whilst our actual objective is Lake Constance on the Swiss border. From Lake Constance, the plan is to head along the Rhine heading east for a short distance and into the forest around Schaffhausen in Switzerland.

The plan sounds easy if, with the forbearance of Hitler Youth search parties, Waffen SS and Gestapo roadblocks, we were able to simply walk on the roads or catch a bus, we would likely be there in a couple of days. However, in reality, it's going to be a tough one hundred and sixty plus kilometres walk through rough country, avoiding contact with the locals as much as possible. Deep in the southern heartlands of Nazi Germany, it's unlikely that we'll be coming across any Allied sympathisers and there won't be any handy safe houses maintained by resistance fighters either.

Albert, whose family live in the Ardennes, has told me he believes his two older brothers have joined the

Maquis Resistance fighters[25]. His father and brothers used to hunt deer and know the forests around Bouillon like the backs of their hands, so, as he tells me, it was an easy step for them to join the Maquis. He's clearly a chip off the old block since his devil-may-care attitude to danger seems to be similar to Gedge's. Albert's knowledge of navigating in forests and his fluent German and native French will mean that we're the 'dumb' partners. Mind you, it's possible to get a long way with a smattering of German, by just repeating 'so [pronounced, zo], ya, ya' and nodding.

We've got minimal gear, just what we're wearing, which, for me, consists of the type of 'denim' breeches that a forestry worker might wear that have been made from a pair of pyjamas, a shirt, a thin sweater and a long overcoat made from a prison blanket. Food supplies are also minimal, just couple of bags of chocolate 'sludge', a kind of high energy hoosh manufactured from cocoa powder, condensed milk and crushed biscuits.

Gedge (Bertrand Masson) is travelling with Ernie (Laurent Garon) who are also both posing as French forestry workers. The plan is to keep together whilst we're out of sight of the populace, but, in the open, we'll split into pairs to avoid attracting unwanted attention and reduce the chance of all of us being taken at once.

---

[25] Maquis were guerrilla bands of resistance fighters operating in the Ardennes region of southern Belgium. Many of the fighters were deer hunters who, apart from being formidable marksmen, they knew the forests and secret traits like the back of their hands and caused havoc with German patrols in the region.

As we're all sitting expectantly, Clem and Douggie Moir, another escapee transferred from Oflag VI-B, are down in the tunnel digging the final two or three feet. It's fitting that these two escape artists get the honour of breaking out, hopefully as planned, they come out into the cover of a farmer's chicken coop situated nearby. Douggie emerges from the entrance shaft with a huge grin on his face.

'Right, this is it, everyone. For those of you who've not been down the tunnel, it's pretty cramped down there, so remove any bulky items of clothing and push them in front of you. If you've got claustrophobia, this is definitely not for you, so if you think you're likely to panic down there, don't risk it; you'll endanger all of us. When you exit the coop, there's what looks like a garden and then open rocky ground to the right that has scattered bushes for cover. Remember, you're heading east. Good luck!'

Although I'd helped to dig the tunnel and had been down there many times before, crawling along the passageway behind Douggie, it all now seems quite different. As we reach the constriction, I notice that Douggie has signed his name and dated it 'D. Moir, June 3rd, 1943'. Now there's a date for the history books!

Douggie stands up into the exit shaft and his legs disappear in a shower of sand and loose stones. Following him up, my head pops out into the straw lying on the floor of the coop. The hens are flustered, the majority have flown up onto the rafters of the coop and are peering at us suspiciously; I feel like a fox eyeing my future supper as I stealthily move across the deep bed of litter on the floor. Clem is standing watch by the door. As we approach, he gives me the nod. 'All clear. Good luck, Freddy.'

We briefly shake hands. I feel quite emotional and feel it in my throat. 'Good luck, Clem.' With Albert close behind, I start running, but turn to check that Gedge and Ernie are emerging from the coop. The feeling of freedom and, an albeit dark, horizon without barbed wire, is quite exhilarating, cathartic even. As we run between the cover of bushes, I've got to pinch myself as a reminder that, instead of being reborn into a friendly place of family and friends, as a realised convict might enjoy, we've just emerged into the hostile world of Nazi Germany full of spies, informers and the dreaded Gestapo.

Gedge checks the compass, and we alter course so that we're heading due east. We can hear, and faintly make out, the sound of water flowing in the Altmühl. It's about four a.m. and an orange glow is appearing ahead of us as we drop down onto the riverbank, keeping as near to the river as possible as a navigation aid.

'We'd better try and wade through the water for a bit when it gets shallower; it'll throw the bloodhounds off the scent. On deer hunts, our dogs often lost the scent if an animal crossed a river, so let's do the same.' No one argues with Albert's logic. Running hard as it's now rapidly getting light, we head into some trees fringing the river. Stopping briefly to catch our breath, I can just about hear the air-raid siren of the camp general alarm sounding.

'Damn it!' Ernie spits out his frustration. 'The alarm's been given already. It's going to mean that every available man, woman and child will be summoned to comb the area. We've got to find some cover before it gets any lighter if we don't want the humiliation of being surrounded by a baying mob of eleven-year-olds from the Hitler Youth!' But we're in luck; a large patch of woodland appears ahead, and we duck into it and lay up for a few minutes while Gedge gets his bearings. I can see the familiar steely look in his eyes; he's obviously enjoying himself immensely.

It's fully light now, and as we approach a single-track road following the river, we spot a truck stopping up ahead. Soldiers leap out followed by two large dogs – bloodhounds! I'm usually very fond of dogs, but the sound of their excited baying stops us dead in our tracks and my blood runs cold.

'We've got to put some distance between them and us and find a place to lay up during the day. We need to get back into the river and swim downstream for a bit, so the dogs lose our scent, otherwise we're finished!' Nobody has a better plan, so we follow Albert.

Running half bent over to avoid being seen, we wade into the freezing water and get out into the current. The river sweeps us quickly downstream and we pass under a road bridge where some local boys are also swimming. They wave enthusiastically at us as we pass by. After a while, I begin to tire and a paroxysm of shivering stifles my breathing; clearly, we're not the fit young men we used to be two years ago, that's for sure.

We swim in towards the bank a few hundred yards after passing under a railway bridge. As we emerge from the water into the open fields again, we're in luck, and, after a few hundred yards, enter a large patch of forest, we're very fortunate, the Germans do love their trees. 'I'm trying to get us to Burgruine Wellheim; it's a landmark of some sort. Then from there we head south and cross the Danube at Schloss Berthldsheim.' Gedge waves us on. Keeping to the woods, as we stumble through the undergrowth, we flush out clouds of mosquitoes and they promptly start feeding on my sweat-slicked arms and bare calves. Despite this discomfort, I look up at the ghostly shafts of light penetrating the canopy overhead. The leaves on the oak and beech trees are still iridescent green since they've not long been fully open. It would be an idyllic spot for a family picnic were it not for mosquitoes and the pack of bloodhounds somewhere behind us.

A rough, low building appears ahead; it looks like it might be an old gamekeeper's hut. On closer inspection, it's clearly been abandoned for some time. Inside, there's a rancid odour of damp and decay, but there's a couple of old chairs and a table. We flop down onto the chairs. 'I'll take the first watch, while you have a breather.' Gedge is in his element; I chuckle to myself. I take out the bag of chocolate goo from my copious coat pocket and pass it around; Ernie produces a pack of dried fruit. For a brief moment, we all take in the tranquillity of our surroundings and a former prisoner's intense feeling of freedom from having broken out of jail.

Fred, Thursday 3rd June 1943, forest north of Schloss Neuburg – Running

The night of our first day on the run steels slowly into the whispering forest canopy as the first tendrils of darkness creep in and merge with shadows under the trees. The evening chorus starts with the otherworldly sound of a fox barking, marking his territory and calling for his mate. The incessant barking is joined by a tentative hooting of owls and the hysterical laughing sound of marsh frogs from a small pond nearby; I've become all too familiar with their raucous sound whilst wandering aimlessly around camp in the evening. Another sound I don't recognise joins the chorus, a continuous, hypnotic chirring. Despite our status as escaped POWs I'm surprised at how soothing the night sounds are.

Gedge appears by my side and startles me. He chuckles to himself. 'A fine lookout you are, sir! If I'd been a Waffen SS Commando, I could have slit your throat ear to ear by now!'

'Thanks for those kind words of encouragement, Sergeant Major! I guess we should make a move and catch some of this twilight to get our bearings before it gets completely dark.' We both look skywards; it's a clear night and the first sliver of the new moon has appeared with its companion Venus poised below its open crescent. I point upwards. 'A moon and Venus in conjunction; it's a good sign. I used to know all the constellations. My father's always been a keen stargazer.'

'We're going to need all the luck we can get.' With that characteristically matter of fact assessment, Gedge turns and moves off back to the hut to rouse the others who've been sleeping the sleep of the dead for the last several hours since I took my turn on watch. I always reckon you can tell if someone's been in the military because every chance a soldier can get, you can be sure he'll grab some shut eye. There's never any halfway house in the army; you're either fighting for your life or bored to tears waiting to fight for your life. I suppose we've been doing the latter sitting around here all afternoon, now it's time for more of the former. At least the baying of bloodhounds hasn't joined in with the other night noises.

Gedge reappears with Ernie and Albert and we hunker down around the unfolded map; all instinctively look to Gedge, the master navigator. 'Right, I reckon we're here, near the village of Rennertshofen. That means we're about two or three clicks from the Danube, which presents something of a barrier if we want to avoid using roads. There's two crossings in the area, both hydroelectric power plants by the look of it; one at Bertoldsheim, the other at Bittenbrunn which looks to be the quieter of the two, but requires a deviation, but we do immediately get into some forest around Oberhausen that's contiguous for quite a stretch almost to Ravensburg where we'll be within striking distance of Lake Constance.'

Gedge pauses and receives nods all around. No doubt encouraged by this, he begins folding the map and checking the compass bearing. Leaving the hut, we immediately pick up a track leading off into the depths of the forest and past the pond where the sound of our footsteps momentarily silences its residents; however, they resume their raucous cackling as we leave them behind.

Picking up the pace, we begin a pretty gruelling yomp to take advantage of easy going on the track. It's now totally dark and the almost total blackness removes all sense of direction. Gedge must have the eyesight of a cat to make anything of it at all. After about two hours, he suddenly stops. 'I think I can see a light up ahead. It's dim, but in this dark, I can just make it out.' Bobbing my head left and right, I convince myself I can see it also. 'I propose we carry on along the track until we can see better what lies up ahead. I'm thinking if it's just an isolated farmhouse, we skirt around it and carry on.'

'Yep, good.' A pejorative agreement, so we move on. After twenty minutes or so, we can clearly see it's a farmhouse with a couple of large barns. There's no dogs barking yet, so we feel encouraged to continue.

As we get level with the first barn, I'm starting to

feel confident that we might just pass it by, but Ernie motions for us to stop, points and whispers, 'Look, a basket of eggs, it's too good an opportunity to miss.' Besides the eggs, there's what appears to be a metal box on the table that also carries some jars of preserves and what appears to be honey, all just sitting there for the taking, so we decide to do just that.

On closer inspection, the tin box is clearly for money since it's fixed to what is clearly a produce stall like you used to see in England before the war. Gedge has a go at opening the box with a screwdriver he's been carrying, but a young boy appears around the corner of the barn right in front of him. Like the crack commando he is, Gedge instinctively chops him in the throat and he falls flat on his back.

Albert rushes up and checks the boy. 'He's stunned but breathing okay.' As he cradles him gently in his arms, the boy comes to and Albert tries to reassure him and speaks softly. 'Es ist in ordnung. Wir sind freunde, die etwas zu essen kaufen wollen' The boy looks petrified and makes to shout out, but Gedge has injured his throat and his shout is inaudible. 'We've got to go, the boy can't be alone, he'll be all right.' Albert's distraught as he looks up at Gedge. 'I think you might have damaged his throat.'

'Hey, hör auf, wer ist da!' The farmer appears at the door of the cottage. Seeing us with his son, he bobs back into the house and reappears with a rifle, but in his haste, he drops his box of shells. None of us want to wait until he's loaded his gun, so, while he's scrabbling around trying to chamber a round, we run for it. 'Crack.' Albert, who's at my side, loses his footing, falls to the ground. 'Crack.' Another shot. I get Albert up and we make into the trees finding a handy firebreak which we follow.

Incredibly, there's still no sound of dogs and the farmer will likely tend to his son rather than follow us. We keep running whilst I support Albert around the waist. 'Where are you hit, Albert?' I prop him up against a tree and assess his condition.

'I'm okay, it just caught my shoulder, nothing serious. He must be a pretty good shot! But my brother Jules would have got me I'm sure.' Albert gives me a grim smile.

'I'm sorry about the boy.' Gedge looks close to tears and his shoulders slump. 'I, I, didn't mean to strike him so hard.' Ernie clasps Gedge's shoulder.

'It's all right, old chap, quite understandable. The lad came out of nowhere.' I pass Albert a pair of woollen socks I've found in my coat pocket and he uses them as a wad to staunch the blood coming from a shoulder wound.

'Are you okay to go on?'

'Yes, Freddy, I'm okay. Let's go.'

We assume a steady trot for what seems like hours. Finally, climbing a small hill into a clearing in the trees, we get a view down to a small town. A wide river glints in the starlight; it's obviously the Danube. We skirt the village and Gedge unerringly brings us down near the road where the river widens below a bridge. Keeping to the undergrowth next to the road we walk nonchalantly onto the bridge. Below, the Danube rushes through the turbines that must be turning under our feet. Walking quickly but not running to avoid attracting attention, we cross the bridge and make it into a wood. I'm exhausted. We briefly stop and share what food we have between us. I've got the shakes; my legs feel like jelly and I wish to hell we'd had the presence of mind to grab some of the food at the farm when we had the chance instead of just dropping everything.

A twig snaps ahead of us, everyone's head turns, and we peer into the darkness. There's scuffling and a sound of grunting. Ahead of us, the squat outline of what looks like a pig wanders into a clearing. I slowly pick up a fist-sized stone, take aim and throw it with every ounce of strength I can muster. A high-pitched squealing sound ensues, and we rush up to find a wild boar thrashing on the ground, blood pouring from a wound on its head. 'My God, Freddy, you got him! Now what?' As if to answer Ernie's question, Gedge leaps forward and grabs the stricken animal around the neck. Using his considerable weight, Gedge pins the boar down.

'Get the screwdriver out of my pocket!' I fumble through his coat to no avail. The animal appears to be regaining his strength and bucks wildly trying to get away. 'Get me a stick then, quick!' I grab a sturdy branch from the ground and hand it to Gedge who immediately places it at the animal's throat. Straining hard, the animal's thrashing briefly intensifies, and then slows to an eventual stop.

'Christ, Gedge, I think you've strangled the poor beast!' Whilst the boar's dead body represents a mountainous source of flesh, searching our pockets all we can muster to butcher it is Gedge's screwdriver and couple of cutlery knives. Undeterred, Gedge and Albert set to work. It's now that Albert's skill at butchering deer comes to the fore and we sit back and watch the man work.

Focussing on the flanks, Albert deftly hacks out a haunch of flesh and places it on a bed of leaves. 'Well, who's going to be le Chef de Cuisine?' Ernie, Gedge and myself set off to collect wood and light a fire.

'We need to cook as much of the meat as possible before dawn so we can carry it with us.' As always, Gedge's logic is unassailable. Using a couple of flat stones, we rig up a makeshift griddle. The aroma of frying pork causes saliva to almost pour out of our mouths in anticipation.

Albert's face is a picture of ecstasy. 'Mon Dieu, quelle fête! 'It reminds me of my days hunting with Jules and Maurice in la Forêt de Boullion, magnifique!'

As I look around the faces of my companions illuminated in the light of the fire all I can see are gleaming eyes as we all tear at the meat with what's left of our teeth. Suddenly, I know I'll never forget this moment. We're on the run and in fear of our lives, but

I've never felt so alive! We've taken back control, we're back in the game and for the first time in more than two years, I feel like we're soldiers again.

Fred, Friday 4th June 1943, Neustadt – Running

We are so close to making a home run I can almost taste the chocolate and hear the cuckoo clocks ticking in Switzerland, but serious exhaustion's set in and it now seems we've drifted off course somewhat. The bus journey to Villingen-Schwenningen was a calculated risk, but it's paid off in spades. A twenty-kilometre dash due south on foot from where we left the bus should have taken us into the forest around Schaffhausen and over the Swiss border. Gedge lets out a small, exasperated sigh and jabs at the map as if accusing it of leading us astray intentionally.

'I think we're too far west. In fact, I think we're somewhere near this lake.' As Gedge's finger jabs again at the offending map, I can just make out the name, Titisee, a tiny excrescence of water in the middle of the Schwarzwald about twenty clicks from the border.

Looking at the vast expanse of green, we appear to be in the back of beyond, so I voice what everyone is clearly thinking. 'Surely we can just try making a dash for it along the main road. We've not seen a soul all day.' Nods from Albert and Ernie; but a scowl from the old soldier who wags his head.

'Jerry will know POWs will be heading here, that is, if they make it this far. The remoteness of the location and density of forest make it a prime location for an attempt to cross the border. I think we should keep to the forest tracks for a bit longer and make a dash for it tonight.'

Ernie nods, but suggests a compromise. 'Look, it's six p.m. in the afternoon; another three or so, hours of light. I vote we test the water a bit and see how we go on this minor road between the two lakes; if we get to the larger one, here, the Schluchsee, and there's still been little, or no traffic or people around, it might be safe for us to just keep going all the way to Stühlingen and penetrate the border this evening.'

The thought of actually reaching safety is incredibly enticing and I can see that Albert agrees with Ernie, so I seem to have the casting vote. All eyes are on me. 'I agree with Ernie. Let's give the road a go for a bit and see how it pans out. If there's too many people about, we go back into the forest and wait it out until nightfall.' Nods all around. 'Okay, let's go.'

Gedge stuffs the map back into his coat pocket and purposefully picks up the pace along the path we're following. There's fresh prints accompanied by those of a dog, so it's likely we're coming up to some kind of habitation. A small house appears ahead as we move into a forest glade. The situation is picturesque, and the little cottage has a quaintly rustic charm. For the lady of the house, it must be washday. A long line laden with sheets, towels and clothing flutters in a stiff breeze.

Walking briskly past, some of the clothing has blown off the line and has been caught on a bush a hundred or so, yards away. I deviate over to it. We've been out for almost forty-eight hours; we could definitely use some different clothing to change our disguise in case our descriptions have been widely distributed. As we pass the garments, we quickly bundle them up and continue swiftly along the track and out of sight of the house.

'Mmmh, it's all women's clothing.' Albert sorts through what's been blown off the line; a dress and a woman's blouse and bra, all pretty large, so she's obviously a pretty groß country frau. I smile to myself. I'd read in a magazine article a few years ago that Hitler was particularly fond of large, big-breasted countrywomen who he sees as the backbone of the Reich, no doubt producing the next generation of Aryans.

Albert holds the dress up to himself. 'Well, what do you think?' I can see Gedge and Ernie are somewhat taken aback to learn that Albert may be thinking of wearing women's clothing. 'Think about it, I reckon I looked pretty good as Vivienne in our production of "Un Jour au Paradis".'

'I'm sorry, Albert, I don't think any of us saw it. Our French isn't up to scratch.' I can see Ernie's a little irritated.

'But what is more suspicious to the Germans, four

men moving together? Or a couple and couple of other men; it changes the group dynamique, non?'

'Oh, you mean a sort of a ménage à trois?' Gedge just looks at me with his arms akimbo.

'What is a ménage à trois when it's at home?'

'Oh, just a French term for a woman sharing her home with two or more men,' Albert laughs. 'But seriously, I'm the only clean-shaven one and I've had plenty of practice at acting a female role and still have the long hair to prove it! The Germans will be looking for groups of men.' I can see Albert's logic and the others are beginning to come around to the idea.

Before any more discussion can be had, Albert has donned the house frau stockings, dress and blouse and there in front of us stands a fairly passable woman. As we watch, Albert finishes off his disguise by stuffing his woollen socks into the commodious bra and places his wide-brimmed hat at a jaunty angle to it looks like a fedora. 'Voila!' Magnifique, non?'

'Okay, Albert, but I think you should carry your ordinary clothes with you just in case you attract too much unwanted male attention.' Gedge isn't usually much of a joker, but we all laugh at this. By the time we reach the road, all of us have had a chance to get used to Albert's new persona. We've voted and decided that I should stay with Albert and make up the other half of a happy couple whilst Ernie and Gedge separate from us.

Almost immediately, a family passes along the road

in a cart, the old man driving the horse touches his hat and smiles at Albert. 'Guten abend, fraulein!' I can't help smirking but manage to wave and smile as the cart passes. Just as we enter a bustling village called Grafenhausen, a dark grey Citroen saloon car passes us and stops up ahead at a market stall selling 'billige zigarren', cheap cigars. The passenger door swings backwards partially blocking our path and a Gestapo officer steps out and over to the kiosk. I've rerun this very scenario so many times in my head, that, for a moment, I can't quite believe what I'm seeing.

Albert and I are ahead of Gedge and Ernie who have dropped back from us and are crossing to the other side of the road, so we do the same. I'm willing myself not to look over in the direction of the kiosk, but my curiosity gets the better of me. As I watch, the officer turns and lounges back on the kiosk counter and puffs on his newly acquired cigar catching my eye as he does so. Taking another puff, he pushes himself off and begins to walk across the street towards us. He looks lean and mean, in his early thirties and he's smiling as he approaches. 'Und wohin gehst du mein hübsches junges Alpenmädchen?'

Without pausing, Albert replies, 'Wir sind gerade für einen abendspaziergang, sir.' I can't believe how well Albert is playing his role and he does sound like a woman. I can see the officer is suspicious, and, as he speaks, the policeman's totenkopf [death's head] badge appears to smirk at us from its position on the Gestapo officer's cap mimicking the insouciant smile of its owner. Passers-by are ignoring us and generally giving us a wide berth; nobody wants to mess with the Gestapo.

At this point, I'm unsure where Gedge and Ernie have got to, but I'm hoping they've managed to get around us and have had time to make their escape. Sure enough, as Albert is talking, I can see that Gedge and Ernie are up ahead, but something's amiss. Two other Gestapo men have got out the car and are walking over to intercept them. Whilst I'm still unsure what to do for the best, the officer speaking to Albert appears to have gone for Albert's disguise and makes to return to his staff car. The feign worked, but it was a gamble from the start and I'm wishing we'd never gone along with the idea in the first place.

Free to continue on our way, we proceed down the street. Looking up, my heart sinks to my bootstraps. Up ahead, I can see Gedge pulling away from one of the officers who's grabbed his arm and he's running out into the street. It's a desperate move. 'Du da drüben! Halt!' As I helplessly watch, the whole scene appears to unfold in slow motion. The officer that Gedge pushed undoes the catch on his flap holster and pulls out a pistol, which he fires, hitting Gedge squarely in the back between his shoulder blades. The big man lurches forward and tries to continue running, but a second shot brings him down.

Ernie is struggling with the other guard and breaks away, obviously wanting to go and check on Gedge.

Another shot rings out and Ernie drops heavily to the ground and lies motionless. The officer with the cigar who'd been speaking with Albert has now also drawn his Luger and he drops slightly behind us and to the right to cover us.

Finished with Gedge and Ernie, the two Gestapo officers run over to us with their guns still drawn. I can see that Albert thinks they're going to open fire. As he tries to get around the back of the shop we're passing, the approaching officers both open fire. I don't care anymore what happens; I just want to do something, to get away and make this stop. I'm about to try and make a run for it, but the next thing I know is I'm sprawling on the ground. Dazed, I roll onto my side to see that the Gestapo officer has been joined by a silver-haired Wehrmacht officer, probably a major, along with two soldiers armed with sub-machine guns pointing in my direction.

The major squares up to the Gestapo officer and looks like he means business. 'Tritt zurück, Hauptmann, das ist eine reine Armeesache. Ich nehme es von hier. dieser mann ist ein gefangener der Wehrmacht.'

'Das ist Herr Hauptmann für Sie, Major! Und zu Ihrer information, diese Männer waren verdächtige Britische spione, die sich als französische arbeiter ausgaben und sich der verhaftung widersetzten.'

'Er wird wegen befragung in gewahrsam genommen.'

'Und ohne Zweifel von dort zu einer folterkammer

der Gestapo und dann zur hinrichtung.'

'Hinterfragen sie unsere methoden, Herr Major? fragen der staatlichen sicherheit und der spionage sind sache der Gestapo. Ich werde mich mit ihrem Kommandanten befassen!' ['Stand down, Hauptmann, this is strictly an army matter. I will take it from here. This man is a prisoner of the Wehrmacht.'

'That is Herr Hauptmann to you, Major! And for your information, these men are suspected British spies posing as French workers and resisting arrest. This man will be taken into custody for questioning.'

'And no doubt from there to a Gestapo torture chamber and then summary execution.'

'Are you questioning our methods, Herr Major? Matters of state security and espionage are the responsibility of the Gestapo. I will be taking this matter up with your commanding officer!'

The major turns to me and speaks in English. 'You have escaped from Oflag VII-B, yes?' The officer reaches out and opens my shirt collar. 'Hah! I thought as much, ein kriegsgefangener[26]! Give me those identity tags.' Turning to the Gestapo captain, the major dangles my POW ID tags triumphantly in front of him. 'Sie sehen, Hauptmann, diese männer sind geflohene kriegsgefangene!' With that, the Gestapo officers back off.

Turning back to me, the major continues speaking

[26] Kriegsgefangener: prisoner of war.

to me. 'This is most regrettable! Your friends should not have resisted arrest. If we had only arrived sooner this might not have happened.' The major shakes his head and examines my POW ID disk and army dog tags. 'And you are?'

I can't find the words and just shake my head for a moment before simply replying, 'Second Lieutenant Frederick Whitton, 95121.' Try as I might, tears well up and I can't stop them; I feel ashamed and look away. The old major's face softens; perhaps it's my youth or that I might remind him of a son back home.

'I am very sorry for what has happened to your companions, Lieutenant, very sorry indeed.' With that, he signals to his men and they leave us, and we walk together to the waiting army truck. With some difficulty I manage to climb inside. In the back there are two other re-captured British POWs. I vaguely recognise them, and all they can manage is a grim-faced nod in my direction before they resume their thousand-yard stare straight ahead, no doubt recalling their few hours of freedom and wondering, as I am, what fate lies ahead.

Fred, Monday 7th June 1943, northern suburbs of Munich

Dark thoughts haunt me in the gloomy confines of our prisoner transport where the seriousness of my situation and the prospect of interrogation by the Gestapo begins to hit home. On the road since early this morning, after being transferred into Gestapo custody at an army barracks heartbreakingly close to the Swiss border and salvation, I've had time to rerun in my mind the deaths of Gedge, Albert and Ernie over and over like a movie on a continuous loop. But tragic and overwhelmingly sad that they met their deaths as they did, I now envy their quick end since it would be preferable to a slow, agonising death under torture.

I search myself for the strength I need to face what lies ahead. Just as I think I'll be engulfed by despair; the soothing lilt of O'Callaghan's Irish voice comes to me reciting the Catholic prayer in the same way he did when he defiantly faced his own death. 'Hail Mary full of grace, the Lord is with thee; blessed art thou amongst woman, and blessed is the fruit of thy womb, Lord Jesus Christ.' As O'Callaghan's voice repeats these lines several times, I lapse into reciting 'Hail Mary full of grace' over and over under my breath.

After a while, my spirits begin to lift as though some of O'Callaghan's courage has transferred itself to me and, as it does so, I raise my head and my eyes meet those of my two companions, both of whom cross themselves and quietly recite what I realise is the same prayer in what could be Russian.

'Zdrowaś Mario, pełna łaski, Pan jest z tobą; błogosławionaś Ty między niewiastami, i błogosławiony owoc żywota Twojego, Panie Jezu Chryste.'

'Język angielski? English?' It's the taller and younger of the two men opposite who's addressing me. It's then that I recognise the Polish language. That makes sense. The Germans treat the Poles, especially Polish Jews, as though they're less than human; untermenschen as the Germans like to refer to them. I manage to smile.

'Yes, English, escaped from prisoner of war camp in Eichstätt.' The older man nods.

'Dachau, uciekliśmy z Dachau.' As he speaks, his mime of running would be comical if our current circumstances weren't so dire. So, I'm guessing they've escaped as well. 'Armia Krajowa.' Both men press the palm of one of their hands to their own chests. I nod.

'Polish Resistance, yes?'

'Tak!' Both men nod again in unison and give a grim smile. Now that they've introduced themselves, the effort required to communicate appears to have been severe as both men fall silent again. But rather than lapsing back into despair, somehow remembering the example of O'Callaghan's Catholic grace seems to have pushed me to look beyond my selfish inner despair and think about what these other two men must be going through. I now notice for the first time what a pitiful state of physical health they're in.

It seems hard to believe that Nazi Germany's Third Reich is so paranoid as to believe that shuffling old men are a threat to its supremacy; but if it is, then Hitler's Third Reich is in serious trouble and must surely be near its end.

As we have now lapsed back into mute silence, the only sound is a hum of tyres on smooth tarmac and the jangle of unused manacles on the other benches as we sway around corners. I wonder how many other doomed prisoners have worn those same manacles; perhaps it's their ghosts not the bends in the road that cause them to jangle so. More frequent stopping and starting, plus the sound of traffic suggests we've entered a city. We finally stop for a while and a feeling of dread twists my gut hard.

As I look across at the Poles, they both cross themselves; they know what lies ahead, after all, they've just escaped from Dachau. Two young Gestapo officers swing open the doors and set about unlocking our manacles whilst two others stand outside, pistols drawn.

'Raus, schnell! Hände hinter dem Kopf!' Following the example set by the two Poles, I step down onto the pavement and put my hands behind my head.

We're in a rundown part of a large town with tawdry shop fronts and a couple of seedy bars visible on the opposite side of the street. Flanked by the officers with pistols, we're led towards the side door of what looks like a disused restaurant. The words, 'Gaststätte Fangerheim' are written above the shopfront in the, now familiar, old-style German cursive lettering. It looks like we're being taken to one of the Gestapo's underground interrogation centres; I'd heard rumours about such places.

As we reach the panelled street door, we're quickly bundled inside and taken down a long corridor to another large door that's recently been reinforced with steel. One of our guards taps once on the door with the butt of his pistol and we enter a small vestibule that gives on to a large, well-lit room furnished with several steel desks. From there, it's down a couple of flights of stone steps and, at the bottom of which, another corridor leads us past a line of cells. As we're pushed into separate neighbouring cells, I notice that we appear to be the only prisoners here this evening, which almost seems worse.

I lay back and try to do the military speed sleeping routine; you're exhausted, tomorrow'll be hell, therefore, get some shut eye. It must've worked, because I wake to the sound of my Polish neighbours quietly talking to each other. I get the impression they've been chatting for some time, so I begin to think that we'll see the night out before our ordeal begins, but four guards enter our corridor and remove the Poles from their cells. As they are being led away, the taller man says something to me. 'Boże, chroń cię, przyjacielu.'

I nod, but not really understanding what he said, I reply, 'Good luck, my friends.'

June 7th, night

I must have fallen asleep again on the steel bench, the only piece of furniture in my cell besides the bucket in the corner I've been using to urinate into, because I wake with a start at the sound of my cell door being opened.

'Up! Come with us, now!' One of the two young Gestapo officers standing at the door appears to be able to speak good English. Steadying myself on the bars of my cell with one of my manacled hands, I manage to get to my feet, pass through the door and out into the corridor where I wait for the second guard to open the main door, which then opens onto the steps leading to the floor above.

I think to myself, 'Now it begins.' Without the benefits of even the meagre rations I've been getting in POW camp, the steps prove to be arduous for my wasted muscles and I pause between flights to catch my breath, which is rewarded with a push in the small of my back and, 'Move, move!'

Waiting for us on the floor above are two other, apparently more senior officers; my knowledge of Gestapo uniforms is sketchy, but one of them might be a captain. Both have removed their tunics and have put them on the back of the chairs of adjoining desks. The two guards with me shove me towards a third chair that's been placed in the centre of the room; this one has leg and arm restraints. At this point, O'Callaghan's voice in my head returns to whisper the Catholic prayer, 'Hail Mary full of grace, the Lord is with thee…'

I'm pushed down into the chair by strong hands, but it's not needed; my body is weak and has no fight left in it. 'Well, Lieutenant.' I suddenly realise that one of the officers is speaking to me. 'Let's see what information you have for us, shall we?'

In time-honoured fashion, I simply reply, 'Second Lieutenant, British Army, Frederick M. Whitton, 95121, being held as a prisoner of war in Oflag VII-B.'

'Your stubbornness will only be rewarded by more unpleasantness, Lieutenant. If, as you want us to believe, you are simply a British Army officer, why were you dressed in civilian clothes and carrying counterfeit identity papers? Surely these are the actions of a person who wishes to conceal himself; a spy for instance, working for British Intelligence. Is that not right, Lieutenant?'

The officer's English is clear and almost without accent, so I can't even feign misunderstanding, so I simply repeat, 'Lieutenant Frederick M. Whitton, 95121.' After repeating this mantra a few more times, I allow my eyes to focus on my shoes which are still caked in dried mud from the forest tracks I'd been walking with my friends just a few days ago.

'If you want to play it that way, Lieutenant, that is up to you, but we do have methods that we can use to loosen your tongue.' The officer signals to an orderly, who's been standing nearby, and they quickly step over to where I'm sitting. He's carrying a steel dish containing a hypodermic syringe and a piece of rubber tubing. 'Since you're in British Intelligence, I'm sure you know all about scopolamine. Its effects on some susceptible subjects can be quite severe; I've personally seen a quite a few people reduced to a pitiful state of stupor from which they never recover. Which will you be, I wonder?'

The orderly wraps a tube around my upper arm and tightens it until a vein appears in the cleft of my elbow. With a clear target now in sight, the orderly proceeds to push the needle of the syringe into my vein.

'Sweet dreams, Lieutenant, let's hope, for your sake, that you're even able to remember your own name, never mind your service number after we've finished with you.'

Looking down at my arm, a small tear of blood appears at the point of entry of the needle. As I watch, it runs into the fold of my arm and I have a sensation of the overpowering effects of the drug rushing up my arm. Like a ripple after a stone's been thrown in a pool of water, an uncontrollable euphoria travels towards me until it breaks over my consciousness and I feel nothing more.

Slowly becoming aware of my surroundings, I

realise I'm back on the steel bench in my cell; however, I'm now completely naked. In fact, the chill in my body is what appears to have brought be round. I look down at red weals on my wrists, but the manacles have been removed. Not having a mirror, I can't check my body for injuries, but when I try to raise my head, my vision begins to swim and I'm forced to return it, with a thud, to the steel surface of the bench.

Slowly, some distorted images bubble to the surface of my consciousness. Endless questions, the same questions, my feet being beaten; I suddenly feel excruciating pain on my soles and ankles and my genitals ache like my testicles have been repeatedly been struck hard. I reach down and feel them, but the pain is sickening and getting worse as the stupefying effect of the drug is now beginning to wear off. Further memories surface, and I feel intense pain in my anus. Balling my fists, I fight to push further recollection away and try to focus just on the physical pain rather than the utter humiliation I'm feeling.

Fred, Wednesday 25th August 1943, Schloss Colditz

'Well, we're with the "bad boys" now, Freddy!' I recognise that booming Scottish lilt immediately.

'Jock! Where in hell did you spring from?' While I'm shaking hands and getting over my surprise at Jock [Hamilton-Baillie] springing out of nowhere, Douggie [Moir] and Frank [Weldon] join us in the little cobbled square in front of the station as it fills up with a ragbag of Americans and British RAF.

We all shake hands while Jock continues, 'When did you get bagged? We thought you'd made a home run[27] for sure. What's the matter, Freddy?' It must be the expression I'm wearing on my face that gives it away. Jock then asks the question I've been dreading. 'What happened to Gedge and Ernie and that Belgian chap, Albert wasn't it?'

I shake my head. 'They were all shot in the street by the Gestapo. It was an absolute mess. A Gestapo officer rumbled us, there was a scuffle and a couple of other officers started shooting. I was knocked on the

[27] Home run: meaning an escape to neutral territory and freedom.

head and avoided a bullet only because an army major appeared, otherwise I guess I'd be dead, or worse, being held in some Gestapo detention centre.'

'That's bad luck, old chap, really bad luck. Sorry to hear about them all, but I know you and Gedge were close, in the same regiment.' Jock shakes his head; he looks genuinely upset, whilst Dougie and Frank listen stone-faced. After a pause, Frank breaks the silence.

'Well, we went as quiet as kittens when we were nabbed. We were pointed out to the police by a little old lady as we were standing on the platform at Stuttgart Hauptbahnhof and were rounded up by a couple of soldiers guarding the station after only being on the loose for forty-eight hours. Not much to show for more than a year's work.' There's a short pause while Frank no doubt ponders that fact before he asks another inevitable question. 'So, where've you been?'

I'd not really told this part of my story to anyone; I feel ashamed by the whole thing, but I can't just keep silent, so, taking a deep breath, I decided to give them a sanitised version, leaving out being stripped naked and the humiliating beatings.

'When I was bagged, although the army intervened, the Gestapo insisted I was questioned before they'd hand me back over to the Wehrmacht. I just assumed the Gestapo'd shoot me as a spy; in fact, I was put against a wall at one point for a mock execution to try and get some information out of me. I'm guessing that the army major who initially took me into custody kept an eye on proceedings. I count myself lucky. I never thought I'd owe my life to a German officer. After that, they laid on a truck especially for me. I was driven back to Eichstätt and put straight into solitary for twelve weeks; I haven't really seen anyone since I was put in the bag.'

'Well, the goons have been bragging that they've picked everyone up. I think we'll find most of them here in Colditz. Like you, we were in solitary for a long time back in Eichstätt before the commandant decided to ship us to a Sonderlager.[28] I guess we should feel honoured!' There are some wry smiles from the others at Douggie's little joke.

The group next to us starts moving off, so we follow them and form a ragged column shuffling through what appears to be an ancient market square. There's hardly any people about, so, apart from a few hard stares, we don't get the same little homecoming 'welcome' we got in Trier the first-time round.

Leaving the square, I look up at the dark looming hulk of Colditz Castle, already illuminated in floodlights in the growing dusk. The ancient-looking edifice dominates the town making it a forbidding and inscrutable presence. As we move away from the centre and cross a wide river, the incline steepens, and I'm reminded how out of condition I am. Puffing hard I can barely keep up with the others. Making an effort to avoid the inevitable rifle butt if I fall behind, the ground

---

[28] Sonderlager: a high security special POW camp.

starts to swim in front of me and suddenly I feel it coming up to meet me. Almost immediately, I feel hands going under my armpits and I'm unceremoniously dragged to my feet.

'Are you okay, Freddy? You lost your footing there, old chap.'

'Sorry, Jock, I haven't eaten in twenty-four hours and sitting around in solitary for weeks hasn't helped!'

I can see that exhaustion is kicking in for everyone as we finally cross the moat and stand in front of the huge wooden gates of Schloss Colditz, a veritable fortress on a rocky outcrop that is surely impossible to escape from. The feeling of impregnability and, therefore, inescapability fills me with dread as we pass through each of two successive heavy gates, finally entering a spacious courtyard which we cross, climb some steps and enter an imposing five-storey building in the far corner, the Kommandantur[29] .

Inside, orderlies rush about taking our names and service numbers. In return, we receive our customary tags stamped with my prisoner number, 387, and an octagonal disk stamped with my name, after which, I'm given a board with my POW number chalked on it and photographed; this time I don't smile.

After processing, our group of maybe forty or so move off through a covered walkway leading to yet another huge wooden gate that opens onto a much

---

[29] Kommandantur: administrative offices.

smaller courtyard where a volleyball game is still in progress despite the growing darkness. A strong sense of hopelessness feels like it's crushing my soul. I neither speak, nor look at any of the other servicemen who have gone through the same process; I'm in a daze and feel physically sick. The thought of spending more time locked up in this forbidding dungeon makes me feel nauseous. Just as I think I might actually vomit, I become aware of someone standing in front of me.

'Are you all right? You look all in. Are you with the lot that's just arrived? Pardon me, my name's Mike Sinclair[30].' Mike extends his hand in greeting. Taking it, I hold onto it like a man who's being swept along by a fast current and past the safety of the riverbank. Snapping out of my daze, I remember my manners.

'Freddy Whitton. Apologies, Mike. I've spent the last couple of months in solitary and I've lost the knack for conversation! I've been transferred from Eichstätt, Oflag VII-B.' Mike's eyes light up in recognition.

'Ah, ha! So, you're part of the group who escaped. We've already had quite a few of you chaps arriving here in dribs and drabs. I'm guessing the goons will be transferring all of you into here in due course. They're saying that more than sixty got away. Great stuff and

---

[30] Lieutenant Michael (Mike) Sinclair, DSO of the King's Royal Rifle Corps was a real person who attempted many escapes from POW camps, including Colditz. A decorated war hero, he was highly respected by the German guards who referred to him as 'der rot Fuchs' (the red fox).

well done; I'm sure it's caused Jerry quite a headache! Well, you've definitely earned your ticket to Colditz! But you're going to find it pretty cramped in here after Eichstätt. There's barely room to swing a cat in the courtyard as you can see.'

I look around and I have to agree; it's tiny for the number of prisoners that are already in here. Mike's friendly good humour is having the effect of seeing off my black dog depression, and I draw a deep breath. After all, I'm not the only one having to accept being bagged and sent back into captivity.

'Look, Freddy, let me show you around a bit. It's a forbidding old place from the outside, but really, it's less impregnable than you might think. Castles were built to keep people out, not in.' Mike winks knowingly. 'The locks are old and easily picked and there's loads of hidden passages. After a while you'll be able to move around the place no problem! Mind you, we recently got a new commandant, Oberstleutnant Prawitt. A bit of a stickler and he knows his stuff when it comes to security. He's made a few changes, but that's not stopping people from finding their way out; where there's a will there's a way!'

Thursday 26th August, 3.00 a.m.

'Gedge? Gedge! I can't understand why he's ignoring me. I angrily grab his shoulder and spin him around. The horrible sight of the twin caverns of Gedge's hollow eye sockets sends me reeling backwards, but Albert and Ernie break my fall. The three of them physically push me back and forth between them like schoolyard bullies. As I bounce from one to the other, their bodies appear to steadily decompose; rotting flesh drops onto the ground. I can hear the wet thud and each piece runs with putrefied blood. I slip on their gore and lose my footing again. Picking myself up, the three of them surround me, their faces now all but unrecognisable in a circle above me.

A voice that sounds like Gedge's shouts angrily, why didn't you do something, Freddy? You panicked. You gave us away. Now we're finished, over, we're nothing, it's down to you, and it's your fault.' My head must've bumped against the steel frame of my bed, quite a crack. I feel for a swelling on my forehead. As I do so, like the Cheshire Cat's smile, Gedge's clenched teeth and the dark holes of his empty eye sockets hang in the air in front of me for a few seconds before they finally disappear.

'I'm sorry, Gedge, I'm so sorry, forgive me…' The sobs come in waves; I can't hold them back any longer.

Fred, Tuesday 31st August 1943, Schloss Colditz

'Well, I can safely say the food's no better here than it was at Eichstätt!' Jock tosses down his bowl of thin porridge and cup of coffee and sits down heavily beside me. 'If anything, it's worse! At least we occasionally got some real coffee instead of this stuff made from acorns!'

'Think yourself lucky you don't have a caffeine allergy. I knew a chap back home who couldn't take caffeine, but he actually got hooked on coffee made with acorns when he was travelling in Portugal.'

'Well, he's welcome to it, that's all I can say.' Jock's light tone and sense of humour is always guaranteed to snap me out of my dark moods; black dogs, I've come to call them and they're becoming more frequent and increasingly difficult to deal with. Since we got here, the cramped conditions in the only outside space we have really brings home the feeling of confinement; there's nowhere to go for a decent walk and Jock's right, the food, if anything is worse than it was at Eichstätt. Between stomach cramps, occasional bouts of dysentery and the interminable roll calls day and night, I seem unable to get off to sleep and the nights pass very, very slowly. God knows how I'm going to get through the long winter nights!

Looking up from my inner grumbling, I spot Mike Sinclair making his way over to us with Douggie and Frank. 'Good morning, gents. How are you this fine morning?' A little conspiratorial party forms round Jock and myself. I'm aware that I'm now in the company of some of the most persistent and successful escape artists anywhere in the British Army, and that's saying something considering the fact that everyone in here has earned his spurs as an escaper. Before saying anything more, Mike takes a quick look about to check for any ferrets that might be sniffing around.

'Look, we've got a run planned in the next few days and we're looking for some extras that might be interested in escaping or acting as lookouts.' Mike pauses and everyone nods. 'Okay, I kind of thought you chaps would be in. Look, I'll keep it short. The plan's rather simple. I'm going to impersonate one of the heads of security, a Stabsfeldwebel [31] called Fritz Rothenberger[32]. Rothenberger's a good choice as he's a decorated war hero and highly respected by the guards who are, therefore, less likely to question his orders.

'The idea is that myself plus two other chaps

---

[31] Stabsfeldwebel: Sergeant Major.

[32] Incredibly, Sinclair's audacious plan became known as the Franz Josef escape after the nickname that the German guards had for Rothenberger whose luxurious moustache made him look like the former Austrian Emperor.

impersonating guards will get out onto the terrace, relieve a couple of the guards on watch and replace them with our lads. Then we'll simply unlock the gates down to the park below and let everyone out. We're thinking that we'll maybe get thirty or forty away before the goons realise what's happening.' I'm quite taken aback by the boldness of Mike's idea and voice what the others are also probably thinking.

'Mike, that's the most incredibly audacious escape plan I've ever heard of! But we've only just arrived here; surely there are many more people who deserve a chance to escape? It must have taken months to get the fake identity papers and civilian clothes run up.'

Sinclair smiles. 'You're right, Freddy. The first twenty or so places on the escape have all been filled, but I'm just making you chaps aware that, if they get away, the plan is for a second and possibly third wave of people to have a go as well. If nothing else, it'll cause further confusion. Besides, Dick Howe's been singing the praises of your lot's escape at Eichstätt, so, in his capacity as escape officer, he's asked me to see if any of you chaps would be interested in joining the second wave. Besides, there's not so much interest in just having a go on spec without all the disguise and identity card paraphernalia, but since you've been out recently and know the ropes back to front, you'd probably have more chance than most. At the very least, why not keep lookout for us?'

Jock can't contain himself. 'Well, you've

convinced me! How could we miss what could be your crowning performance?'

Sinclair smiles wryly and jokes, 'Or perhaps it'll be a short engagement.' Everyone laughs, but we all know that Mike's plan is potentially very dangerous and that he and his two other impersonators are taking a very big risk.

Fred, Saturday 4th September 1943, Schloss Colditz

In the gathering dusk, I can see the first bats swooping around the clock tower as they pass through the powerful beams of the security lights. After a bit of a flap over a small fire in the kitchen, evening roll call is running pretty late. Perhaps because of the fire, and rather ironically considering what we're going to be doing later on this evening, Stabsfeldwebel Rothenberger is the NCO in charge of proceedings and he keeps a keen eye on us as his corporals perform the count, no doubt to catch any devious moving around at the back that might signal some attempt at covering for someone who's missing.

I can clearly see Rothenberger's trademark handlebar moustache illuminated in the parade ground lamps as they come on for the night shift, which makes him vaguely resemble Lord Kitchener in his famous WWI poster urging the last lot of doomed young men to sign up for the Great War. Impatiently tapping his palm with his swagger stick the old soldier looks up at the clock tower and then back to our serried ranks in front of him; things are running late, and he doesn't like it. Finally, his adjutants report on the count. There appears to be nothing amiss, so, without further ado, Rothenberger signals to the SBO to carry on and we're dismissed to go about our nefarious business!

Walking back over to our billets for the night, I can't see anyone from the escape party, so I just go back to my bunk and immediately bump into Jock and Douggie. 'The show starts in half an hour, so let's get ourselves over to the chapel and make our way through to sickbay.' Following Jock, we nonchalantly walk across the courtyard towards the chapel and let ourselves in. It's now that the old familiar butterflies are fluttering around in my stomach. Will we make it out? I'm ready to go, no matter what, but, if anything, we're further from neutral territory than we were in Eichstätt. This time, walking's going to be out of the question.

I suddenly feel lost without Gedge, Ernie and Albert. I try and push the horror of their final moments out of my mind; this time it'll be different, or I'll die trying. The thought of, one way or another, just ending it tonight feels very tempting. Death by guard, at least it would be quick. Walking through the cool air inside the chapel, the ecclesiastical mix of mouldy hymn books and wood polish reminds me of the smell of the school library where I used to pound my head with my fist trying to remember my times tables. At the back of the chapel, we pass through a door into the infirmary. You've got to hand it to Jerry, they're nothing but not efficient; if you die in the infirmary, they can have you on the slab and on the way to burial more or less all in the same building.

At the top of the steps, we carefully make our way to a storeroom where, sure enough, there's a knotted rope dangling from the open loft hatch. I go first; might as well since I'm the lightest. The effort of getting into the loft is absolutely killing and I'm puffing like an old man as I wait for the others. Tiptoeing over the creaking loft floorboards, I can see a few dark figures at the far end, their ghostly faces illuminated by a shaft of moonlight.

A disembodied voice. 'Sinclair, Hyde-Thompson and Pope have just relieved one of the guards. We're going to get into position now.'

'Okay, we've got your back. Good luck!' Groups of five or six men move through a window created in the roof for the escape and let themselves down onto the terrace below. Myself, Douggie and Jock drop down behind them. Once I'm on the roof of the infirmary, I run over to the far side so I can observe the other end of the terrace and also look down into the guard's courtyard. All looks quiet, so I give the thumbs up to Douggie who'll in turn let Sinclair and his 'guards' know it's clear to move on. Sure enough, the guard tower door below swings open and Sinclair strides out and along the lower terrace where he relieves the guard at the watch tower, replacing him with one of our ersatz guards before continuing out of sight under the machine gun post disappearing from view on his way to the fence. So far so good.

The first wave group of twenty escapers now move down and past our friendly guard moving underneath the machine-gun tower and along the terrace and out of sight. 'Right, come on, Freddy, let's get ourselves in position so we can watch their backs.' Following Moir, we walk down the steps to the lower terrace and through some trees keeping an eye out for further guards. All that stands between us and freedom is the terrace fence and then a six-foot wall in the park below the castle. All's clear, so we get into position near the main group of would-be escapees.

As we arrive at the final corner, I can just make out a sentry box and the wire where an altercation is going on between Sinclair and the guard on duty. There's raised voices, the door to the right opens and Sinclair's party is joined by four other Germans plus what looks like Rothenberger himself.

'Freddy, it's blown, there's nothing we can do. Come on back!'

'Jock, there must be something we can do. We can't just leave them to it.' Caught in a dilemma I watch helplessly as a scuffle breaks out between Sinclair and the guards. 'Crack.' A single shot rings out and echoes around the walls.

'Come on, now, Freddy!' Jock yanks my arm hard and I follow him back the way we came. As Jock is letting himself down the rope from the loft, two guards appear, their MP 40s at the ready.

'Halt! Or I'll shoot! Move, this way!' Jock,

Douggie and a few others who have now appeared from the roof space above, put their hands behind their heads and walk slowly ahead of the guards. One of the lads behind me is whispering something about Sinclair.

'I think he's been shot; I saw him go down.' The guards lock us in a prison cell adjoining the senior officers' quarters. No doubt we'll be getting a spell in solitary confinement for our troubles this evening. I've got to admit to myself that I've never felt so utterly beaten as I slide slowly down onto the floor of the cell. Sinclair played it to the end; his was a short engagement after all. A bitter smile plays on my lips. At least he's left this godforsaken place.

Turning my head and looking into the corridor leading away from the cells, light through a window causes a shadow of the prison bars to fall across my legs as I stretch them out in front of me. I don't feel like I have any more fight left in me. I wish to hell I'd had the guts to just make a run for it and end it all then and there like Sinclair. On a single night, my fate seems sealed; I'm here for the duration, I can feel it in my bones.

Postscript
George & Fred, Saturday 19th July 1952, Lakes Hotel, River Derwent, Lake District

Freddy steps from his battered old Triumph and our eyes meet. His sallow face and hollow cheeks in stark contrast to the familiar bushy eyebrows – a family trait – sitting above his haunted eyes.

'Well, Freddy, you look like you've lost more weight.'

'And you look like you've borrowed it!' We both laugh; the ice is broken, and we walk over to the hotel together with an arm around each other's shoulders just like old times.

The interior of the hotel hasn't changed a bit since we used to stay here with our parents before the war. Wood panelling and leather armchairs line the reception area along with various fishing-related conversation pieces on the wall; a fishing rod here, a gaff there and the odd photograph with various happy fishermen holding a large trout. Perfect! We approach the little bar near the reception.

'I'll get the first one in, George, what'll it be?' I

catch sight of Freddy's threadbare wallet and two single pound notes therein.

'I'll get these, Freddy. You can buy the next one. After all we've got the whole weekend!' Mulling over our pints of Cumberland Ale, the freshly caught trout with creamed potatoes and seasonal vegetables stands out from the rationing-constrained menu; after all, we're here to catch them, so why not start the weekend by eating them?

'The brown trout looks good, Freddy; two of those?'

'That'll do for me, George!' Waiting for the barmaid, I steal a glance at my brother; he's lost none of the haunted look he brought back with him from Colditz. His listless stare and wasted look is worrying and I wonder how life is for him living on his own in his spartan garret at Bamburgh Castle. Ironically, he left Nazi captivity in one castle for self-imposed captivity in another. Perhaps none of us ever truly leave our past behind.

For me, there isn't a day that goes past that I don't think of Ylena and the life together we could've had. Is that why I just flopped into the easy chair of an older woman, a widow with money no less? I'd never love again, so why not be comfortably off at least? I had hoped that coming to the Lake District would bring back memories of happier times for both of us, but I'm beginning to have my doubts. We used to have such a laugh together. It's almost as though Fred's suffering from some kind of facial rictus as he struggles to appear outwardly cheerful. I fear that rigor mortis has set in to his life and there's no going back for him.

At that moment, I resolve to use our time together to push Freddy to open up to me; he needs to step out of his self-imposed life of a recluse. The woman from the bar self-consciously enters our brotherly enclave for a moment to set our plates before us. Steam rises from our dishes of trout. I take a deep breath, and dive in.

'Freddy, I hope you don't mind me asking, but are you getting out and about much these days? What do you do for Lord Armstrong? Is it still mainly the shoot or are there other duties?' Fred continues to chew his food and cocks his head to one side in the manner of someone considering his options and weighing the consequences.

'I'm really still just a glorified gillie. Of course, that suits old Shotty[33] down to the ground; I only need to get my gun down to give it a clean and he's already scratching at the door! Really, George, I'm fine. I know why you're asking these questions. Mother is worried and Father thinks I'm just wasting my time, but I'm happy with my lot, I don't need anything more. I don't think I could cope with any complications.'

'By complications, do you mean women? Did you ever contact that woman you met in Wales, Rowena?'

'Oh, Roanna, no, I couldn't face it. I mean, after all

---

[33] Fred's faithful Springer Spaniel

these years. I know so many of the lads in POW camps were disappointed when they got home to find girlfriends and even wives hitched up with some suave Canadian or US serviceman, I didn't think I could take any more disappointment either.' Ylena's face pops into my mind for a second time in as many minutes; the beautiful shape of her mouth as its corners turn upwards into the smile that will haunt me forever.

'I never told you this, Freddy, but… Ylena, the Maltese woman I was seeing, she was pregnant.' My voice wavers for a moment; it feels like a confession.

'George, I never knew. I never guessed. Why didn't you say anything before?'

'Too ashamed. I got her pregnant, I left her there, and she died. I lost myself to her in a way that's impossible to describe. Every day I wish it'd come out differently.' As I search his face for a glimmer of empathy and concern, it becomes clear that Fred isn't going to acknowledge or respond further or engage in swapping secrets. Instead, I change the subject. 'Freddy, you're not eating?'

'I'm sorry, George, it's gastric trouble. It comes in waves, sometimes acid reflux, cramps and then there's the nausea. Having been deprived of it for so long, it seems I'm doomed to a life of being unable to enjoy food.' Fred glances up from the table, a look of despair briefly flickers across his face; I suddenly see the torment that sits behind his impassive façade.

'Come on, Fred, let's finish up and get out there.

The sun's shining and the Derwent beckons. So, what if we don't catch anything, it'll be great to just get out there!'

Climbing a stile in the fence and heading along the well-beaten track across a farmer's field, we reach our fishing beat; a little boarded platform sitting in the shallows of the riverbank. We're at a spot on the Derwent upstream of Cockermouth where the river bends at its closest to the Lakes Hotel. The hedgerows are alive with songbirds, several yellowhammers call to each other; our father always used to say it sounded like, 'a little bit of bread and no cheeeeese!' The fringing trees dip their lower branches into the water upstream sending ripples and eddies down to us. In the shadows, a small cloud of gnats dance about above the surface of the water and mayflies' flit around the reed beds.

Whilst I'm taking in this bucolic scene, Freddy is quietly unpacking his equipment from a large wicker fishing basket, putting together his rod and methodically threading fishing line through the little hoops. As I continue to observe him, he's wrapped in concentration as he opens a large wooden cigar box with, 'El Merito, Manila', boldly printed in red lettering framing a colourful drawing of a native hut and palm trees sitting at the far end of a field of what must be tobacco. I recognise it as one of Father's old cigar boxes. Opening the lid, Freddy surprises me with a collection of flies. Serried ranks of them sit hooked onto four rows of rectangular cushioning; clearly the box has been lovingly adapted for the purpose.

'Well, Freddy, you've got an impressive collection of flies there! Did you make them yourself?'

'Yes, as a matter of fact I did. By sheer luck, there was a book written in English on fly fishing in the library at Eichstätt. I used to often look over at the river running near the camp, the Altmühl, and think it would be an excellent trout river, so, to pass the time, I would make flies using feathers, thread and bits and pieces of steel wire.' Sweeping his palm over the contents of the cigar box in the manner of a magician conducting a magic trick, Fred continues, 'there are the dry flies, and the larger wet flies are here. Since it's mid-season and the brook dun are about, I'm thinking of trying some dry flies, see here, the "Adams". I've a couple of types, why not have a go with one, you'll need to use a reel of dry line though.'

Impressed again, this time by Freddy's seemingly encyclopaedic knowledge of fly fishing, I decide to take his advice. Having spent some time setting up, we settle after a while into a time-honoured routine of casting and reeling, casting and reeling as we attempt to mimic a fly landing on the water's surface. As the day wears on, fish are beginning to rise, and it looks like there's a possibility one of us will soon be reeling in some trout. Having been absorbed for some time in trying to improve my casting technique, I glance over to see how Fred's getting on. To my surprise, he's simply standing stock still intently staring at a spot on the riverbank. The end of his rod is trailing in the water and his face the very picture of horror and surprise.

'Freddy! Are you all right?' Throwing down my own rod, I rush over to where he's standing. I take his shoulders and gently shake him to try and snap him out of it. His body is stiff and tense. Following his gaze, it seems that he's staring at something in the shallows downstream of where he's been fishing. 'What's the matter? What do you see there?'

'George, do you see them, there in the water? Oh God, George, it's horrible! Do you see them? The bodies in the water. Look over there!' Panic rises in his voice and his hands appear to wrestle with each other in the extremis of his anguish.

'You must be hallucinating, Freddy, there's nothing there, just the riverbank.' I take him in my arms and gently sit him down on his little folding chair where, after a while, his eyes seem to regain their focus.

'Oh, George, they come to me, these horrible visions. They seem so real. I sometimes think I'm going mad. O'Callaghan, Jimmy Pile, the bodies in the Somme River. Other times it's just faces, or I see someone I recognise in a crowd, but I know they can't be there; I saw them die. I'll never be free of it, George, the shame, the guilt, the horror. I feel like they're watching me, judging me.'

I intently watch his face as his features eventually recompose themselves into an impassive gaze as he comes back from whatever private torment that he's living. We remain together side by side on the riverbank for some time, but eventually I start packing up our gear and we walk back to the lane and the hotel. The day has lost its magic and whist it's still a bright summer's day, like Fred, I can now see only shadows.

George, Thursday November 16th, 1972, Beacon House, Western Way, Whitley Bay, Newcastle

For the sake of exercise, I've left Dora reading through a stack of women's magazines and I'm walking down the stairs to the lobby to collect the mail. The stairwell has an ever-present aroma of boiled potatoes and cabbage hanging in the air. Despite the fact that we're supposed to be living in a 'luxury' block of flats, it seems that even the residents of North Tyneside who have pretensions to being upper class, still cling to their need to consume over-boiled vegetables on a daily basis. Come Friday, the boiled veg will be replaced by the smell of deep-fried fish and chips; old habits die hard.

The wind and rain are, yet again, swirling around the building. From our airy perch on the eleventh floor, the slate grey of the sea and the black clouds merge into the horizon, broken only by the solitary white pillar of St Mary's Lighthouse in the kind of seascape beloved by poets and painters. However, at ground level, the view of rain bouncing off the dark street is deeply depressing.

Aware that I need to be on the road to my first customer of the day – a carpet salesman's work is never done – I find our mail box and, as I rummage through its contents, a blue envelope drops onto the floor. Neatly framed by the edges of the tile onto which it's fallen, I experience a familiar reluctance to retrieve it, my sixth sense kicking in.

Picking it up and turning it over, Freddy's scrawl is unmistakable. It's postmarked Bamburgh, date stamped November 14th and Freddy's used a second-class stamp. Well, he could have just come over to visit, why send a letter? Even whilst these thoughts are passing through my mind, I know that Fred would never come and visit. Before I even start to read what's written on the little square of blue notepaper, I know what it's about.

I manage to find one of the lobby chairs before my legs give from under me; I feel like I've just received a physical blow. Whilst I read, part of me wants to believe that I'm peering over someone else's shoulder and reading their brother's suicide note and not one from my dear Freddy.

George

My dear brother and dearest friend, by the time you read this, I will have embarked on my final journey. I've spent several hours composing this letter to you, but all I've managed is a few sentences, hard though they have been to write. I know I have not been the perfect brother to you these last few years, and God knows, I know you have tried to coax me out and get me back into the world, but the urge to stray more than an easy walk from my lodgings has all but vanished; a bitter irony for a man who has spent as much time in a prison cell as I have. I have come to the conclusion that going on is pointless and I can no longer see any hope that things will improve for me. The baggage of the past, the shame of my inaction whilst so many gallant comrades died around me, fills every waking hour and many of my nightmares. I want you to know that I love you, brother, and I hope that you will forgive me this final selfish act. And, as someone once eloquently wrote, 'I shall miss this place in the interval that sits between living and death. Dying is an abomination, but immortality would be much worse. The fates put us all in the firing line between a rock and a hard place. All that any of us can do in this life is to at least make the best fist of it we can.'

Adieu

Your loving brother, Fred

Resources:

George's Cigar Box: personal photographs and WWII memorabilia collected by the late George Anderson Whitton, kindly provided by the Estate of the Whitton Family.

Forces War Records: https://www.forces-war-records.co.uk.

Air Sea Rescue During the Siege of Malta. Bill Jackson, Troubadour Publishing Ltd. ISBN 978 1848764729.

Fortress Malta. James Holland, Weidenfeld & Nicholson Ltd., 2003. ISBN 978 0304366545.

Colditz: Oflag IV-C. Michael McNally, Osprey Publishing Ltd., 2010. ISBN 978 1849082914.

Guests of The Third Reich. Anthony Richards, Imperial War Museum, 2019. ISBN 978 1912423064.

Colditz: The Definitive History. Henry Chancellor, Hodder & Stoughton Ltd., 2001. ISBN 0 3407941.